PE… …S

'Would you be my po… …asked, hesitantly.

I nodded, looking u… …him. The words 'pony-girl' doubled my excitement, putting a name to my fantasy. It was a beautiful way of putting it. I found myself thinking of how it could really happen. I'd be stripped, put in a harness, a plug shoved rudely up my bottom, tied to a cart, my bare cheeks smacked with a riding whip, used as a pony-girl . . .

Other Nexus Classics:

THE IMAGE
AGONY AUNT
THE INSTITUTE
OBSESSION
HIS MISTRESS'S VOICE
BOUND TO SERVE
BOUND TO SUBMIT
SISTERHOOD OF THE INSTITUTE
SISTERS OF SEVERCY
THE PLEASURE PRINCIPLE
SERVING TIME
THE TRAINING GROUNDS
DIFFERENT STROKES
LINGERING LESSONS
EDEN UNVEILED
UNDERWORLD
PLEASURE ISLAND
LETTERS TO CHLOE
PARADISE BAY
EROTICON 1
EROTICON 2
EROTICON 3
EROTICON 4

A NEXUS CLASSIC

PENNY IN HARNESS

Penny Birch

This book is a work of fiction.
In real life, make sure you practise safe sex.

First published in 1998 by
Nexus
Thames Wharf Studios
Rainville Road
London W6 9HA

This Nexus Classic edition 2001

www.nexus-books.co.uk

ISBN 0 352 33651 X

All characters in this publication are fictitious and any resemblance to real persons, living or dead, is purely coincidental.

Typeset by TW Typesetting, Plymouth, Devon

Printed and bound by
Clays Ltd, St Ives PLC

Penny Birch is among the founding members of the BB&L pony-girl club and has been doing it for real since 1994. There is almost nothing in her novel that is not drawn from true experience.

I would like to dedicate this book to Boudicea, Palomina, Abigail, Tarragon, the real Pinky and the rest of my stable mates – Penny Birch

One

There are few things more embarrassing than getting caught short in the middle of nowhere. With hindsight, I knew I shouldn't have had the second pint of cider when I stopped for lunch at the King Billy. Hindsight was a fat lot of good now, when I was squeezing my thighs together and looking desperately around for somewhere where I could get two minutes' privacy.

You'd think it would be easy: in the middle of the Wiltshire countryside, without a town for miles. It was high summer too and the woods and hedgerows were green and lush. Potential hiding places abounded on every side. Hiding places that looked as if they'd lain undisturbed for years, never mind the time it would take me to get my jeans and knickers down long enough to relieve myself. Appearances can be deceptive. The path I was on ran between a high wall to one side and an enormous cornfield on the other. The wall had a wood beyond it, but I couldn't even reach the top, let alone climb over. The cornfield offered no real concealment. Also, a combine harvester was working slowly towards me, preventing me from nipping across to the inviting-looking line of trees and scrub on the far side. Worse still, there were just enough people using the path to make it impractical for me to whip my panties down and crouch by the wall.

It was getting to the point when it was a choice between risking getting caught doing it and wetting myself; either one was unthinkable. Determined to reach the distant hedge that marked the end of the corn field, I kept going. I made it, scampering the last few yards, only to find that the hedge bordered a field occupied by the most enormous bull I had ever seen. I squirmed in desperation, crossing my legs. Back down the path, a group of walkers was approaching in the distance: army, by the look of it. In the other direction the path stretched away, the hedge at the far side of the bull's field offering a last, desperate chance to save my blushes.

I ran, dodging around an elderberry bush to discover a collapsed section of wall. It was no more than four feet high, with flint and brick rubble making a little ramp. I was through it in an instant, finding myself in a dim wood of massive oaks and blackthorn underbrush. It was perfect. I had dropped my map and was struggling with my belt buckle even as I identified a nice clear space of ground by one of the oaks. An instant later, my jeans were around my thighs; then my panties were down and my back was pressed against the rough bark of the tree, the air deliciously cool on my bare pussy.

A sensation of utter bliss went through me as I let go, my pee gushing out onto the leaf mould underneath me and splashing my legs and jeans. I didn't care; at least I hadn't wet myself or had the unendurably embarrassing experience of being seen with my panties down by a load of army boys. I finished and wriggled my bum to shake the last few drops off, then stood to pull up my pants and for the first time really took in the details of my surroundings.

I was in a fairly thick wood. Once, perhaps, it had been neat parkland, but now the undergrowth had been allowed to spread unchecked. Blackthorn, holly, smaller bushes and plants grew in profusion, the gap in the wall I had come through now barely discernible among the foliage. Broken sunlight came through the high canopy, creating a cool green space that was a pleasant contrast to the heat of the footpath and open fields. Beyond the wall I could hear voices, evidently the army boys I had seen before. I paused, suddenly in no hurry to go back to the path.

The wood was obviously private property, but it had an empty, disused look about it and I decided to explore. Moving through the dappled sunlight, I felt a bit like Alice stepping into Wonderland. Not that my surroundings were weird in any way: quite the opposite, in fact. Quiet, peaceful – serene, almost; yet curiously detached from the rest of the world.

My discovery of a path brought me sharply back down to earth. It had the same look of abandonment as the wood: pressed gravel with worn areas filled by half-dry puddles. There were bicycle tracks too, but there was something odd about them. Instead of the normal criss-cross of tyre imprints where the rear wheel has followed the front, the tracks were parallel and a line of footprints ran between them; or rather shoe-prints, shoe-prints made by dainty high heels. As I studied the marks I heard noises coming from somewhere along the path, outside my range of vision.

I stepped back into the bushes, suddenly very aware that I was on private property but too curious to simply leave. The noises I had heard had been laughter and a curious smacking noise. Now came the sound of footsteps, moving at a smart jog. I crouched down and pushed a big dock leaf aside so that I could see the path. My mouth fell open as the strangest sight I had ever seen appeared around the corner.

The first shock was to see a naked girl jogging towards me – or, rather, trotting, as her legs were moving with neat, precise steps. She was trotting like a horse. Also, she wasn't entirely naked. The bits that mattered were; there wasn't a stitch to cover the little furry triangle between her legs, while her breasts were bare and bouncing as she went, her nipples stiff with excitement. She had a corset on, black leather and very tight, which nipped her waist in and exaggerated her chest and hips. Boots, too: smart little high-heeled numbers that came just above the ankle, also in black leather and fastened with big shiny metal buckles. The strangest thing was the harness she was wearing; heavy leather belts secured her waist and wrists and she wore a complete bridle, including a bit set between her bright red lips. The top of the bridle caught up her long tawny blonde hair in a beautiful ponytail which had been tied with a smart red ribbon.

The second shock was what her harness was attached to. Her wrists and waist were shackled to a cart, painted a jaunty yellow and built like a gig, only in miniature. In it sat a handsome young man in full hunting gear: hard hat, pink coat and all, despite the heat. He held a short riding whip in one hand and, as I watched, he used it to flick the girl's bottom, drawing a muffled squeak from her and an increase in her pace. His expression was one of calm amusement, his eyes fixed on the girl's rear view.

As they drew nearer, I noticed a hank of golden hair swishing from side to side between her legs and realised that she had some sort of tail to complete her outrageous appearance. My eyes were riveted to her and, as they drew parallel to my hiding place, I saw that the tail projected up from the base of her spine in a wonderfully realistic manner. It was the same rich tawny colour as her hair and stuck out an inch or two, falling in a graceful arc over her bottom and down to the backs of her knees.

They went past, my stare following them as they went; her tail swished from side to side across the bouncing cheeks of her bottom. Her buttocks were covered in little red marks where he had used the whip, and she was running with sweat, making her skin damp and glossy. It wasn't obvious how the tail stayed on but, as he gave her another taste of the whip, the tail swished aside further than normal and I caught a glimpse of a black spine running between the cheeks of her bottom. I knew she wore nothing at the front, which meant that it was somehow plugged up her pussy – or worse, up her bottom.

I found myself shivering as they passed out of sight. She had all too obviously been enjoying herself – the blissful expression on her face had shown that – yet I found myself wondering how she could allow herself to be subjected to such indignity, in the name of sexual pleasure. I mean: stripped, made to wear a tail that plugged into her vagina or even her anus, fastened to a cart to be used as a draught animal, whipped across her naked bottom and in all probability thoroughly shafted when her 'driver' had finished humiliating her. He'd probably have her from the rear, I considered, while she knelt on the stable floor, still in harness, her bottom stuck up in the air while his cock hardened as he looked at her rear view, the tail falling across her open buttocks, the plug showing in –

Shaking myself to disperse the disturbing fantasy, I got to my feet and began to retrace my steps. I felt confused: at once shocked and turned on, horrified and delighted. I had always thought of myself as open-minded, an unshockable modern girl, but this was something else. As I made my way back through the wood, the vision of the naked sweat-soaked girl and her cool, poised driver kept coming back to me with increasing force. Stepping through the partially collapsed wall and back into the open sunlight calmed my fevered imagination a little, but only until I looked back into the dim interior of the wood.

Inevitably, now that I didn't need to pee anymore, there was nobody in sight; the footpath stretched away in both directions, empty. Even the combine harvester driver had stopped for a break, his massive machine looming over the hedge of the bull's field, silent in the bright sunlight. Now I could have stripped naked and danced the hornpipe, never mind had a quick pee, and nobody would have been any the wiser. To add to the irony, the next field along proved to be planted with maize: tall, ripe and offering ample concealment. It was as I stood looking at the maize that a sneaky little thought came into my head.

I might not need to pee anymore, but I could certainly do with a good orgasm. Perhaps I could find somewhere quiet and masturbate? No, the idea was too dirty; besides, I was bound to get caught and, if the idea of being seen relieving myself was unendurable, that of being found frigging myself, by some farmer, defied description. On the other hand, I could think about it and work up a really good fantasy for later, when I could do it in safety. I would imagine myself the subject of attention from that cool, handsome young man, allowing him unrestricted access to my body.

He'd amuse himself with my breasts, fondling them casually, possessively; he'd take his whip to my bottom, just for sport of it, then watch while I lubricated the tight little hole between my buttocks . . .

If I didn't stop, my panties were going to be soaking, and for a quite different reason than before. On the other hand, why restrain myself? I wasn't doing any harm, and it was stupid to feel guilty about fantasising – or masturbating, for that matter. Beyond the maize field was the stand of trees and scrub I had seen earlier. Surely it would provide enough concealment for a quick frig? Surely the scrub was dense enough? Why would anybody be there, anyway? Trousers and knickers down, ten minutes on my back with my eyes closed and my legs apart, and I'd be there; nobody would see.

I took my map and unfolded it, which brought home

a sudden reality to the idea. A pang of guilt shot through me. Masturbating? In a wood? You little slut, I thought to myself. Yes, a little slut, what a delicious thought. Imagine getting caught, though. Found with my jeans and knickers in a tangle around my ankles, my top up so that I could play with my tits, with one hand on my pussy and the other on a nipple. Any farm boy who found me like that would undoubtedly expect to fuck me then and there. The thought was terrifying – but also thrilling, just so long as it didn't actually happen.

Looking at the map, I saw that getting caught was very unlikely. The trees I could see hid a stream in a gully, beyond which were more fields. There was no farm building nearby, nor any track marked in the woods. The idea was becoming more and more compelling. I glanced to where the map showed the woods I had seen the couple in. There was a roughly square area of woodland with a lake at the centre and a symbol marking the site of a ruin, nothing more.

Determined to carry out my intentions before common sense got the better of me, I glanced hastily to either side to check that the path was empty and climbed the fence into the maize field. The act of leaving the public right of way sent a new thrill through me, a deliciously naughty feeling of anticipation and rudeness. The maize stood to the height of my head, the hedge shielding me from the other side. I ran light-footed down the channel between the two, dodging to avoid the occasional muddy patch. I quickly reached the far end, finding myself in a broad channel between the high maize and the dense scrub. The solitude was absolute; droning insects and the distant bark of a dog were the only sounds. I waited, standing still and listening for possible signs that I had been seen and followed, but none came.

The next task was to find a quiet place, a really quiet

place where I could concentrate. Maybe it would be possible to titillate myself a little first though, to do something rude that would help me to my eventual climax. An idea came to me as I looked around. The thing that had affected me the most had been the girl's tail and the utterly dirty way it appeared to have been held in up her anus. I didn't have a lovely black tail to match my hair, but that didn't mean my bottom had to stay empty. A maize cob would provide the perfect natural dildo; phallic, bumpy, yet clean and abundantly available.

Most of the cobs were far too large for my unfortunate bottom but a search quickly found one that was just daringly large. I began to peel the husk away, and decided that I ought to perform the whole operation with my knickers down to increase the thrill. I put the cob between my teeth, and my heart was in my mouth as I again fiddled with my belt and slid my jeans and panties down around my thighs, exposing my pussy and bum to the hot sun. My fingers were trembling as I peeled away the rest of the husk, glancing nervously out from among the maize plants. The cob was quickly peeled, the surface pale yellow and lumpy as I stroked it and wondered if I could really be that dirty.

Yes, I could, I decided, popping the cob into my mouth and sucking it. I left it in my mouth for a moment, licking at it while my hands went behind me to feel the soft orbs of my bottom. Trembling more strongly than ever, I let a hand sneak down between my cheeks, finding the tight hole of my anus already wet with sweat. My finger went in easily, the feeling making me catch my breath.

Part of me was yelling not to be so filthy, as I took the cob out of my mouth with my spare hand. I paid no attention, instead sticking my bottom out and preparing the target. The little hole closed as my finger came out. I put the tip of the cob a little way in, relaxed, pushed and then my anus was gaping around the rough surface as it slid up my bottom. There was that wonderful feeling of being entered, and it was more than I could resist not to slide it in and out a few times. The sensation made me pant but I forced myself to stop and stood up, feeling the cob between my thighs, my anus filled just like the girl's had been, experiencing the same deliciously dirty feeling she must have had. Part of it, at least; for the whole feeling, I needed some extremely fancy equipment and a good-looking young man with a riding whip.

Still, it was plenty for now and I pulled up my pants and wriggled into my jeans with a feeling of exquisite rudeness. For a moment, I considered returning to the path and continuing my walk to experience the thrill of passing people quite casually while, unknown to them, I had a small maize cob inserted in my anus. My need to come was too strong and as I emerged from the maize I was already looking around for a way into the scrub.

This wasn't so easy; a great bank of bramble and thorn barred my way for the whole length of the maize field. I walked up and down, becoming increasingly frustrated – and increasingly turned on by that very frustration and the motion of the cob in my pants. Finally, I decided on a place and forced my way through, arriving scratched and sweaty in the interior of the wood. The growth was even thicker than in the other wood; a rank tangle of thorn and elder grew low over a carpet of sodden leaves. For a while I had to go along in a crouch, but finally found a place where one of the bigger elders had fallen. It had created a small clearing, carpeted in soft grass and hemmed in on all sides by thick vegetation.

It was perfect. Not only could I not be seen but, if anybody should approach, I would hear them long before they saw me. The atmosphere was wonderful as well: quiet, secretive, somehow special. It was also pleasantly warm rather than hot, and faintly scented with pine, elder and woodland smells.

Emboldened by the secrecy of my hiding place, I stood and stretched, then began to strip. As I undressed, I imagined the man I had seen driving the girl watching me, inspecting my body and commenting on it. His expression had been so calm, so arrogant, and I imagined that same look as I lifted my top with mock timidity. My bra followed, the air cool on my breasts as I lifted them in my hands and ran my fingers over the nipples. He'd tell me to do that, of course, instructing me to make a display of myself as he looked on. The girl would be watching too, an amused sneer on her face because it was my turn to be utterly humiliated. She was perfect for my fantasy: tall and blonde with big breasts, the opposite of my own petite figure.

Naked from the waist up, I undid my belt, popped the button on my jeans and slowly slid the zip down, opening my fly and holding the front of my panties out and down to show my pubic hair. He'd know I was embarrassed about the size of my bum, and he'd want to see me expose it, to add to my shame. I turned to my imaginary onlooker, sticking my bum out and sliding my jeans down ever so slowly. The girl would laugh and remark that I had a fat bottom, even though hers was a good deal fleshier than mine. The jeans fell to my ankles and I was left with just my pants to cover my modesty, and of course to conceal the fact that I had already been thoroughly dirty and put a maize cob up my bottom.

He'd laugh, telling me to touch my toes and pull my back in, thrusting my bottom up for their inspection. He'd walk up to me and pull down my pants. No – he'd make her do it, doubling my humiliation as another girl peeled the little scrap of pink cotton down over my bum. He'd laugh when he saw the base of the cob protruding obscenely from my rear. She'd give an exclamation of disgust, planting a firm smack across my buttocks to make them bounce and wobble. He'd tell her to do it again, to spank me well for such disgusting behaviour. He'd also order me to masturbate while I was beaten.

My panties joined my jeans at ankle level as I slipped a hand between my legs, finding my clitoris and beginning to rub. The other went back and I began to smack my bum, imagining it was her doing it while he watched. She'd spank me hard, aiming at the fullest part of my cheeks so that the cob was rammed home each time she hit me. He'd pull his cock out as he watched my pussy begin to juice, casually getting his erection ready for me as I was beaten in front of him.

I'd look back between my legs and see him as he stood up, an enormous erection rearing out of his fly, his dress otherwise undisturbed. She'd step aside, leaving my buttocks red and sore, the maize cob still sticking out of my anus. I'd grip my ankles as he got behind me, watching her bend and take his erection briefly in her mouth, leaving it glistening with her saliva. I'd feel another wave of humiliation as she turned her attention to the rear of my vulva, avoiding my frantically rubbing fingers as she dampened my pussy lips with her tongue.

He'd be casually ordering her to go and fetch the cart and harness as his cock touched my pussy. Then he'd be in me, filling me, my pussy stretched around his erection, his first push catching the base of the cob so that it was shoved yet deeper into my anus. Everything would be full to bursting, my fingers working desperately at my clit, his big hands locked onto my hips, my little titties naked in the warm air. Finally he'd orgasm, filling me with sperm, the sticky come squelching out around my pussy to trickle down my thighs and over my vulva. As my fingers became coated with sticky hot sperm, I'd come myself – which is exactly what I did.

The standing position was too much, and I sank

down onto my haunches and lay back in the grass, finishing myself off with my eyes shut and my mind focused on my fantasy and the feel of the cob as my anus contracted around it in orgasm. I was holding my pussy lips open with two fingers, frigging with a third while my spare hand gave a nipple her share of attention. My orgasm seemed to last an age, draining me of strength and breath and leaving me panting on the grass.

I lay there for a long time, pussy and anus both rather sore, the cob still lodged up my bottom. I rolled over into a kneeling position and drew the cob out, throwing it into the woods. I felt sweaty, sticky and badly in need of a wash but utterly satisfied. The sense of solitude was stronger than ever. Remembering the stream marked on the map, I undressed completely, bundled my clothes together and began to make my way carefully towards it. The ground quickly began to slope, then became steeper. I was soon plastered in leaf mould and mud. Finally, I lost my footing and slid the last few feet on my bum.

I ended up sitting in the stream, my clothes around me, absolutely soaked. I got out and hung them up to dry in a sunny patch, then climbed back into the water to wash. It was wonderfully cold against my body, easing my soreness as I lowered myself onto the sandy bottom. Sitting in a little pool, I was quite enclosed and was able to wash at leisure, then relax in the cool water, watching the patterns of light through the leaves high above me.

As I lay there, I began to think about what I had seen. Now that the knot of sexual tension it had caused had been eased, that any girl should allow herself to be treated that way seemed incredible. I had often fantasised about being controlled by lovers – had even been tied up once or twice, spanked occasionally, buggered not infrequently. Being used as a draught animal represented a whole new level of submission to a lover's will. Unless of course, the girl had been the instigator of the game. It was possible, after all, as most of the supposedly degrading things I'd done had been at my own instigation. A lot of men didn't dare ask for that sort of thing, even when they wanted it. Actually, it's remarkable how many men won't do that sort of thing, even if the woman does ask. More than once I'd tried to tease a man into spanking me, only to be told he had too much respect for me. I'd have thought that the offer of a squirming girl over your lap with her bare, hot bottom stuck up in the air would be more than any man could resist, but apparently not.

So maybe it wasn't so much a question of submission to a lover's will, but of lovers having mutually compatible sexual fantasies. In any case, they would have to be extremely intimate and very trusting of each other. After all, one of the problems of indulging in the more outrageous sexual pleasures was that it could become embarrassing when a boyfriend became an ex-boyfriend and the fact that you liked it up the bum was being broadcast among your friends. This was worse when you worked in the rather closed environment of a university research facility, as I did. It had happened to me, so I knew.

On the other hand, it looked wonderful fun; given the right man, I felt I could manage it and really enjoy it. Given the right man, of course. Someone discreet; also trustworthy enough not to overstep the mark when I was helpless; rich enough to own a suitable location to play; inventive enough to make the fantasy work; cute enough to turn me on; into petite, dark-haired girls and without a partner already.

I laughed at myself as I sat up in the pool. I'd never met a man who filled even half the necessary requirements. The chance of one cropping up, just because I fancied a bit of unusual sex, had to be close to zero. I stood and stepped out onto the lower bank at the far side of the stream. My clothes were still wet, but the area was quite enclosed and my feeling of safety absolute, so I walked naked down the clear space along the bank, wondering if it really was practical to make anything more than a fantasy out of my experience.

Ten minutes later, I was sitting on a log, still stark naked and still thinking about the couple in the woods. I had long since ceased to have the slightest worry about being caught when a sharp crack from upstream brought me to my senses. Suddenly acutely aware of my nudity, I scrambled back to where my clothes were hanging and began to dress hurriedly, despite the dampness of the fabric. There were no more noises, but the moment had gone and the lonely beauty of the wood had faded, replaced by a sinister atmosphere that had me imagining eyes peering out of every thicket, as I struggled to make myself decent.

After what seemed an eternity I was finished, my boots alone proving really uncomfortable. I climbed back up the slope, pushing under the elders and emerging into the maize field to find it as quiet and sultry as it had been before. The heat of the day had barely begun to fade. Although the shadows were getting longer, I had plenty of time to get back to my car, which I had left outside the King Billy. That was only three miles away, so I decided to skirt the wood. When my boots were dry, that was, I decided as I bent to undo the laces.

The map showed the footpath running along one side of the wood and the other three sides bordering fields, except where a track ran up to it from the road. Having been running around in the nude for the best part of an hour and having got away with it, I felt bold enough to risk the minor piece of trespassing necessary to investigate the wood. Whether I would dare enter it again was another matter, given that I now knew that it was being used, and how!

Eventually, my boots were dry enough to be bearable and I pulled them back on. I walked along the side of the maize field and checked carefully that the coast was clear, before climbing over the fence. As I had felt a thrill of disobedience when I crossed onto private land, so the thrill went as I crossed back, and I looked back at the maize field with a curious sense of missing something and a lovely sense of having been really naughty and got away with it.

Oddly enough, it was harder to pluck up the courage to climb the fence at the far end of the wood than it had been to climb into the maize field. Maybe this was because I no longer desperately wanted to masturbate. On the other hand, it may have been because I was stepping into a big open field with no cover and because I was spying rather than trying to avoid being spied on.

The first side was frustratingly blank. The wall stretched away, taller than my head; the flint and brick construction made it impossible to get a good toe-hold. Even if I had been able to see over, the wood on the far side was as thick as it had been where I had first got through. The wall turned at an angle then thrust out into the open field, leaving me feeling completely exposed and thankful for the moderate camouflage of faded jeans and a green T-shirt.

Along the next section of wall, I could see banks that presumably marked the position of the track and therefore the gate. I stole towards it, bent over and undoubtedly looking extremely guilty. The gate proved to be set between massive stone pillars, its ancient black paint flaking to reveal rusty iron-work beneath. There was a little stone lodge inside the gate, the window-panes long gone and the thatch of the roof sagging and moss-grown, in keeping with the general air of dilapidation. Despite this, the gravel showed scrape marks where the gates had been swung open recently.

I listened for a moment but heard nothing. The gate was shut and held closed with a rusty chain. The padlock was shiny and suspiciously modern, quite clearly not part of the ancient construction it guarded.

Did that mean they had left? Not necessarily, but the padlock was outside the gate and would certainly be awkward to get at from the interior. Intent on taking my piece of detective work a little further, I walked boldly over to the gate. Tyre tracks showed clearly in a muddy area of the path: one set in, no sets out. They were still there.

Not only that, but the general state of the track showed that the place was used infrequently at best. Whatever the place had been, it had obviously fallen into disuse years ago. I was fascinated; the whole situation filled me with such curiosity that I knew I could never just leave it. I was even thinking of going boldly in and offering my services as a spare plaything, but quickly chickened out when I turned to look at the forbidding, and pointedly locked, gates.

Still, I decided, I could spy a little more. The woods inside were made for skulking about in and if the wall was a serious obstacle, then the gate would be easy to climb. Reasoning that I would hear their car in enough time to hide, I began to climb the gate, using the fancy wrought-iron decorations as holds. I was soon swinging myself over the top and down the far side, then nipping behind the lodge and again listening for noise.

Nothing happened, so I peered gingerly in at one of the windows. The interior was disappointingly empty, containing only a decaying table and a few ferns that had taken root among the soggy mess of leaf mould and glass on the floor. Emerging from hiding, I started cautiously down the drive, ready to dive into the bushes at the first hint of sound. I jumped at the sudden call of a pheasant, which made me realise just how nervous I was. The drive curved, leaving the shelter of the wood to emerge on an area of badly overgrown lawn, beyond which stood a house.

The remains of a house, I should say. There was no roof, and what was left of the walls was in an advanced state of decay, the occasional area of blackened stone or charred wood hinting at the fire that must have destroyed it. I walked cautiously forward to get a closer look, only then catching a glimpse of bright red, a colour entirely out of place in the rotting grandeur of the setting. It must be their car, I realised, as I stepped back into the bushes.

It was parked among a group of buildings that stood to the side of the main house. I guessed they had once been stables: long, low structures with rows of tall doors facing a compound. If the house was ruined, the stables were anything but. The buildings were in good order and the yard even looked freshly scrubbed. The car, a big, bright red Rover, stood in the middle, empty. I shifted position, bringing more of the yard into my view. The little cart I had seen the girl pulling was parked at the far end, an untidy tangle of harness hanging from the shafts and a pile of clothes thrown across the seat.

I was considering the implication of this when a noise attracted my attention. It came from beyond the main stable building and sounded suspiciously like a squeak of pleasure. I began to make my way around the back of the stable, staying well concealed and ready to bolt if I was seen. I wasn't, and presently found myself in a position from which I could see them. She was on her back on a little grassy area, her legs thrown up and open as he mounted her and thrust away vigorously. Her black corset was still on, and her high-heeled ankle boots, along with the red ribbon in her hair; otherwise, she was naked. So was he; his back heaved and his muscular buttocks moved rhythmically as they fucked.

They were locked in each other's arms, oblivious to their surroundings; their sighs turned to squeals and then grunts as his pace quickened and her grip tightened around his back. My hand had gone between my legs as I watched, feeling the shape of my pussy under my jeans. He was thrusting furiously, making her pant and gasp. At what must have been the last possible instant he pulled out, knelt up, grabbed his erection and jerked frantically at it to send a spray of white sperm splashing out over her face and breasts as she leant forward.

He sank back on his haunches, cock still proud in his hand as she put her hands up to her big breasts and spread the come over them, rubbing it into her nipples. Her face was towards me, her eyes shut and a trickle of white running down one cheek. He came forward again, this time burying his head between her thighs. She groaned loudly, still smearing his come over her breasts as he licked at her. I felt close to orgasm myself, wishing I had a skirt on so that I could get at my pussy and masturbate again.

Suddenly she screamed, then screamed again as she came under his tongue, her thighs locked around his head, her nipples sticking up from between her fingers and sticky with male come. My head was swimming with my own pleasure, but caution got the better of me and I sank back into the bushes as he got to his feet and stretched in the warm air.

I made for the gate, keen to get clear before they dressed and left the wood. My last glimpse was of them walking into the stable yard, hand in hand, and it was only then that I realised that the girl's whole bottom was flushed red. Obviously, at some stage during the afternoon, she had been soundly spanked.

So great was my state of nervous excitement that I ran most of the way to my car. I got in and sat back, puffing to recover my breath. I desperately wanted to get my jeans and pants down and give myself another orgasm, but it was impossible, with people already arriving at the King Billy for an evening drink. I went and had a drink myself instead, a pint of cold orange, by the end of which I felt ready for the drive back to my flat.

Two

That should have been that, but it wasn't. On the few other occasions that I'd unexpectedly come across something really erotic, I'd fantasised about it a few times, had some lovely orgasms and then moved on to something else.

One had been watching a couple make love among a patch of rocks in the Welsh hills during a field trip. From their point of view, it must have just been a hurried knee-trembler. She'd had her trousers and pants down and been taking him behind her. We'd been a long way off and hadn't even had a clear view, but it had really got to me.

Another had been coming into a friend's room unexpectedly at college. She had been kneeling between a man's legs with his cock in her mouth and her top pulled up over her breasts. That had provided me with a week's happy masturbation and greatly increased the frequency with which my own boyfriend of the time had his cock sucked.

This was different. The image of that woman in harness and the cool, amused way he had taken his pleasure just wouldn't go away. My fantasy developed over the week, starting with me being in her position, then exploring various related ideas and lastly turning the tables on the man. By the end of the week, I realised that I wasn't going to be satisfied until I had found out more. The question was, how?

Despite never having heard of the particular kink they had been indulging in, it occurred to me that it might not be as rare as all that. Following this reasoning, I bought a contact magazine for the first time in my life. The things people did want from each other opened my eyes considerably, but there was no mention of what I wanted. Of course, I had no idea what the technical term for it might be; with the amount of euphemism and jargon used, I quickly realised that I needed more knowledge to get anywhere.

That really left me with the option of going back to where I had seen them and asking a straight question. Unfortunately, this was easier said than done. First of all, when it came to the crunch I didn't know if I'd have the guts to walk up to them and ask if I could join in their fun. That was assuming I could find them again. Actually, given the condition of the stables and the sheer complexity of their sex play, it seemed fair to assume that they did it on a fairly regular basis.

I spent most of the week thinking about it and then drove down to Wiltshire again on the Saturday. As I pulled into the car park of the King Billy, I was already feeling nervous. Rationally, I kept telling myself, all I had to do was wait outside the gate of the old park and speak to them when they arrived or left. The worst thing that could happen would be that they told me to get lost. Emotionally, it was a very different matter. The idea of accosting a couple of complete strangers and attempting to butt into their sex life filled me with a feeling of social impropriety so strong that it gave me butterflies in my stomach. Also, there was the chance that I would waste my day sitting around by the park gates and that they wouldn't turn up.

I decided that a spot of Dutch courage would help and ordered brandy in the pub, instead of my customary glass of cider. The day was even hotter than it had been the previous weekend, but with enough breeze to make the trees shiver. As I sat in a window seat and tried to get up enough courage, a gust caught the skirt of a girl in the car park. I caught a brief glimpse of pale-blue panties and found myself smiling as she hastily smoothed the material down and glanced around her.

For some reason, the incident made me feel braver, and also more inventive. As I ordered my second brandy, a new line of enquiry occurred to me. The barman was a big, bearded man of about sixty with the look of someone who knew everything that had happened locally for the last half-century. He was also garrulous and clearly disposed to chat to me.

'Have you lived in this area long, then?' I asked with all the insouciance I could muster.

'All my life,' he replied with evident pride.

'It's very beautiful,' I continued. 'I come out here to walk quite often. It would be great to live here, but I expect all the best houses have belonged to local families for generations.'

'Some,' he agreed, 'but there've been more newcomers recently.'

'I passed a wonderful-looking estate near here, the other day,' I said. 'By the footpath that runs up to the plain. Dense woods, no neighbours at all and it shows a lake on the map. I'd love to live somewhere like that. Do you know it?'

'That would be the old Linslade place,' he answered, his voice carrying a hint of confidentiality. 'Nobody lives there now. The house burnt down. In around sixty-eight, if memory serves me right. Old man Linslade was too mean to insure it properly and couldn't afford to rebuild it.'

'Who owns it now, then?'

'His son, Arthur, but he lives at the farm out along Broadheath way.'

'Oh right, that's sad. I suppose it goes to show that things aren't always as idyllic as they seem. It's a nice walk that way, anyway.'

‘That it is,’ he replied and turned to serve another customer.

I walked back to my seat feeling thoroughly pleased with myself. The man I had seen had been thirty or so, which might fit the age of Arthur Linslade. A quick browse through the local phone book and I had the address of the farm, which was no more than four miles away.

With the brandy nestling warmly in my tummy and adding greatly to my confidence, I set off towards Broadheath, turning onto a convenient footpath after a mile of country lane. As I walked, the delicious feeling of naughtiness that I had had the previous week began to return. The route I was on was pretty lonely and I kept remembering now nice it had felt to stretch naked in the warm air and bathe in the stream without a stitch on. It also occurred to me that if I was going to succeed in my venture it would help to look as attractive as possible.

Attractive, yes, but also harmless, as it wouldn’t do to antagonise the girl by appearing to be a threat. Fortunately, being five foot three, lightly built and with my hair cut in a practical bob, looking unthreatening is something I am naturally good at. Besides, I’m always being told I have an innocent face, even if it generally is by men who are hoping to see it wrapped around their cocks.

I stopped and considered how I could best rearrange my clothing to best advantage. The obvious step was to take my bra off and stuff it into my rucksack, leaving my nipples just discernible through the cotton of my blouse. I then undid all the buttons and knotted the loose ends between my breasts, hopefully showing them off nicely and also leaving my midriff bare. Nothing else seemed practical, given that my jeans were already tight over my bottom and slightly caught between the lips of my pussy.

I carried on walking, presently passing a group of young male hikers and noting with satisfaction that every one of them turned his eyes surreptitiously towards me. I resisted the temptation to look back when they had passed, but as I turned a corner I caught a comment that I suppose was complimentary if unexpectedly rude.

The path passed through a long stretch of scrubby woodland, punctuated with small fields. The heat of the day was still building and that and the alcohol were beginning to make me feel drowsy when I came out onto a ridge that looked down on a farm. Beyond it, the more open chalk downland rose in a steep scarp, and I realised that this had to be the Linslade farm. The footpath joined the farm track and I turned towards the buildings, determined not to back out now that I had come this far.

There was nobody visible, just an ancient dog lazing in the sun. It didn't even bother to bark as I approached, merely opening one eye and watching me with a minimum of interest. I crossed the yard and knocked boldly at the front door, standing back with a lump in my throat. There were noises from inside and then the door opened, revealing a heavy-set man with a brush of dirty blonde hair and a ruddy complexion, about as different from the man I had expected as it was possible to be.

'Yes?' he asked, with a hint of irritation that utterly deflated my expectations. Still, it was too late to back out now.

'Are you Arthur Linslade?' I asked.

'Yes,' he repeated, no more friendly than the first time.

'I'm sorry,' I continued, feeling completely ridiculous. 'I think there's been a mistake.'

'What do you want?' he demanded. Another man appeared behind him, younger and taller but also definitely not who I had been expecting.

'I'm sorry,' I said again, searching desperately for something to say and feeling incredibly self-conscious. I hesitated for a moment, both men looking at me as if viewing a particularly stupid child, then inspiration struck me.

'You don't own a red Rover 800, do you?' I asked. 'Only I accidentally knocked into one the other day in the car park at the King Billy and someone told me it belonged to you. The guy left before I could get a chance to speak to him, but he was tall and had dark hair, so I must have got it wrong.'

My impromptu story was pretty garbled, but it seemed to make sense to them as Arthur Linslade turned to the younger man and spoke.

'That'd maybe be Michael's car?' he suggested.

'Sounds like it,' the other replied. 'He didn't say anything about a knock.'

'It was only a nudge,' I said, 'but a bit of paint came off so I thought I'd better speak to him.'

'He lives down in Broadheath,' Arthur Linslade said, now more friendly. 'He's in Swindon, today. Perhaps you could leave a name and number.'

I complied, not really having a great deal of option and reasoning that I might eventually get to speak to him.

'Is he a relative?' I asked when I had dictated my name and number to them.

'Our brother-in-law,' the younger man told me.

I thanked them and left, feeling thoroughly embarrassed as I walked away up the track. I knew they were looking at me and felt intensely self-conscious, not daring to turn round until I had reached the shelter of the woods. When I did, there was no sign of Arthur Linslade. The younger man, who I took to be his brother, was walking down the track with an armload of wooden stakes.

Feeling rather muddled, slightly drunk and in need of

sorting my thoughts out, I left the path and went a little way into the wood, then sat down on the trunk of a fallen beech. On reflection, it didn't seem likely that the man called Michael would ring me. After all, there was no damage to his car. In fact, I had no reason to think his car had been in the pub car park, except that it would have been the best place for them to have had a drink before going up to the old park. I did feel quite pleased with myself for having had the guts to ask and knew that if I could do that, then I could probably ask Michael about his erotic sport if I ever managed to find him.

The copse I was in was rather like the place where I had dried off after my little bit of nude bathing the previous week. Dappled sunlight came through the canopy and a thick understory sheltered the clearing left by the great beech. The buzz of insects and the occasional distant bleat of a sheep on the slope up to the downs were the only sounds, creating a drowsy atmosphere. I tilted my head back and closed my eyes, looking at the pattern of orange and red where the bright sunlight came through my eyelids. I exhaled slowly, enjoying the gentle warmth of the air on my skin, spoilt only by the less comfortable sensation where my clothing covered me.

The temptation to strip off and sit nude in the sunlight was considerable, especially when I had done it the week before and got away with it. In fact I had got away with a lot more, masturbating to orgasm in my private place, virtually nude and with the small maize cob up my bottom. The thought of what I had done sent a deliciously naughty thrill through me and I began to wonder if I could repeat the experience. There seemed little chance that anyone from the farm would come my way, but I was too close to it to feel really comfortable. I took out my map and began to study it, feeling thoroughly dirty as I searched for what might prove a safe place to strip and play with myself.

The area I was in was a maze of little fields and woods running along the base of the downs. A river and a railway cut through it, creating a long thin piece of no-man's-land which looked promising. To get to it, I would need to run across a railway bridge; but that meant that, once I was on the other side, the chances of being disturbed would be close to zero.

Ten minutes later, I was scrambling down the railway embankment into the shelter of a stand of willow. The ground was boggy and the shelter less good than I had hoped, but I persevered, moving along between the tracks and the river in the hope of finding somewhere better.

I didn't have to go very far. After not more than a hundred yards, I came across a brick shed at the base of the railway embankment. It looked like it had been built as something to do with the railway but it had obviously been out of use for a long time. Behind it was a pile of old sleepers, high enough to form a convenient seat and completely sheltered from all angles. It was perfect, the very realisation of which increased my excitement. Despite this, I felt the same pang of guilt and uncertainty that I had before. Could I really be so dirty? Was the place really as secure from intrusion as it seemed? I climbed to the top of the sleepers, looking around and straining my ears for any sound, one hand already on the knot that held my blouse closed over my breasts.

There was neither sound nor sight to cause me concern and I realised that I really was going to do it again. In fact, I knew I couldn't help it; the memory of how much I had enjoyed it before made it an urgent need. This time, I would strip first and enjoy being nude for a while, before starting to masturbate.

I was tugging at the knot as I climbed down. It came open and the blouse fell aside, baring my breasts to the warm air. My nipples were already hard as I took a small breast in each hand and began to caress them, the firm little mounds of dark red flesh peeping through my fingers as I squeezed. It felt wonderful, more so when I had shrugged my blouse off and the daring feeling of being topless in the open was added to the physical sensation.

I undid my laces and kicked my walking boots off; my socks followed and then my jeans, leaving me standing in just my panties. I folded my discarded clothes neatly, making a pile on top of the sleepers, forcing myself to take it slowly and not rush. There was plenty of time to work myself up before getting down to the messy bit. I decided to keep my pants on for a while, knowing that doing so would enhance the thrill when it finally came to exposing my pussy and bum.

I sat down on the sleepers, relishing the feeling of being nearly naked and occasionally stroking a nipple or the front of my panties. Stretching luxuriantly in the warm sunlight, I decided not to take off my pants until the next train passed. When it did, then I would have to, creating a new sense of anticipation and irresponsibility. As I waited, a fantasy began to form in my mind. I imagined I'd been hired to strip for some sort of railwayman's do. Afterwards I'd been persuaded to come back to their hut for a private performance and was now waiting outside in nothing but a pair of over-tight white panties. They'd soon be coming outside, one by one, for promised blow-jobs. One by one, their cocks stiff in my mouth, then coming in it . . .

One hand was on a nipple, the other pushing the damp cotton of my panties in between my pussy lips. I desperately wanted to pull down my pants and finish off, but was determined to wait for the train.

In my mind the first railwayman had me on my knees in front of him and was holding me by the hair, guiding my mouth to the enormous erection sprouting from his trousers. I took his shaft in one hand, my fingers not quite meeting around it, starting to tug at him as my mouth opened expectantly . . .

A sharp crack brought me instantly to my senses. There was the unmistakable sound of a footstep on gravel from the far side of the shed. I grabbed at my clothes, but only succeeded in knocking them down the far side of the pile of sleepers. Panicking, I threw myself flat against the shed wall, praying that whoever it was would carry on past and knowing damn well that they wouldn't.

There was a pause and then the younger Linslade brother appeared around the corner of the shed. I froze, covering myself as best I could and feeling utterly ashamed and embarrassed. Fear quickly supplanted that feeling. He was a big, powerful man and had caught me next to naked in a really remote place.

Hc shrugged, spreading his hands in a gesture that conveyed more sympathy than anything and giving me a lopsided grin that was anything but threatening. I relaxed a bit and tried to return his smile, acknowledging that the embarrassment of the situation was not only on my side.

'I'm sorry,' he began, after a moment's silence. 'I didn't realise . . .'

'Could you pass me my clothes, please?' I asked.

'Yeah, of course,' he managed, grabbing up the garments from the ground and passing them to me. 'Um . . . Sorry, I did want to talk to you, though.'

'Right, er . . . could you go away while I dress?' I replied, managing at least a touch of assertiveness now that I was sure he had no intention of interfering with me.

'Yeah, sure,' he said, disappearing behind the shed, his voice then continuing from the far side of it. 'I'm really sorry; I just thought you wanted a walk where you could get a bit of peace. I needed to talk to you, so I followed.'

'What did you want?' I asked as I pulled my jeans on and felt at least some of my embarrassment go.

'You were looking for Michael . . .' he began rather slowly, as if testing the water.

'Yes,' I replied cautiously.

'You say you saw him last weekend?' he asked.

'Yes,' I repeated as I began to do up the buttons on my blouse.

'Was he with a woman?' he continued. 'Quite tall, honey-coloured hair, in her mid-twenties.'

'Yes,' I admitted, continuing with my buttons as I realised where his questions were leading. Evidently he was sounding me out, and presumably he was wondering if I'd seen Michael and the woman in the park. I felt a thrill of excitement. Surely that had to be what he was getting at?

'That was my sister, Virginia,' he was saying. 'I'm Matthew, by the way, Matthew Linslade. Look, it's hard to know how to put this, but let's say that we both know that Michael and Ginny weren't at the King Billy.'

His tone was eager but uncertain, the same tone men use when they're about to ask for some sexual favour but feel guilty about it and aren't sure if you'll agree.

'That's true,' I admitted. 'I'm called Penny; hi.'

I'd heard the same tone many times before: "Would you let me come in your mouth?", "Can I put it up your bottom?", "Can I tie you up?". He knew full well what I'd seen.

'You can come round now; I'm decent,' I added as I straightened my blouse.

'And I'm sure you didn't scratch their car,' he said as he came back to where I was. Now there was a new tone to his voice, as if he'd caught me out – which he had.

'No,' I said, unable to prevent myself blushing as he looked at me and smiled.

'So, Penny, why did you want to find him?' he asked.

My cheeks flushed hotly and I found myself looking

down at the ground. I'd already been caught by him in just my knickers and he must have guessed I'd been playing with myself. Now I was going to have to admit to him that I'd been peeping at his sister and brother-in-law. My main feeling was of utter abashment, but there was a lump of excitement in my throat that went with it.

'I . . . I wanted to find out more about what they were doing,' I stammered.

'And what were they doing?' he asked in an amused tone.

'You know full well, don't you?' I asked, unwilling to be further manipulated into humiliating myself by describing what I had seen.

'Yes, but tell me anyway,' he insisted.

'You'd like that, wouldn't you?' I retorted, giving him a dose of his own medicine.

'Did you want to do it yourself?' he asked, dropping his attempt to make me put it in words and reverting to his hopeful "I'd like to do something rude with you" tone.

I nodded, the knot of sexual tension tight in my stomach.

'Would you . . . with me? Be my pony-girl?' he asked, now really hesitant.

I nodded again, looking up at him. The word 'pony-girl' doubled my excitement, putting a name to my fantasy. It was a beautiful way of putting it. I found myself thinking of what could now be reality. I'd be stripped, put in harness, a plug shoved rudely up my bottom, tied to a cart, my bare cheeks smacked with a riding whip, used as a pony-girl . . .

I could see that he was excited, too, partially by the tension in his body but mainly by the bulge in the front of his trousers.

'I . . .' he began and then swallowed hard. I knew exactly what he wanted. Me, on the spot.

He took a step forward and I lifted my face to accept

his kiss. His arms went around me, one hand stroking the nape of my neck and the other in the small of my back. I responded eagerly, feeling the swell of his cock pushing against my belly. My hand went between our bodies and squeezed his shaft through his trousers, searching for his zip as he cupped my bottom.

His other hand had moved down from my neck and began to fumble for my bra catch, clumsily in his eagerness to get at my breasts. Suddenly it went and he was pulling my top up, exposing me even as I freed his cock from his trousers. I pulled back a little, wanting to see the lovely thick cock I was holding in my hand. It was fully erect, looking fit to burst as I pulled up and down on the loose skin of the shaft.

He sighed and I let go as he moved back to sit down on the sleepers, his legs apart and his cock sticking up like a flagpole. Typical, I thought; he wants it sucked while all I've had is my tits and bum felt. Then, when he'd come in my mouth and I'd swallowed it for him, he'd get bored and I'd have to do without my own fun.

I was wrong. Instead of making the expected hopeful gesture towards his cock, he took my hand and began to pull me towards him.

'Hey!' I protested as I felt myself drawn down, not into his arms but over his lap.

'I'd like to spank you, Penny,' he breathed, pulling me across his knee and wrapping an arm around my waist so that I was held helplessly in place with my bum stuck up in the air. It felt wonderful. I was going to be spanked across his lap, bum up high, little tits dangling bare beneath me and his cock pressed against me to remind me of what I was going to get afterwards.

'What for?' I squeaked in a deliberately pathetic voice, glad that he wanted to give my bottom some attention before coming.

'Trespassing,' he said, planting a firm smack on the seat of my jeans. It was hard and made me squeak.

'Peeping,' he added, giving me a second smack on the fullest part of my bottom and again making me cry out.

'Playing with yourself,' he continued, the third smack landing where my bum cheeks met my thighs and shoving against my pussy from the rear.

'I suppose you'll want to take down my trousers, then?' I asked hopefully, after I had caught my breath.

'I suppose I'll have to,' he agreed, his hand already groping at my belt buckle, 'and your knickers too, I'm afraid.'

'Please, sir, no, not my panties, not on the bare bottom!' I joked, just to make sure that he knew it was exactly what I wanted him to do.

He laughed and I relaxed over his lap, lifting my hips obligingly to let him expose my bottom for its spanking. I closed my eyes, relishing the feeling of my jeans being eased down over my bum, the denim tickling my buttocks and then the backs of my thighs as he pulled them well down and arranged them around my knees. He spent a moment caressing my bottom, his hand squeezing my cheeks and stroking the seat of my pants. Then his thumbs were in the waistband and my pants were coming down, filling me with the delicious sense of erotic shame that always comes with being prepared for a spanking. As they slid down over my bum, the air felt cool on my freshly smacked cheeks. I knew my bottom would already be rosy pink and hoped that it would soon be very red indeed.

He settled my pants around my thighs, far enough down so that I could feel the air on my pussy lips and knew they'd be showing from behind. I braced myself for my spanking, but he had decided to have a good feel before punishing me. First he took hold of my buttocks and pulled them open, redoubling my sense of shame as I knew he'd be examining my bottom hole. He made a leisurely inspection, treating me with outrageous intimacy, considering that we'd only just met. I was too turned on to care, instead shivering as his finger tips traced a slow line between the cheeks of my bum. He was obviously either unaware or indifferent to the liberties he was taking with me. I felt a finger touch my anus, then invade it, working slowly up my bottom.

'Hey!' I protested half-heartedly, torn between telling him not to be so rude and asking to have his finger replaced with his cock once he'd given me a good spanking.

That was what he had been waiting for. His finger was pulled sharply out of my bum and, the next instant, a heavy smack landed across my bare cheeks. The arm around my waist locked tight as the second smack fell. These were hard, knocking the breath out of me and making me squeal. A third fell and then he set to work, spanking me in earnest. In a moment my bottom was on fire and I was kicking and wriggling over his knee. It went on for ages, and I was soon indifferent to the display I was making of myself but concerned only for the pain in my bottom and the fact that I was helpless and being thoroughly beaten.

Finally he stopped, leaving me sobbing and limp over his knee. My bottom was a ball of fire, bare, stuck high in the air and throbbing with pain. I was breathing heavily, well and truly spanked and so turned on that I knew a few deft touches to my clit would be all that was needed to bring me to orgasm.

He lifted me and turned, setting me gently down where he had been sitting. The concrete of the sleeper felt hard against my smarting bottom. He stood in front of me, his cock sticking up, inches in front of my face. I grabbed it and began to suck, my mouth filling with the salty male taste as I opened my legs and my free hand found my pussy, delving between the lips for my clit. I was swollen and wet, on the very edge of orgasm, tugging frantically at his cock in an effort to get a mouthful of sperm at the exact instant I hit my peak. I was rubbing hard at my clit, wishing his cock could be in my mouth, my pussy and up my bum at the same time. My mind went to the way he'd spanked me: hard, bare-bottomed, over his knee with my pussy and bum-hole showing. That was too much for me and suddenly I was coming.

It was a moment too early. I felt my muscles contract as I went into orgasm, my thighs closing and locking around my hand. I sucked hard on the ridged pole of flesh in my mouth as I came, only to have him take me gently by the hair and pull half-way out and begin to masturbate furiously into my mouth as my orgasm subsided. I managed a muffled squeak and then his cock started to spasm and my mouth was filling with his come.

He groaned, pushing his cock well in and holding it there until he was finished. I swallowed, but too late, his last thrust forced a good measure of sperm out around his cock to dribble down my chin and splash on my blouse.

He was apologising even as he took his cock out of my mouth, then asked me if he had spanked me too hard.

'Slow down,' I managed, trying to get my breath back. 'It was fine, don't worry.'

'Are you sure?' he insisted, showing that sudden post-coital concern that is so common in men who like to dominate when they have sex.

'Fine, really,' I assured him. 'Lovely, in fact. I've never been spanked so hard. You're really strong.'

I stood up and rubbed at my bottom, unable to avoid a grimace at the soreness now that I'd had my orgasm. It would be sore for a week, but that was well worth it.

'You've been spanked before, then?' he asked, sounding slightly disappointed.

'A few times,' I admitted, turning to show him my red bum. 'I like it, but a lot of men won't do it. I can see even you feel a bit guilty.'

'Yeah,' he admitted. 'Thanks, anyway; that was great. Your poor bottom!'

I shrugged and smiled, starting to tidy myself up as he made the last rearrangements to his clothing. Now that the heat of passion was past, he seemed shyer and less certain of himself, as if he couldn't quite accept that what had happened had been what I wanted as well. Nothing was said for a period, while I did my best to make myself look presentable.

'So can I see you again?' he finally asked.

'Sure; I'm going to be your pony-girl, aren't I?' I replied.

'Yeah,' he said, 'if you're sure you want to be.'

'Come on,' I laughed. 'I drove all the way out here, took the trouble to find your farm, embarrassed myself in front of your brother and shared the most wonderful sex with you. Of course I want to be a pony-girl.'

'Great,' he said, looking as if he couldn't believe his luck. 'Arthur doesn't know about Michael and Ginny. It's all a bit delicate. He's a lot older than Ginny and I, and a bit straight-laced. It's actually Ginny who owns the park where they go. Dad left it to her and the farm to Arthur and me. Would you like to meet there, next weekend?'

I readily agreed and we walked back as far as the footpath together, chatting with an intimacy that would normally take weeks to build up but which seemed completely natural.

Three

I spent the whole of the following week with butterflies in my stomach. It was like being a teenager again; waiting for Saturday night after making an important date. Also reminiscent of my teenage years was the worry over what I should wear when Saturday morning finally arrived. Unlike teenage dates, though, I was definitely going to end up undressing. From the point of view of practicality, a short dress with neither bra nor knickers underneath would have been best. It didn't give me enough opportunity to show off, though, and I ended up in lacy black underwear with a light summer skirt and a cotton blouse.

Outside, the day was warm and sultry, even at nine o'clock in the morning, so I stopped at a service station and stocked up on water and sun cream. The drive to Wiltshire seemed to take twice as long as normal, but I eventually found myself at the turning I needed. GATED ROAD – PRIVATE said a large sign, followed by some information about public access. I drove through, presently reaching the first gate.

As I shut it behind me, I felt a strengthening of the sense of detachment that had been building ever since I had left the service station. Ahead, the ground rose in a broad sweep of grass, parched by the sun to a dun colour. Beyond that the tops of trees were visible, trees that stood in the Linslade's park. I drove on and, a few minutes later, I was pulling up in front of the gates I had climbed only two short weeks before. They were padlocked, as before.

I stopped the car and got out. There was no sign that anybody else had been there, but with the ground packed hard after two weeks without rain, it was hard to tell. On the far side of the gate was an envelope pinned to a stake. By peering through the bars, I could just make out the word 'Penny' written on it. I was about to climb the gate when I realised that the padlock might not actually be holding the gate shut. It wasn't, allowing me to unwrap the chain and drive through. Once parked on the inside, I took the envelope, wondering why Matthew hadn't simply met me at the gate. Inside was a padlock key and a lengthy note.

'Dear Penny,' – it began. 'Please lock the gate behind you. If you want to drive in and meet me at the stable yard, that's fine. I would prefer you to follow the instructions underneath.'

I glanced quickly down the page to see what was expected of me. The idea seemed to be to get the most out of the fantasy and I decided to play along. The first instruction was simple: strip.

The idea certainly worked; even while I was locking the gate properly I was beginning to feel the exciting combination of apprehension and urgency produced by undressing where I might be seen. Once the gate was shut, I stood by my car for a while, listening to the sounds of the wood and wondering if Matthew was watching me from some concealed place. It seemed likely. In fact, I was sure I'd seen a movement among the dense rhododendron bushes that lined the drive. For a moment, I considered undressing in the old lodge, thus depriving him of the pleasure of watching and probably earning me a spanking.

As it seemed unlikely that I would get to the end of the day without a smacked bottom anyway, I decided to pretend innocence instead and began to undress with exaggerated shyness. I took my skirt off first, undoing the buttons and stepping out of it hurriedly as if being seen stripping were more embarrassing than being seen stripped. I knew this left my black knickers showing under the tail of my blouse, and so made a big deal of folding the skirt and putting it in the car, taking care to bend right over as I did so, with my bum stuck out towards the place I thought he was most likely to be. I stayed in position while I took off my shoes, imagining his eyes feasting on the scrap of black lace that was all that covered my bottom. My blouse followed, each button undone gingerly, then pulled open and quickly shrugged off to join my skirt. I went to check that nobody was visible through the gate before taking off my bra, part for show and part just in case some farm-hand or walker was about to get an eyeful of my breasts.

They weren't, so I unsnipped the catch and held the cups on for a moment before dropping them to bare my titties to the wood and, hopefully, to Matthew Linslade. I resisted the temptation to play with my nipples as it would have completely destroyed any pretence of shyness. Instead, I put the bra with my other clothes and hooked my thumbs into the waistband of my panties, turning my back to where I thought Matthew was, easing them slowly down my legs and kicking them off to stand naked in the sunlight. The sun felt hot on my bare skin and I realised that not only was a good coating of sunblock necessary, but putting it on would give me more opportunity to show off to Matthew.

I spent a good ten minutes creaming myself, concentrating on my breasts and bum for his benefit but making sure I got a good even coating as well. By the time I was finished, I was thoroughly turned on, with my nipples sticking out and glistening with cream while my pussy felt wet and ready. I locked the car and hid the key, then took the note and strode boldly down the drive, stark naked and ready to become a pony-girl.

When I was some way past the clump of rhododendrons in which I suspected Matthew to be concealed, I heard a rustle behind me, confirming my suspicions. I smiled to myself and wondered how long he'd be able to hold out before having full sex with me. The next instruction in the note told me to walk down the drive until I found a table and put on whatever had been laid out for me. Given that Ginny Scott had been nude except for her boots and harness, I wasn't quite sure what to expect. Certainly a harness – the very idea of which sent a new thrill through me – but possibly also a few touches to suit whatever Matthew's own preferences were.

The table stood in the curve of the drive, a small trestle set with complicated-looking pieces of black leather, plenty of yellow ribbons and a pair of boots like the ones I had seen Ginny Scott wearing. I studied the pieces in an effort to work out how to put them on, aware that I was being watched and not wanting to make a fool of myself. The note gave instructions but, as I didn't understand the terminology these were less than helpful.

The bridle at least was fairly obvious, a leather bit running between two brass rings with several straps and buckles attached. I picked it up, trying to remember how Ginny Scott had worn hers. I wondered if it was actually her harness. It was clean but looked worn and obviously wasn't new. She was a lot taller than me and more curvy, making me wonder if it would fit. If they were her things, then the only item obviously missing was the tail, which set me to thinking how sweet it had looked, waving behind her as she trotted.

At that moment, there was a sound behind me and I turned, expecting to find Matthew. Instead there was the person I had been thinking about a moment before, Ginny Scott. My first reaction was annoyance that Matthew had told his sister what we were planning to do; I hastily covered my breasts and opened my mouth to say something.

Even as I started to speak, it occurred to me that I was being completely unfair. I had been peeping at her, and Matthew must have told her about it. He'd probably also told her that he'd spanked me for it, which turned my anger into embarrassment and I found myself blushing furiously. She smiled and held out her hand in greeting. I took it, only to be drawn forward and kissed.

'Hi,' she said, stepping back again. 'I'm Ginny Scott.'

'Penny Birch,' I responded, still unsure how to take her or why she was there. 'I was expecting Matthew.'

'He'll be along soon enough,' she answered, still smiling as she went to the table and picked up the largest piece of leather. 'I volunteered to help you with the tack.'

'Thanks, I . . . er . . .' I began, unsure how I felt about being done up as a pony-girl by another woman, even one I knew was into it herself. It would have been easier if she'd been in the nude too, or in a riding outfit or something, but she was dressed in cream slacks and a loose blouse which made her look completely mundane.

'Don't be shy,' she said brightly. 'After all, you've seen me in harness, haven't you?'

'Yes,' I admitted.

'And with my tail in,' she continued.

'Yes,' I said, accepting the situation. After all, she was obviously quite at home joining in and it seemed prissy to object; especially when I was the one in the nude. I wondered just how much she knew. She and her brother were obviously close enough to share the secrets of her and her husband's sexual preferences, and I'd told Matthew everything, even how I'd masturbated after seeing Ginny and Michael. I found myself blushing again at the thought but realised that the reason she was so at ease was probably that she was as bad as I was.

'I'm sorry there's no tail for you,' she remarked, adjusting a set of brass pins and eyelets with a glance at my waist. 'They take about a month to order and we'd need to match your hair, anyway. What's your waist, about twenty-four?'

'Twenty-two,' I answered as she came towards me with the belt.

'This goes down to eighteen; I'll see if I can pull you in that far,' she said, wrapping the thick belt around me and slotting together another set of eyelets and pegs. 'Breathe in,' she ordered and tugged the lacing at the back of the belt closed, constricting my waist. 'Do you normally undress like that, by the way?'

'No!' I protested. 'I thought it was Matthew watching.'

'It was me,' she answered, sounding thoroughly pleased with herself. 'So we're even, now. I liked the bit with the sun cream; he'll be sorry to have missed that.'

I was too embarrassed to reply, but stood quietly while she tied the laces and stepped back to admire her handiwork.

'There we are: eighteen inches,' she said. 'Lucky thing. You're in harness now, so no talking. We do have what we call a safety word, though. If things are getting a bit much say "Amber" and Matthew'll ease off; say "Red" and he'll stop immediately and take you out of harness. OK?'

'Got it,' I replied.

'I said, no talking,' she snapped in mock annoyance and gave me a gentle but familiar smack on my bottom. 'Whoever heard of a talking pony?'

I shut up and stood obediently while she fixed the harness on to me. The main piece consisted of the waist belt and straps that went over my shoulders to a brass ring, just below my breasts. A thin black rope hung from this, which I vaguely remembered as attaching to eyes on the ends of the cart's shafts. Wrist-cuffs followed, which she snapped together behind my back to make me helpless. The bridle followed, the bit going in my mouth and the straps enfolding my head with the long leather rein hanging down my back and tickling the bare skin of my buttocks. The ribbons went into my hair, Ginny tying four in bows down the back of my head; my hair stuck out from the hair rings in little tufts. The boots completed my outfit, leaving me standing helpless and feeling more turned on than I ever had in my life.

Ginny had stood back and was smiling at me, a wicked look in her eyes. Up until then, my experience of sex with other women had been confined to my fantasies and a couple of drunken fumbles at college. From the look in Ginny's eyes, I didn't think things were going to be staying that way for long.

'You look very pretty,' she was saying. 'Stamp once, if you may.'

I stamped without hesitation and saw her smile broaden to a grin as she reached out and touched one of my nipples. As her fingers closed on the little bud of flesh, a shiver went through me and I gulped involuntarily. She stroked, her eyes locked on mine as she explored my breasts. Long fingernails traced lines across my skin, too gently to mark. She tweaked each nipple and then began to trace a slow line down the centre of my tummy, crossing the harness to touch my belly-button. I shivered again as she reached my pubic hair, then squeaked out loud as her finger burrowed in between my pussy lips and found my clit, rubbing gently. It wouldn't have taken much to make me come, and I was pushing my hips out for it, but she withdrew, stepping back to leave me in an agony of wanting.

'We mustn't spoil it for the boys, must we?' she taunted and then popped her finger into her mouth and made a great show of sucking my juice off it. 'Now, run along to the stable yard and we'll get you hitched up.'

Walking down the drive to the stable yard, I began to realise just how strong the experience of being a pony-girl was. I'm still not sure why, but it's a far more intense experience than the other exotic sexual practices that I've tried. Maybe it's because it combines so many things that are normally separate: bondage, control, physical punishment, exhibitionism, leather, heels . . . It really doesn't leave much out. In any case, by the time I reached the stable yard I was well into my role and ready for just about anything.

The last instruction on the note had been to attach my reins to a hitching ring and wait. This was impossible with my hands fastened behind my back and I supposed that that had been an addition of Ginny's. I found the hitching ring and stood next to it, waiting as ordered. It was hot, my position leaving me in the full sun. As I stood waiting to be used, the last thing Ginny had said came back to me. 'The boys,' she had said, quite distinctly. Presumably that meant that Michael was around as well as Matthew. That didn't altogether surprise me; and, after all, it had been Michael Scott who had first attracted me. Could she mean more than just Matthew and Michael? I began to wonder just how many people were going to have the use of my body that day. Was I going to be pawed by half a dozen farm-hands? Made to perform in front of a crowd? The idea was rather more than I had expected but intensely exciting. I was already wondering how much truth there was in stories about girls taking an entire gang of bikers or something, one after the other, when Matthew and Michael walked into the yard.

Both were in full riding gear: shiny black boots, jodhpurs, hard hats, white shirts and scarlet jackets, these last thrown across their shoulders in the heat of the day. Each also carried a riding whip, Michael's the black length of plaited leather he had used before, and Matthew's an elegant bone-handled affair. Matthew was drawing the cart and set it standing in the very centre of the yard. To my mingled relief and disappointment, nobody else appeared, but neither of the men paid me the slightest attention.

Instead they stood and chatted, discussing the state of the tack and whether it would be pleasant to bathe in the lake after they had driven me. Their casual indifference to my presence was beginning to annoy me when I realised that they were behaving exactly as they should. After all, I was there as a pony-girl for their use; why should they worry what I thought?

I stamped and shook my head to draw their attention, at which Matthew turned and began to walk over to me. He stood over me, looking straight into my eyes and then reaching out to stroke my cheek. I shivered and he smiled, taking my reins and turning to walk back towards Michael, the reins slung casually over his shoulder. I walked behind, relishing the feeling of complete subjection to him.

'What do you think?' he asked Michael as we reached the cart.

'Hmm,' Michael replied, walking forward and giving me an appraising glance. 'Pretty, definitely pretty. Small, of course, I don't imagine she has much pulling power.'

He had walked around me and, the next moment, I felt a large, male hand cup one of my buttocks and begin to fondle, quite casually.

'I don't know, she has quite a muscular little behind,' he continued. 'Yes, better for shows than races, I dare say, but not bad . . . not bad.'

He finished his exploration of my bottom with a firm smack that made me start, spent a moment idly stroking one of my breasts, and then stood back.

'We'll see how she does on the circuit, shall we?' Matthew said. 'I think you'll be surprised.'

Michael nodded and took my reins from Matthew,

leading me over and placing me between the shafts of the cart. Matthew unfastened my wrists and attached each strap to the steel eye at the tip of the shaft, allowing me to take hold of the leather grips that covered the last six inches or so of each shaft. Michael completed my harnessing by running the rope from my ring to the shaft eyes and then stood back, admiring me with that cool detached arrogance that had so excited me in the first place.

'Kneel,' Matthew said.

I was a fraction slow to realise that he was ordering me and the tip of his whip caught the left cheek of my bum. It stung and I knelt hastily on the smooth cobbles of the yard.

'Moderate,' Michael remarked, from where he was leaning against the wall in the shade.

'Knees apart, bottom stuck out,' Matthew ordered tersely.

I obeyed, opening my legs and pulling my back in. Matthew adjusted my pose with gentle taps of the whip. This put me in a completely obscene position that left my cheeks parted and gave anyone behind me a fine view of my pussy and bum-hole.

'Better,' Michael commented with little apparent interest, but I noted that he had moved round to get a better view between my legs.

'Stay still,' Matthew said as he began to trace a line down my spine with the tip of his whip. I knew where the whip end was going, down between my buttocks. It touched my anus and I whimpered as he moved it up and down, then squeaked as he flicked the tip against my exposed pussy lips.

'Much better,' Michael said from behind me.

I wiggled my bottom, drawing a laugh from Michael and another smack from Matthew, this time across the fleshy part of my cheeks. It stung and I knew that it would have left a red line across the plumpest part of my bottom, making me wish I had a mirror.

I waited while Matthew stepped over the shafts. I responded to the order to rise fast enough to avoid any further punishment. I braced myself for the added strain as he lowered himself onto the seat but it made surprisingly little difference.

'Walk,' he ordered and I started forward, finding pulling the cart and his not inconsiderable weight a lot easier than I had expected. I felt the tug of the bit in my mouth and responded to it, allowing him to angle me towards the stable gates. I quickened my pace in response to an unexpected flick of the whip and crossed in front of the house at what I hoped was a smart trot. Ginny Scott was seated on the stone balustrade that flanked the carriage sweep. She clapped as I passed, laughing with pleasure at the sight of me pulling her cart.

Beyond the carriage sweep, the path crossed an area of long-neglected lawn and then entered the woods, all at a slight downhill incline which made the going easy. I passed the point where I had seen Ginny before, after which the track began to climb again. This was much harder and I was soon running with sweat. Matthew said nothing, using the reins on corners and occasionally applying the whip if I slowed. The smacks were fairly hard, if infrequent, and quickly began to smart, making me very aware of my naked bottom and my vulnerability to the whip.

I trotted on, paying attention to my surroundings but with my mind focused on my throbbing bottom. The experience was bliss, better even than it had been in my imagination. I felt completely controlled and completely without restraint, only wishing I had a tail plugged into my bottom to complete the sensation.

It was halfway through the second lap that Matthew ordered me to slow and steered me on to an area of soft grass in the shade of a vast oak. I came to rest facing the tree, panting, muscles burning, wet with sweat and very much on heat.

'Kneel,' he ordered and I sank to my knees, spreading my legs and thrusting out my bottom as I had been taught.

'Head to the ground,' he added and, as I obeyed, I found myself with my bottom the highest part of my body, feeling utterly vulnerable and helpless with my wrists strapped to the shafts. My breasts were touching the ground, the nipples rubbing against the grass, which produced an exquisite tickling sensation. My position left my bottom completely available, either for beating or rear entry. I imagined he'd probably want to whip me first and was waiting for the first stroke.

I could only see his boots from my position, but I heard the rasp of his zip and other noises as he prepared his cock. I realised that I was not going to get my anticipated punishment but was going to be entered without preamble. He was humming to himself, quite casually, as he stepped between the shafts and out of my vision. I expected to be immediately filled with his prick, but nothing happened and I found myself whimpering in anticipation. I could hear him behind me, his breathing heavy despite his pose of complete cool. I knew he'd be drinking in the details of my sex, probably stroking his erection so that it would be rock-solid when he chose to fill my vagina.

He put his hands on my sore bottom, moulding the cheeks and pulling them further open. His thumbs were on either side of my anus, stretching it open, and I wondered if he was about to bugger me. I braced myself, preparing to yell, 'Red,' if he didn't open me up properly first, but instead I felt his cock touch my pussy, nestling in the wet folds. One hand left my bottom and he began to rub himself against my clit. It was unbearably sensitive and I screamed and wriggled, only to have his hands go to my hips. He held me firmly, his cock prodding my pussy and searching for the opening. Then it was in, sliding up me in one easy motion and pulling out a little as he began to fuck me with slow, powerful strokes. His hips would smack against my bottom with each stroke, his balls banging on my vulva, the weight of each shove sending a shock through my entire body. His strokes began to quicken and I was soon panting, then gasping as he fucked me.

Despite the ecstasy of intercourse, my frustration at not being able to get at my clit was unbearable. I knew I'd never come without it being touched, but I was being held constantly on the edge of orgasm. He slowed his pace for a moment and I found myself begging him, my voice muffled through the bit. All I got for my pains was a hard smack on my bottom and a renewal of his pace. Once more, his hands locked hard on my hips and his front began to slam against my buttocks. He was grunting and I knew he was about to come. I stuck my bottom out as his cock exploded inside me, a final thrust knocking the breath out of me as he came.

Then he was pulling out and I was left kneeling on the ground, in absolute ecstasy, naked but for my harness, sodden with sweat and with my pussy gaping for attention. I squirmed my bottom, praying he'd put a finger to my clit and let me rub myself against him. He didn't, and I heard him laugh, presumably at the exhibition I was making of myself.

For a horrible moment, I thought he was going to leave me like that, but then I felt the delicious sensation of his tongue on my pussy as he buried his face between my legs and began to lick me. The muscular firmness of his tongue found my clit almost immediately and I began to squirm myself against his face, immediately feeling the first tingle of orgasm. It went right up my spine, exploding in my head and making me scream, then clench my teeth hard on the leather bit. Suddenly I could feel every bit of rope and leather that secured me in place, my limbs straining against them as I came again.

I'm not sure how long my orgasm lasted but, by the time I was finished, I had collapsed in a sobbing heap on the grass. I finally looked up to find Matthew standing beside me with a knowing grin on his face. He had tidied himself up and looked quite at ease, certainly infinitely more than I did. I managed to pull myself into a kneeling position but my legs felt too weak to rise and I was trembling with the after-effects of sex. My bottom was smarting and my pussy felt sore and sensitive. I also knew that there would be bruises on my hips where he had held me, but I didn't care; it would just be a nice reminder of what we had done.

'Would you like to come out of role?' he was saying, again showing the change in his manner that came after orgasm.

I nodded my head and then changed my mind, shaking it and indicating the direction of the stables with a nod.

'Lead me back, please,' I managed through the bit, drawing a big grin from Matthew.

He helped me to my feet and took the reins, giving my bum the gentlest of pats for speaking and then starting off towards the house. I was exhausted but determined not to come out of my role as a pony-girl until I'd had the full experience. Somehow, stopping just because I'd come seemed not to do justice to the fantasy. Matthew walked me slowly, the cart being easy to pull uphill now that it was empty.

We came into the stable yard to find Michael and Ginny waiting for us, leaning against their car and eating sandwiches. They clapped when I appeared and I saw Ginny run her eyes down my body. She looked up and smiled, obviously guessing what had happened from the dirt on my knees and chest.

Matthew greeted them and stopped, detaching my wrist cuffs and the rope to leave me standing in the centre of the yard. I waited while he filled a zinc bucket from a tap. I knew what was coming, but the bucketful of cold water thrown over me was still a shock. Three more followed, until I was dripping wet and standing in a pool of water.

'There we are, then,' Matthew said, the subtle change in his tone telling me that my experience was over.

'Hang on,' Ginny called and I looked over to see her digging in her handbag. She found something and walked over to me, pulling the bit from between my teeth and holding out her palm. There was a peppermint on it, a gesture I found at once sweet and deliciously humiliating. I nuzzled it up from her hand, Ginny smiling and stroking my wet hair as I sucked on the delicacy.

They waited until I had finished my peppermint and then undid my straps, grinning and laughing as I sank down in exhaustion.

'That was ... incredible,' I managed after a while. 'Thanks.'

'My pleasure,' Matthew answered, but it was Ginny who knelt down and hugged me, indifferent to her clothes getting wet.

They had fetched my own clothes from the drive and we talked while I dressed. They had set the day up to leave me with two options. If I had chosen to walk down to the stable yard fully dressed, then Michael and Ginny would have melted quietly into the woods and left Matthew to give me a less ritualised introduction to being a pony-girl. As it was, they had felt that the three of them being there was risking losing me but had taken the chance anyway.

The rest of the day was spent picnicking, swimming in the lake and discussing the fantasy. Michael put Ginny in harness late in the afternoon and took her for a drive around the park. She came back flushed and happy and had obviously been served much the same way as I had. I found myself envying her tail, which looked so beautiful, and also her strength, as she managed three laps with ease when one and a bit had had me close to dropping. I also couldn't help feeling that while Matthew was attractive, Michael was more so and was definitely the driving force among them. My feelings for Ginny were also disturbingly strong, as I had never felt myself so attracted to another woman. I considered asking to drive her but wasn't sure if it would be acceptable, so I left my feelings unvoiced. What I really wanted to do was have her kneel between the shafts as I had done, pull her tail aside and lick her pussy. Unfortunately, I didn't have the courage to ask.

I did ask if I might have my own tail and a set of tack like hers. They were pleased with my enthusiasm and agreed to take me to the saddler who made the tack. I asked how they'd managed to find a saddler prepared to make harness for a human and was told that it had actually worked the other way.

The saddler, apparently, was a woman called Amber Oakley. She had been at school with Ginny and they had stayed friends after leaving school. It was Amber's enthusiasm for pony-girls that had infected Ginny. Michael, on beginning to date someone he thought was a demure young Englishwoman, had been delighted to discover just how exotic her sexual tastes were. Matthew had always been close to his sister and had known about what she and Amber Oakley got up to long before Michael appeared. He had always been intrigued by the idea but unable to find a partner, hence his delight in meeting me and finally getting a chance to have his own pony-girl.

I left that evening with a warm glow inside me and a very sore bottom for the second week running.

Four

Visiting Amber Oakley wasn't a simple matter of turning up and selecting a few suitable pieces of pony-girl tack from a rack. During the week, she ran a perfectly ordinary shop in a village in the Hertfordshire green belt. A saddlery, it was true, but for real horses and with no hint of sexual behaviour. As we drove across the countryside on the Sunday morning, I learnt that she had a fair client base for her erotic sideline but that visits were by appointment only and invariably at weekends.

I had been expecting to spend the Saturday night in bed with Matthew. In my experience the first night of a relationship generally means sex with everything, breakfast included. I'd been rather surprised when he'd made his excuses and left to go back to the farm. The explanation for this was apparently that his brother was something of a tyrant and also a terrible moralist, which rather shattered my image of Matthew as the dominant male. I went back with the Scotts instead, spending a comfortable night in their cottage in the village.

Why Matthew couldn't have come and rogered me senseless at the Scotts' was beyond me. Michael and Ginny were good company and I was half-expecting an invitation into their bed, which I would have gladly accepted. It didn't come and I ended up playing with myself instead and even got a good night's sleep.

Matthew joined us again in the morning and my

slight annoyance was soon forgotten as the air of erotic expectation built up again on the drive. From the onset, I was the centre of attention. First, they teased me into taking my panties off under my skirt, then into pulling my skirt up so that my bum was bare on the seat. Ginny, in particular, seemed to enjoy having me make a display of myself and suggested that I ought to strip, only to have Michael point out that getting arrested on the way to Amber's wasn't going to make a good start to the day. I compromised by taking my skirt off completely and sitting there bare from the waist down.

I was in the back with Matthew and it didn't surprise me at all when, a few minutes later, he guided my hand to his fly. I gave him a look of mock surprise but drew his zip down. Ginny had turned back to the map and was busy helping Michael find his way around a new bypass. Matthew's cock was already half-stiff as I pulled it out, squeezing the thick shaft in my hand and then starting to pull up and down. It quickly became hard and I couldn't help smiling at the expression of bliss on his face as I stroked him to full erection.

We were in fairly heavy traffic and it was a great thrill to be half-naked and fondling Matthew while other people could see our top halves through the window. I checked around us to make sure there were no high-cabbed vehicles near us and then leant over, taking his cock in my mouth. He groaned and took me by the hair, attracting his sister's attention.

'Matthew!' I heard her exclaim.

'What are they doing?' Michael asked.

'The little tart's sucking him off!' Ginny answered, obviously delighted by what I was doing.

Michael laughed and a delicious thrill of humiliation went through me even as I promised myself that I would get even with Ginny. She seemed to take a particular pleasure in my exposure and immodest behaviour, and I didn't see why she should get away with being so cool and demure. I returned to my task of sucking Matthew off, ignoring Ginny's occasional taunting remark from the front seat.

'You two better hurry up,' Michael remarked after a while. 'We'll be going through a town in a few minutes.'

I began to suck harder and faster, holding the base of Matthew's cock tightly with one hand and squeezing his balls with the other. After less than a minute I felt his muscles tighten and was rewarded with a mouthful of come, which I dutifully swallowed. Looking up, I found buildings around us and a set of traffic lights ahead, on red and with several people milling about on the pavement.

Matthew managed to get his cock out of sight fast enough, but I was still struggling with my skirt when we stopped. A man on the pavement gazed at me non-committally through the window and then gave me a look of complete amazement as he caught sight of the puff of black pussy hair that I was trying to cover up. At his exclamation, his wife turned and gave me a look of utter disgust as I finally managed to cover myself.

The lights changed and I caught the single word 'slut' as we drove off. All three of my companions were laughing and I was blushing furiously as we drove down the main street of the little town. I stayed quiet, feeling extremely embarrassed and thoroughly turned on. Risking making an exhibition of myself in public had always appealed to me, but I'd never been brave enough to actually take a serious risk of getting caught. I'd also fantasised about flashing, but had never dared do more than sunbathe topless in a park, which was pretty much acceptable anyway.

The result of all this was that, by the time we pulled up outside Amber's saddlery, my pussy was soaking and I was seriously hoping that the process of getting my tack was going to involve plenty of physical attention to my body.

Amber Oakley surprised me. I knew she preferred other women to men and so had been expecting someone pretty butch. I'd like to think that I'm fairly immune to the popular image of lesbians as gargoyle-faced viragos with potato-sack bodies. Amber Oakley, though, looked like she'd stepped out of the pages of *Horse and Hound*. A little above average height, her face was pretty, cheerful and framed by tawny curls. Her figure looked compact and was indistinct beneath a loose cream jumper and a long skirt, but hinted at firmness and muscularity coupled with undoubtedly feminine chest and hips.

She greeted Ginny with a hug and shook hands with each of the men, only then turning her attention to me. Her first glance told me that she was keen on me and I found myself blushing slightly as she kissed me on each cheek. The feeling was mutual, and I found myself guiltily watching the swell of her bottom move under her skirt as she turned and went into the house.

'So,' she addressed me when we were settled around her kitchen table with coffee or glasses of beer, 'what would you like?'

'A set of tack,' I replied uncertainly, as I assumed that Matthew would already have told her what we needed. 'Like Ginny's . . . and a tail.'

'Tails take a bit of time, especially if you want the design that goes up your bottom,' she replied in a matter-of-fact voice. 'Do you?'

I hesitated before answering, rather taken aback by the completely casual way in which she was discussing something so intimate. 'Yes, please,' I managed after a moment, realising that my voice sounded quiet and shy and wishing I could be a bit more assertive.

'Good,' Amber replied, taking a sip of beer from her glass. 'I'll need to take a few measurements and I should have everything ready for you by next week. The tail will take a little longer, but I'll do it as fast as I can. If you just want a harness like Ginny's, that's great, but there are other options and lots of extra bits and pieces.'

'Like what?' I asked.

'Blinkers, martingales, hobbles, saddles . . . lots, really. I can show you, if you like?'

'Good idea,' Ginny put in before I could answer.

Amber swallowed the last of her beer and we followed her out of the kitchen. Behind her house was an area of concrete and a large red brick building with big double doors and a smaller door at the end. Across the yard, a thick hedge blocked our view, the sole gap in it revealing only another line of hedge a few feet beyond.

Amber unlocked the small door in the brick building and ushered us in. It was like stepping into another world. The interior was scrubbed red brick, square and high, the ceiling lost in the shadows. A bench occupied one wall, covered with pieces of leather and tools. More leather lay in skins on a rack and an old tea chest full of scraps stood in one corner. The sweet, faintly animal smell of the cured skins pervaded the place, a rich, heady aroma that I found intensely erotic.

Above the desk a line of pegs held a variety of instruments, some familiar, some not. To either side the pegs continued, but held complete items of harness, rope, lengths of chain, whips of every sort I'd heard of and several I hadn't. Finally, on the last peg, hung a long implement of dark brown wood with a curved handle; an old-fashioned school cane.

I found myself swallowing as I eyed the implements and cast a nervous glance at Amber. She smiled back, and glanced up towards the ceiling. I followed her gaze into the dim heights of the room. Above me, barely visible in the gloom, hung a set of iron manacles suspended from a pulley in the very peak of the roof. I starred open-mouthed at the device for a moment, then looked back down to find myself staring directly into Amber's eyes. She gave me a wicked smile that told me exactly where she would like me to be.

A very odd feeling indeed was going through me. Half of me wanted to run away; the other half wanted to be hung in the manacles and whipped – naked, with everyone watching. I also felt very alone and vulnerable. Matthew and Michael were studying the pictures of pony-girls in various harness that decorated the walls. Ginny was leafing through the skins, feeling their texture and sniffing each in turn.

All I could do was lower my head and look at the ground. I had been completely unprepared for the effect Amber was having on me. I'd found Ginny attractive and felt a little guilty about it, but with Amber both feelings were far stronger. I wanted to be at her feet, or kneeling naked between her thighs, licking her pussy. Her hand would be tangled in my hair. My bottom would be spread and vulnerable to flicks from one of the long whips that hung on her wall. I'd be in a collar, my ankles and wrists secured with cuffs . . .

'Right, this won't take long,' she said, shattering my daydream. 'Penny, have a look at this and tell me if you prefer any of the styles of harness or if you fancy any of the bits and pieces.'

She handed me an album which I opened to find pictures of pony-girls done up in various styles. I immediately recognised Ginny but there were around five different girls in total, mostly standing elegantly in their harness but some in close-up or in positions that showed off various bits of tack. I found myself shivering as I turned the pages. I kept thinking how exposed and rude the girls looked, then how I must have looked just the same, the previous day.

One harness in particular appealed to me. It was a sort of cross between the waist belt Ginny had and a corset, done in soft-looking black leather and giving a wonderful curve to the model's waist. It seemed ideal and I ordered it, drawing appreciative agreement from everyone. I also chose a bridle exactly like Ginny's, but with a single hair ring for my shorter hair. That was the basics, but I wanted to be as smart as possible and so chose a hobble to fit around my thighs, wrist and ankle cuffs, and bells to attach to my cheek rings.

'How about some for your nipples?' Amber asked, turning a couple of pages to show me a picture of a full-breasted girl with sweet little strings of tiny bells clipped onto each nipple. 'I've actually got some finished. They're for another order, but you can try them on, if you like.'

I nodded and it felt the most natural thing in the world to peel my top off and undo my bra, baring my breasts to all four of them. My nipples were already erect, but Matthew walked round behind me and took a breast in each hand and ran his fingers over them anyway. I sighed and closed my eyes, relaxing into the feeling of having my breasts fondled.

'Ready,' I heard Amber say, and opened my eyes to find her standing in front of me with a clip in each hand. Matthew cupped my breasts, holding them up for Amber to clip the bells onto my nipples. I squeaked when the little clips took hold but the initial shock quickly subsided, replaced by a pleasant sensation of pressure.

Matthew jiggled my breasts to make the bells ring and Amber smiled at me, reaching out and tapping a clip so that my stiff nipple wobbled slightly under the weight of the bells.

'She looks really sweet,' Ginny put in, also reaching out to stroke one of my breasts. 'I'd like some of those too, please.'

I closed my eyes again, lapping up the feeling of three people playing with my breasts at the same time. Matthew's hands were under my breasts, holding them up while Amber and Ginny played with the bells on my nipples.

I really thought they were just going to have me on

the spot, all four of them. Unfortunately, it didn't happen. Matthew's hands left my breasts and Ginny and Amber took the nipple bells off. Amber then started to measure me, trying to be calm and professional as she plied the tape measure. Still, her fingers trembled every time she touched me and I could tell that I was having just as strong an effect on her as she was on me.

Given how well the four of them obviously knew each other, I was a bit surprised that they hadn't taken advantage of my obvious state of sexual arousal and clear willingness to play. I did detect a slight tension between Amber and the men though: not dislike, but a lack of complete ease. I suspected that, had I come on my own or with just Ginny, the play with my breasts would have gone a lot further. I wished it had, but held my peace, letting Amber measure me and enjoying the intimate touch of her fingers.

She did it slowly, logging the measurements neatly into a little red notebook. After a while, I had to lift up my skirt so that she could measure my thighs. Having her hands between my thighs made my head spin with pleasure and I deliberately pulled the skirt up higher, exposing my bum to her, complete with marks from the previous day's pony-carting.

'I see you've already been driven,' Amber said. 'Those don't look like you've been whipped for being naughty.'

'They took me out yesterday,' I answered. From what she had said, it was evident that there was an element of ritual in the relationship between the four of them. It was as if, by playing their roles, they could lose the inhibitions that normally make physical intimacy between more than two people difficult, if not impossible. There had been something of the same, the previous day, although in Amber's presence there seemed to be more need for it. Well, if they could play psychological games, then so could I.

'Was she good?' Amber asked the others. I felt a

finger touch the sensitive skin of one of the spots where Matthew's whip had caught me. I had admired my bottom in the mirror that morning and knew that one or two marks had lasted.

'Excellent,' Matthew answered, but I could tell it wasn't the answer Amber had been looking for.

'A good pony-girl, very cute indeed,' Michael supplied. 'As for her behaviour: fair to middling, I suppose.'

'I was really obedient!' I protested automatically.

'Fair to middling,' Michael repeated. I could see where the conversation was leading – to my bottom getting whacked.

'Didn't you say she found out about you by watching you in the park?' Amber asked.

'I've already been spanked for that,' I pointed out, deciding to play compliant yet tart. 'Over Matthew's knee, with my pants down.'

'Just a spanking?' Amber said derisively as she got to her feet.

'It was jolly hard!' I protested, dropping my dress and putting my hands protectively over my bottom.

'I would have caned you,' Amber continued. 'Have you ever been caned, Penny?'

'Oh, yes, let's cane her!' Ginny said enthusiastically, rather spoiling the air of cool authority Amber had been trying to build up.

'No,' I admitted.

'Would you like to be?' Amber asked.

I hesitated. The idea of being punished appealed to me, but the cane looked wicked and I was sure it would be very painful. Physically, I'd always enjoyed the sensation of being spanked. Mentally, it was always best if it was for something, even if my sin was largely imaginary. I didn't suppose for an instant that any of them actually thought I deserved punishment for trespassing and peeping, but I was still going to get beaten for it and it would hurt just as much. Done properly, I knew the sensation would be bliss. The question was, could I take it?

'OK, but start me gently,' I answered, not feeling entirely sure of myself.

'Is that all right, Matthew?' Amber asked.

'Fine,' Matthew replied. 'We've told her the normal stop words. Shall we go out into the field?'

'Yes,' Ginny said, 'with Penny in harness and tied over a jump!'

'Let Penny choose her own punishment,' Amber said and then turned to me. 'Would you like to be done up in any special way? You can use anything I've got.'

I looked around, feeling like a child let loose in a toy shop. There was a wealth of things to choose from, all either designed to keep me in place while I was beaten or to enhance my exposure. I was tempted to try absolute restraint, so that I would feel completely helpless. On the other hand I like to kick and wriggle when I'm spanked, and imagined it would be the same with the cane. The nipple bells seemed a good idea and a sort of pole with cuffs on the end that was obviously intended to stop a girl closing her legs. I took both items and passed them to Matthew, who was standing behind me and had taken the cane from its peg. Then I remembered how good it had felt with my hands tied in the small of my back and added a pair of wrist cuffs and a length of rope to my selection.

'OK, I'm all yours,' I said, trying to sound brave as I handed the last items over. 'I'd like to be done in here; and bent over, please. I'm not sure I can handle the manacles.'

I stepped into the middle of the room and bowed my head, shivering at the thrill of what was about to be done to me. They pulled down my skirt to leave me standing naked in a puddle of cloth. Amber produced a thing like a tall padded trestle from under the bench, obviously designed for bending girls over to be punished. The sight of it made my trembling more pronounced and, oddly enough, if I hadn't half-thought that they expected me to back out, I don't think I'd have been able to go through with it.

Matthew took me by the wrist and led me gently forward, helping me get comfortable over the whipping stool. My bum stuck right up in the air, feeling rude and vulnerable, the cheeks a bit open so that the air was cool down between them. Nobody said a word as my ankles were pulled apart and cuffed. It left my legs almost at right angles and my feet off the ground so that my whole weight was on the stool. I knew what they could see and found myself blushing, despite my acquiescence to the caning. After all, there were four of them, all fully dressed, while I was naked and upended, with my pussy stuck out for inspection.

Amber kissed me as she clipped the bells onto my nipples, continuing to fondle my breasts as Matthew pulled my hands up into the small of my back and clipped the wrist cuffs on. The rope followed, looped around my wrists and the stool, leaving me utterly helpless – able to kick and wriggle, but in no way to shield my bottom from the cane. I knew they must be able to see how badly I was trembling.

'Are you ready?' Amber asked gently.

'Please turn me on a bit more, first,' I asked, not feeling at all sure if I could take the whacking that was coming, 'and start gently.'

'Yes, of course,' she answered. 'I could cuddle you while you're beaten, if you like?'

'Yes, please,' I said. I was already having to breathe deeply and I hadn't even taken a stroke yet. Amber knelt again and put her arms around me, a hand on each of my tits and my head upside down between her breasts. Suddenly, it was all right. I felt secure and comforted, the coming caning something that I needed and deserved.

I'd been spanked often enough to recognise the feeling. In addition to the simple sexual thrill of a hot, bare bottom, punishment produces a wonderful feeling of release – redemption, even. A good spanking always leaves me wanting to cuddle the person who's just beaten me: the opposite response to what many people would expect. The feeling was stronger now, though. Being beaten by the three of them seemed just, as was my nudity, my legs spread and my pussy and bum-hole on show to them, adding shame to my well-deserved punishment.

A finger touched my pussy. I didn't know whose, but it didn't matter. If they wanted to explore me, that was their privilege. After all, I was being punished and didn't feel I had any right to privacy until my punishment was complete. I felt the finger tease open my pussy and slide inside me, move in my vagina and then withdraw.

'Six, I think,' I heard Matthew's voice. 'Two each, that is; and Ginny had better go first.'

I found myself whimpering softly as they stood back from me. Six strokes! More, if Amber chose to join in. My poor bottom was going to be in a dreadful state. I heard the cane make an experimental swish through the air. The next stroke of the implement was going to be brought down on to my bare bottom and I had begun to kick even as Amber pulled my head closer in between her breasts. I could feel the texture of her bra through her jumper, lace over yielding flesh. Then there was another swish and a sharp pain exploded in my bottom. I cried out and flung my legs up in a futile effort to protect myself.

Ginny giggled and waited until my wriggling had subsided. I heard the cane swish again and another line of fire sprang up on my bottom, lower than the first.

'Two,' I heard her say.

I felt her hand on my bottom, stroking my cheeks and lingering on the two cane marks she had made. My skin felt hot and rough where the cane had struck, Ginny's caresses accentuating my awareness of the state of my bottom.

'OK?' Matthew asked and I knew that he had taken the cane from his sister.

'Yes,' I managed.

'Hang on,' Amber said.

There was a murmur of appreciation, I think from Michael, as Amber pulled her jumper up and once more cradled my head between her breasts. Her flesh was against my face, firm and smooth. I nuzzled her, nipping the edge of her bra in a mute plea for more. She hesitated, but only for a moment, then undid her bra catch and pulled the cups up to join her jumper. Her arms came back and now the bare flesh of her breasts was against my face.

I saw her signal to them and, the next instant, the cane came down hard across my bum. I had been imagining that Ginny's strokes gave the measure of how much a cane hurt. I had been wrong. This was much harder and had me kicking and whimpering into Amber's boobs. Ginny laughed even as the second stroke caught me, again making me kick and squirm over the stool, indifferent to the display I was making of myself.

'Four,' Matthew announced, 'there we are, Michael: one wriggling little backside, all for you.'

Amber held a nipple out for my mouth and I began to suckle her as I braced myself to take Michael's share of my punishment. The first stroke landed and, even as I gave my first kick, the second followed. I yelped at the unexpected double stroke and Michael laughed.

That was it. I lay panting and sobbing over the whipping stool, my skin wet with sweat and my bottom a mass of fire. I had been well and truly punished: stripped, tied and beaten, to my own order. Amber continued to let me suckle her nipple, stroking my head to soothe me. Just being cuddled by her was ecstasy, her big, soft breasts providing me immeasurable comfort.

'Make her come,' Amber said, reading my mind. 'There's a vibrator in the drawer under the desk. You'd like that, Penny, wouldn't you?'

I nodded around my mouthful of nipple, trying to push my bottom up further for the welcome contact of the vibrator. I had begun to shake with the after-effects of the caning and my whip marks had started to smart with an odd, prickly sensation that made me more conscious than ever of my bottom. I heard the drawer open and then shut, followed by a brief buzzing sound as someone tested the vibrator.

A moment later the cold hard plastic touched my pussy. It was rubbed among the folds of my vulva, finding my clit and then humming to life. That unique electric thrill went right through me and I found myself tensing my buttocks and thighs immediately. In my upside down position, all I could see were the curves of Amber's breasts and belly, and not who was working my pussy. Whoever it was certainly knew how to frig a girl. The vibrator was pressed against my clit and held steady so that I could set my own rhythm in squirming against it. The bells on my nipples were jingling, Amber's finger caressing one distended bud of flesh. A hand was stroking my bottom, touching the ridges of rough skin where the cane had fallen, to constantly remind me of my beating.

My mind began to run on my punishment. The stripping, being put in bondage and having nipple bells clipped on, being held and then caned: caned methodically while they laughed at my squirming bottom, at my pouting pussy lips, at the vulgar display of my bottom hole.

It didn't take long. My muscles began to contract faster and my breathing became heavy as I approached orgasm. A hand cupped the vibrator against me and a thumb was slipped into my pussy. The other hand left the surface of my aching bum cheeks and slipped between them, finding my anus and sliding a finger inside. I came, feeling both holes contract onto the intruding digits, thrusting my pussy hard against the vibrator and screaming my ecstasy out between Amber's breasts.

I was barely aware of them untying me and, when I was free, I just sat panting on the floor, stark naked and not caring a bit. When I eventually climbed to my feet, they showed me my bum in a mirror. Red lines criss-crossed the white cheeks, each cane mark two parallel scarlet scratches surrounded by an area of deeper red. The flesh was slick and moist, with a tuft of wet pussy hair showing between my thighs. My first thoughts were how sore my poor bottom was, and how humiliating it was to be standing in the nude, with my bum cheeks covered in cane marks. I had given them the right to make those marks, though, and I wouldn't have missed the experience for anything.

Afterwards, as we drank wine in Amber's kitchen, I was surprised at the way their attitudes had changed towards me. Matthew had always treated me rather as if I were made of cut glass; that is, when he wasn't intent on filling me with cock or turning my bum the colour of a cherry. Now, his respect was tinged with awe, as if he found my very willingness intimidating. Michael and Ginny had always been friendly and made no secret of enjoying my body. While I was dressing, I had caught a look of real lust from Michael and I suspected that both of them were wondering what it would be like to have me as their plaything.

As for Amber, she didn't seem to be able to keep still. Talking animatedly and sipping her wine, as if scared that someone was going to try to take her glass away, she was obviously strongly affected by what we'd done. Despite feeling drowsy and satisfied, my own thoughts were very much turned in her direction. She had been both strict and cuddly towards me, a wonderful combination. The thought of being under her control made me melt. My guilt was there, too, stronger than ever because now I wasn't just playing along: I wanted it badly.

'I'll bring the tack down to you next week, if you like,' she was saying, addressing Matthew.

'I can't really keep it at the farm,' he answered. 'Could you bring it to Michael and Ginny's?'

'Fine,' she replied. 'In fact, how about a challenge?'

'What sort?' Matthew asked.

'A pony-girl race,' Amber continued. 'Around your park.'

'Great!' Ginny enthused. 'With a good punishment session for the loser.'

'Hey!' I protested. 'There's no way I can beat you. I'll take my medicine if I lose, but only if it's a fair race.'

'Actually, I was thinking of a prize for the winner,' Amber said.

'That doesn't really give the ponies the same incentive,' Michael remarked, 'and, as Penny says, she and Matthew haven't a fair chance against Ginny and I.'

'We could work out a handicap,' Matthew suggested.

'Or put Ginny in a partial hobble,' Michael added.

'With the loser's punishment worked out in advance and the details pinned to the stable door,' Matthew said.

'Good idea,' Ginny put in. 'Penny and I could read it out before getting into harness . . .'

'Hold on, hold on,' Amber said. 'I want to make a specific challenge. Listen to me. You four can put together any team you like. If I manage to beat you over five laps of the park, I get my prize.'

'Five laps?' Ginny asked.

'You can do that,' Michael replied. 'You've done seven before.'

'Yes, but not racing.'

'Five laps,' Amber continued, 'let's make a decent race of it. If I win, I get Penny as my pony-girl for a day. If that's all right, Penny?'

Her last sentence had been spoken with just a hint of doubt. I smiled and nodded, immediately restoring Amber's confident tone as she continued. 'Alone, that is. What do you say?'

I could see that Matthew wasn't too happy with the bet. Michael and Ginny seemed more amused than anything, but it was Michael who decided to haggle.

'And if we win?' he asked.

'You get my pony to play with, of course,' Amber replied.

'So all four of us get to share one pony-girl who we've not met or you get to play with our delectable new filly all on your own?' Michael went on. 'That's not a very good deal, Amber.'

'What else can I offer?' Amber asked.

There was silence for a moment as each considered the other.

'Yourself,' Ginny spoke suddenly.

'Me!' Amber exclaimed. 'But . . .'

'Matthew and I won't touch,' Michael put in quickly, 'but we do get to look.'

'I . . .' Amber began. She was stuck. Michael obviously wasn't going to back down and she either had to call the whole thing off or accept his offer. She looked out of the window, then at me. It seemed to me that I won either way and that I ought to encourage her to take the risk. I returned her look and gave my upper lip the smallest of dabs with my tongue, then lowered my eyes.

'You're on,' she said to Michael.

Five

I was sure Amber had something up her sleeve. As we had driven back after visiting her, all of them had expressed astonishment at her acceptance of Michael's offer. Ginny knew that she had occasionally been a pony-girl before, but not often and only for other women. In fact, baring her boobs with two men present was regarded as pretty unusual. The assumption was that she had fallen in love with me on the spot, and there was a lot of teasing about what she'd do, once she got hold of me. Matthew I would have expected to be less enthusiastic – jealous, even – but he seemed happy to go along with the idea. They intended to win, after all.

Personally, I doubted we would. I was intent on doing my best, and once we had agreed that Ginny and I would run as a pair, I spent as much time as I could training.

When Amber arrived at the park the following Saturday, it was in a horsebox. She wouldn't open the back, which confirmed my suspicions, but did present me with my tack. She had made it in thick black textured leather which still had a rich scent to it. The fittings were shiny new brass, which Matthew immediately told me to keep polished, with the threat of a spanking if I didn't. It was beautiful work and I was looking forward to showing off in it.

I thanked Amber with a kiss, letting my mouth open

briefly under hers. I was already beginning to feel the unique excitement of being under control as a pony-girl, even before really being in role. Ginny and I had been warming up and Michael and Matthew's method of warming up was enough to get anybody going. First they had had Ginny and I undress each other, then made us run naked on the spot with a carriage whip handy to make sure we kept it up.

We had just finished that when Amber arrived and so, when I kissed her, she got an armful of naked girl into the bargain. She, like Matthew and Michael, was in full kit: shiny black riding boots, jodhpurs and a loose white blouse. The three of them together, with Ginny and I totally nude, made an erotic scene straight out of fantasy. Not only was it real, but I was the main subject of it.

Michael made short work of tying Ginny's and my hands behind our backs and attaching us to the hitching post, then went to talk to Amber while Matthew rigged the cart. I watched as he attached two poles to the eyelets on the shafts and fixed them in place with rope. I could see how it worked. Ginny and I would be pulling on either side of the cart. Thus our heels would be free to kick up without risk of hitting the cart, while both our bottoms would be freely available to his whip. The ropes distributed the strain evenly, the whole design allowing us to run much faster than normal. It looked good to me and I turned to see if our engineering skills were worrying Amber.

They weren't; or at least, if they were, she didn't show it. Instead, she was chatting to Michael and admiring the surrounding park. I had to admire her calm. In her place, I would have been trembling in anticipation of erotic humiliation. As Ginny had told us, part of Amber's philosophy was that you should never do what you weren't prepared to accept yourself. We knew she would accept defeat with good grace, and I privately expected that she would thoroughly enjoy it, as long as we didn't realise it. Still, her attitude betrayed not the slightest hint of apprehension.

She and Michael were discussing the technicalities of the race. He offered to reduce the distance but, as before, she insisted on five laps. With Michael weighing some three stone more than her, they agreed to weight the undercarriage of her cart to make up the difference. They also agreed to dispense with tails; having a plug up one's bottom made running unreasonably difficult. Most of the terms they used were lost on me and I realised that there was more to being a pony-girl master or mistress than simply giving commands and applying whips to bottoms.

Only when they had the cart fully rigged and the race terms agreed did they come over to Ginny and me. Amber watched as we were put in harness, making the occasional remark about the attachments for my new kit.

The corset waist belt was particularly fine, hugging my midriff and bringing my breasts and hips into prominence. Our hands were untied and the wrist cuffs put on, then the bridles, with an adjustable strap running between our cheek rings. The reins looped back, also attached to our cheek rings so that both of us would receive the signals. There were no bells or other bits of decoration that might distract us. Once harnessed, we were led over to the cart and hitched in place by our wrists and waists. As before, there was the delicious feeling of being under control, only made more intense by the excitement of the coming race.

Matthew led us into the shade and we stood patiently while Amber undid the rear door of her horsebox. I couldn't see inside, but Amber whistled and there was a noise, then her pony-girl emerged, walking smartly down the ramp, already in full harness and hitched to a cart.

'May I introduce you to Hippolyta,' Amber addressed the men, smiling proudly as she took the pony-girl's reins and began to stroke her hair.

I was impressed and it was obvious that Michael and Matthew were as well. 'Hippolyta', which was presumably a pet name, was pure elegance. She stood a good three inches taller than Amber, a pillar of firm, hard muscle, naked except for her harness and shoes. Her breasts were small and high, tipped with dark nipples in contrast to her pale skin. Long black hair was drawn back into a pony-tail, tied with a scarlet ribbon and falling to the small of her back. I felt an unexpected pang of jealously as Amber's hand moved from her hair to squeeze a pert buttock.

'Very impressive,' Matthew said, eyeing Hippolyta with undisguised relish. 'Draw your teams up to the line, then.'

As Hippolyta paced forward, I could actually see the outlines of her muscles working in her legs. She was magnificent, it was true, and looking at her made me feel very small and girly. There seemed little doubt that she could outrun Ginny and me in a sprint, but over any distance she might have less of an advantage. Why, then, had Amber been so insistent on the five laps?

The reins flicked against my back and I took a step forward, following Hippolyta's sweetly rotating rump towards the starting line. Michael was walking behind us, holding the reins. As we were not allowed to talk, and were supposed only to obey commands from voice, reins and whip, we had discussed tactics in advance. The idea was for us to start as fast as possible and get ahead by the start of the narrow track. With our two-abreast formation, it would be next to impossible to overtake us on the first circuit and, from there, we hoped being in a pair would tell.

Of course, it didn't work like that. As soon as Matthew dropped his handkerchief to signal the start,

Hippolyta was off like a shot. At the far end of the carriage sweep, she had enough of a lead to pull in front of us and leave us trailing as we descended the shallow slope into the woods. She was still drawing ahead and we quickly lost sight of them on the curved track.

It wasn't that we were going slowly. In fact, compared with my previous experience of pony-carting, we were going at an impressive pace. Having proper shoes with grips instead of high-heeled ankle boots was most important, but the whole experience was very different. For a start, Michael made little use of the whip or reins and gave most of his commands verbally. He had also abandoned his cool, devil-may-care attitude, which was mainly done for the benefit of Ginny. Instead, he drove us with a fevered determination, abandoning the finer points of the fantasy in favour of efficiency. The difference was that, where the pleasure in pony-girl fantasy usually comes from actually doing it, with racing the really erotic part comes with the prize.

For all Hippolyta's athleticism, we managed to gain a little on the rising ground. By the end of the first lap, we were only ten yards or so behind her, but I was already beginning to feel tired and was wondering if any of us would be able to finish five laps at all. She pulled ahead again on the down slope a little less and, by the time we reached the stable yard for the second time, we were right on their heels.

My legs were burning and I could hear Ginny panting through her bit. We'd kept up, though, and that had greatly increased my confidence. As we entered the carriage sweep, Michael shouted to us to go flat out, his whip landing plum across my bottom as he called. I sprinted, pulling to the side, our wheel-housing touching theirs as we drew level. Then we were past, dashing through the gate and forcing Amber to turn Hippolyta aside to avoid running into a pillar.

By the time they managed to sort themselves out, we

were twenty yards ahead; thirty, by the time Hippolyta had matched our pace. As before, she gained on the downhill track but lost as we rose and, when we returned to the stable yard, they were well behind us. Still, there were two laps to go and Ginny and I were both flagging. Michael slowed us, knowing that we couldn't be overtaken on the track and keen to conserve our energies.

There was neither sight nor sound of Amber and I started to wonder if she had pulled up and admitted defeat. We were nearly back at the stable yard and I decided that we were actually going to win. Even when I heard Amber's voice raised in encouragement behind us, I wasn't really worried but responded to Michael's gentle tap of the whip with only a small increase in speed.

We passed through the gates again and I realised that we had done it. They were well behind and couldn't overtake us anyway. I was also exhausted, but reasoned that even a girl as obviously athletic as Hippolyta had to be tired as well. We slowed to a comfortable trot, saving our energy in case it was needed for a last dash across the stable yard to the winning line.

Amber's voice came again, closer this time, but I only realised that something was wrong when Michael suddenly began to yell for more speed and Ginny jumped as a whip stroke caught her bum. I could hear Amber behind us but dared not turn around as we gathered pace once again. My legs quickly began to burn and I felt the first twinge of a stitch coming on. We were emerging from the wood, crossing a broad strip of what had once been lawn but was now a great expanse of nettles. Suddenly I heard a new noise to the left of us and realised that Amber was driving poor Hippolyta through the nettle bed, and at a crazy pace.

The entrance to the stable yard was visible ahead and I tried to strain for more speed but couldn't, my muscles refusing to give me anything. A dark shape came up in the corner of my eye and then drew level, rushing headlong through the nettles. Something was wrong – the shape black where Hippolyta was pale-skinned. Only when they started to draw ahead in earnest did I realise that the pony was not Hippolyta. In fact, Amber was driving not a pony-girl, but a pony-boy, a tall man who might have been Hippolyta's brother in looks and was clad head to toe in a black, shiny material.

I knew we were lost and so did Ginny. As we were overtaken all the fight went out of us and we came into the stable yard several yards behind, staggering over the finish line to drop to our knees on the ground. I could hear Michael and Amber arguing but was too tired to care, waiting passively while Matthew detached us from the cart and then laying myself full length on a grassy area in the shade. Ginny joined me, handing me a bottle of water, taking my hand and squeezing it but saying nothing as she too collapsed in exhaustion. Like me, she hadn't the energy to even take off her bridle, contenting herself with loosening the chin strap and releasing the bit from her mouth.

I closed my eyes and let my body go limp. My legs ached terribly and I was soaked with sweat. If it hadn't been for a light breeze cooling my skin, I don't think I'd have been aware that I was naked, and I certainly didn't care.

After a while, I realised that the others were still arguing. Matthew had joined in and there were two other voices, one male, one female. They weren't angry, but were having a bizarre discussion of pony-carting etiquette that would have been completely surreal if I hadn't been involved myself.

The point at issue was not whether it had been acceptable for Amber to change ponies halfway through the race; that would have been far too simple. Instead, Michael was arguing that you couldn't have a pony-boy in what had been agreed was a pony-girl race. Amber's response was that if you could switch species in a fantasy then a switch of sex was a relatively minor affair. There were other details, but that was the point they kept coming back to. Actually, it was a pointless argument, as both of them were far too stubborn to give in, regardless of the other's logic.

'You cheated, Amber,' Ginny suddenly called over. 'Get your clothes off and crawl to my feet. Now!'

'I'll deal with you later, Miss Virginia Linslade,' Amber retorted. She had such a commanding edge to her voice that she would have had me contrite in an instant.

Ginny was less easy to subdue. 'Amber's due for a spanking and she doesn't like it,' Ginny informed me in a voice loud enough to be heard by everyone. 'But then, she always did try and squirm out of her punishments. She'll be obedient enough, once her bum's warm; you'll see.'

I opened my eyes and propped myself up on one elbow to see what was happening. Amber was glaring at Ginny with a look that would have had me straight on my knees. Ginny just giggled and stuck her tongue out. Michael and Matthew were standing together, with Hippolyta and the man who had been Amber's pony-boy to one side. Hippolyta was stark naked and dripping wet, having presumably been hosing herself down. The man, who actually looked like a younger version of Michael, had a rubber body suit rolled down to his waist, exposing a smooth, well-muscled torso. All in all, it was a fine view and was likely to get better, if Amber ended up admitting defeat.

She wasn't going to and it occurred to me that, unless someone stepped in, the rest of the day was going to be wasted arguing. As nobody else seemed inclined to reach a compromise, it seemed to be up to me. There was also a chance for me to arrange things for my own pleasure.

'How do you mean, she'll be obedient enough, once her bottom's warm?' I asked Ginny quietly, pulling the bit free of my teeth.

'What Amber likes when it comes to men,' Ginny replied, now speaking quietly, 'and you're not to tell the boys this, is for them to think she's being made to take punishment or whatever. That's why I suggested she be the prize herself; I knew she wouldn't be able to resist.'

'I thought she was lesbian?' I answered.

'Her lovers have all been women,' Ginny replied. 'She's not completely averse to men, though, under the right circumstances. She'd never normally suck a man off for instance, but find her an excuse and it's a different matter, especially after a spanking. How do you think she persuaded Anderson to be a pony-boy?'

'Anderson?' I asked.

'Vicky . . . Hippolyta's . . . boyfriend. To get him to do that, I reckon Amber's had a smacked bum from her and a mouthful of spunk from him, at the least.'

'You know them then?'

'Vicky models for Amber. I met Anderson when we were posing together for her catalogue. I'd guessed Vicky would be her pony-girl, but he took me by surprise. If it wasn't for the fact that she'll lose her chance to play with you, she'd have backed down by now. Reluctantly, and with no end of fuss, but she'd have done it.'

'I actually rather want to be hers, tomorrow,' I answered.

'Go and do something about it, then. She'll take a punishment, if you suggest it.'

'You're sure?'

'I've known her for years, Penny. She'd love to be punished in front of everyone, but she'd never ask for it, especially not from the men.'

I sat up and loosened my bridle, undoing the straps as I walked over to them. Amber turned to me as I approached. 'What do you think, Penny?' she asked.

'I think we should compromise,' I answered.

Amber nodded and Michael looked relieved; now, neither of them had to back down.

'We lost,' I continued. 'I'd like to be Amber's pony-girl for a day anyway, so it's really my choice, isn't it?'

Amber smiled warmly; Michael opened his mouth to say something and then thought better of it.

'But,' I said, 'Amber did break the rules of the race. Not the spirit, though, and so to compromise I think she ought to be punished but to choose her own punishment.'

Michael looked doubtful and then began to smile, as did Matthew. Anderson gave an amused chuckle; Vicky nodded approval.

Amber didn't answer but turned to me with her mouth slightly open. 'I . . . All right,' she answered. 'Let me think about it for a bit while you lot have a hose down.'

She went to sit on her cart, chin in her hand. Having a hose down seemed an excellent idea. I stripped off my harness and took the hose, the others watching as I made a big show of washing myself. It wasn't long before Ginny joined me, naked and with a bar of coarse soap. Inevitably, she couldn't keep her hands to herself and was soon soaping my back, occasionally letting her hands sneak down to my bottom. I felt my familiar pang of guilt but relaxed and gave no resistance when her arms went around me and she cupped my breasts in her hands. The hose fell to the ground and curled back on itself, running cool water over my feet as Ginny explored my breasts.

I let her play with them, squeezing gently and pinching my nipples between her fingers and thumbs. Not having too much in the way of tits, I had always had a sneaking fascination with large-breasted girls. Ginny's were pressed against my back, naked and wet.

I wanted to touch them, but felt a bit shy with everyone watching. Strangely, it's a lot easier to show off when I'm tied up or being given orders.

What Ginny was doing to my nipples was driving me wild. I gave in, reasoning that if I could be caned in front of four people then I could play with another girl's breasts in front of six. I turned and hugged her, getting a warm response. She kissed me and drew back a little, leaving her lovely breasts right in front of me and clearly available. I swallowed and reached out, touching the smooth curve of one globe of pink flesh. She sighed and pursed her lips as my finger brushed a nipple, pushing her chest out to offer them to me.

I complied and was soon having a good feel of Ginny's heavy round breasts. I took one in each hand, weighing them and stroking her nipples with my thumbs. She had put her hands on her head and closed her eyes, letting me play without hindrance. I took my fill, exploring her and feeling my own excitement rising with hers.

Everybody was watching us and, I imagine, hoping we'd go further, but I didn't feel ready for it. Not that I didn't enjoy the idea of full sex with Ginny; but it was just a bit too public and somehow the atmosphere wasn't perfect. Besides, I wanted to see what Amber would choose for her punishment.

'Another time,' I whispered, letting go of her breasts and picking up the hose to wash the last suds off.

She made a small sound of disappointment but gave me an understanding look. I stepped away, suddenly feeling chilled as the water evaporated. Matthew threw me a towel and I was still drying myself when Amber got to her feet. I was wondering what she would choose. Ginny had suggested that she liked to suck men's cocks. Despite my desire to be under her control, the idea of seeing her on her knees with Matthew's penis in her mouth appealed to me. Seeing her spanked would be just as good, though. She might even ask to be passed around for spankings, and I'd get a turn myself. Would I dare? The idea of taking Amber across my knee and pulling down her jodhpurs and knickers was outrageous but immensely exciting, let alone the thought of actually smacking her bottom.

She had walked into the centre of the yard and was standing with her hands on her hips. The expression on her face was anything but meek and I began to wonder if she was just going to call the whole thing off.

'Well, boys,' she began, looking pointedly at Matthew and Michael. 'What would you like to do to me? Each of you, and the girls too: we mustn't play favourites, must we?'

Matthew looked slightly abashed but Michael gave his coolest smile and steepled his fingers. 'I'd like you as my pony-girl: the full role, of course,' he answered her, quite unaffected by her tone of voice, which I could see was carefully calculated to embarrass them.

'Fair enough,' she answered. 'Matthew?'

'The same for me,' Matthew answered, following Michael's lead.

'Ginny?' Amber asked.

'I'm going to sit on your face, Miss Amber Oakley, till you make me come,' Ginny replied.

'You'd like that, wouldn't you?' Amber retorted. 'Anderson?'

'A difficult choice,' he answered, smiling thoughtfully. 'I have often felt you would make a good pony-girl but, if you're going to do that anyway, then I'll take my pleasure from watching. Then I think I'd like to bugger you, if that's OK?'

'Fine,' Amber replied, although I noticed Vicky smack Anderson's arm. Amber was being far too nonchalant and I think everybody realised it, but we were all too interested to see what she was leading up to.

'Vicky?' Amber continued, looking sweetly at the tall girl.

'Well, you drove me pretty hard,' she answered, 'but, if Anderson's going to insist on being such a dirty bastard, I suppose I shouldn't be too hard on you. I'll have a sixty-nine, I think, with me on top.'

'Thank you,' Amber went on. 'Penny?'

'I, er . . .' I began. It was hard to choose, especially when they all seemed so much more experienced and confident than me. Still, there were one or two interesting fantasies I'd built up on the odd occasions when I'd masturbated over the thought of sex with another woman. OK, so in my fantasies I was always on the receiving end, but the opportunity was too good to miss. If she went for it – not that I was at all sure she would – then she was going to be a pony-girl anyway, as Anderson had said. If I asked for my pussy licked, I'd just look as if I was following the other girls. Ginny had suggested that she liked to be humiliated and so one option presented itself.

'Actually, I'd like to pee on you,' I said, trying to keep my voice as matter-of-fact as the others had been.

'You would, would you?' Amber retorted. She looked flustered for the first time and I saw that I'd hit a soft spot, especially as Ginny had started laughing. 'Good,' she continued, 'well, you're going to get what you want: or one of you is. You're going to draw straws for it, five short and one long, and I promise to take my punishment from whoever gets the long straw.'

She walked away to find a suitable length of grass. I had been dressing and was still doing my blouse up when Ginny approached, also dressed. 'She'll cheat,' Ginny confided in me quietly. 'Just watch, Vicky or I will win. As for your idea, I can guarantee she'll take it out on you tomorrow, just for suggesting it.'

'That's why I said it,' I admitted.

'You're a disgrace and a manipulative little tart,' she replied, giving my bottom a playful slap.

'I know,' I answered.

Amber had chosen a tall grass stem and was methodically breaking it into pieces. I knew that the next twenty-four hours were going to see me seriously put through my paces and determined to make it even worse for myself.

'Someone else should draw the straws,' I announced. 'That way Amber couldn't be accused of cheating and there'll be no argument.'

Everyone agreed with me, except Amber herself, who gave me an absolutely filthy look. She reluctantly passed the straws to Vicky, who took them and shuffled them in her hand. Personally, I was hoping she'd get Anderson; partially because I wanted to see her lovely bottom fucked and partly because it was sure to mean my own wouldn't go empty the next day.

Vicky went first, drawing a straw from her own hand and taking a short one. Anderson followed and did the same, then Vicky held her hand out to me. The four pieces of grass stem were almost indistinguishable, but not quite. Those from lower down were just a tiny bit thicker. It seemed reasonable to me that she would have broken off five equal lengths to leave a long one, which was therefore going to be one end or the other and probably the lower end. That meant that the thickest straw would be the long one. I picked, pulling my choice slowly up. Sure enough, it kept coming and I was holding the long straw.

'No!' Amber exclaimed, but it was obvious that her horror was put on.

Ginny was laughing, Michael grinning, and the others exchanging looks of amusement and pleasure.

'OK,' Amber sighed in mock resignation. 'How do you want me?'

'Have her keep her clothes on,' Ginny suggested.

'Do you have a change?' I asked.

'Yes,' Amber sighed, 'I've got things in the cab.'

'Then take your bra off under your blouse,' I ordered.

We watched as she unclipped her bra and extracted it down a sleeve. There was a knot of tension forming in my throat, but very different from the one I'd felt when I was about to be caned. This was pure excitement and, for the first time, I felt a flush of what could only have been sadistic pleasure. Amber's nipples showed through her top, dark under the white cotton, and erect.

'Now your boots and jodhpurs,' I continued, 'but not your knickers.'

She complied, tugging off her boots and then turning her back to us to pull down her jodhpurs. Her panties were plain white cotton, the type that's see-through when wet.

'Turn around slowly, then kneel down,' I said when she was down to just her blouse and panties. She looked really sweet, her legs bare and with a triangle of white cotton covering the bulge of her pussy. As she knelt, the blouse rode up her back, leaving the broad seat of her panties showing, the material stretched taut across her bottom. I walked round her, watching her big eyes looking up at me uncertainly from underneath her fringe of pale brown curls.

'Lift your top,' I said, unable to resist the opportunity to see more of her.

She did as she was told, revealing her tight waist, the soft swell of her tummy and her naked breasts.

'Stay like that,' I added as I began to undress myself. Everybody else was absolutely quiet, watching Amber and me. Michael's arm was round Ginny's waist; Anderson's hand laid gently on Vicky's bottom.

I took off everything below my waist, going deliberately slowly and piling each garment neatly on top of the last. Amber watched me, her eyes wide and bright, occasionally nipping her lower lip with her teeth. I knew how she felt: much as I had, the first time I had been put across Matthew's knee.

'Drop your blouse,' I said, stepping nearer. 'Hold your tits up for me.'

She was trembling as I straddled her and pushed my hips forward, my pussy inches away from her face. I pulled my lips apart and closed my eyes, concentrating on building up the need to pee. I wasn't sure I could do it at first, then felt the familiar ache start to build and knew I could.

I opened my eyes as I let go, watching a splash of pale golden liquid catch the front of Amber's blouse. She sighed as it hit, the cotton immediately soaking my pee up and starting to cling to her breasts. Her nipples showed, every little bump of the areolae now visible through the wet cotton. I stood back a little, my stream catching her lower down and plastering the blouse against her tummy. Her mouth was open and her eyes shut, her hands massaging her breasts, the pee running through her fingers and down her arms. It was more than I could resist. I moved forward again, close to her face, filling her mouth with my pee. She opened wide, sticking her tongue out and lapping at my pussy as the stream died to a trickle. For a moment I felt the touch of her tongue on my clit, then she had drawn away, golden pee running down her face in rivulets. I stood back, watching her. She was sitting in a pool of it, her blouse and knickers sodden, still kneading her breasts and with her eyes shut tight. The front of her pants was soaking, the thick bush of her pubic hair plainly visible through the sodden material.

'Sit your bottom in it,' I ordered, 'then stand up.'

She did it, wriggling her bum against the ground then getting unsteadily to her feet and turning so that I could see the wet patch spreading across the seat of her knickers. The wet cotton clung to her bottom, making a very pretty sight indeed. I left her standing, keen to let her humiliation really sink in and wondering if I should order her to sit back in the pool of my pee and masturbate in front of us. I hesitated and then decided that not to make her do it would spoil it for her.

'Get back in it and you can come,' I said, reasoning that she always had her stop word if she didn't want to.

She obeyed, sitting down in the middle of the puddle with her legs at right angles. I could see every detail of her pussy through her knickers until she slid a hand down the front and started to play with herself. Her eyes were still shut and the other hand on her breasts, rubbing her nipples through the wet material. Her breath quickened and I knew she was going to come, but was taken by surprise when she called my name as she reached orgasm.

I quickly went forward to cuddle her, holding her head as her orgasm peaked again and then subsided. As she let out her breath, someone started clapping and then, the next thing I knew, the hose had been turned on us. It didn't take long to clean up, although I had to take off my soaking blouse and bra and settle for staying topless for the rest of the afternoon. Amber had other ideas, as I discovered when she emerged from the horsebox, now fully dressed in corduroy trousers and a fresh blouse.

'Right,' she announced calmly, as if we hadn't just watched her make an utterly filthy exhibition of herself, 'I hope you all enjoyed the show and you can be very sure I'll remember it, for future reference. Revenge will be sweet.'

'Well, just make sure we don't catch you cheating again,' Ginny retorted.

'And as for you, Miss Birch,' Amber continued, once more the cool, haughty mistress, 'you can start by undressing again. Then you can put your harness on, all of it, and get in the back of the horsebox.'

My hands went to my jeans button and popped it open. This was what I'd been manipulating myself into, and now I was going to get what I deserved.

Six

If you don't enjoy erotic pain and sexual humiliation, it's impossible to understand either. I'd always enjoyed the fantasy of both and occasionally the practice. Now I was really starting to explore my sexuality, yet I couldn't really claim to understand my feelings. As I lay in the back of the van in full pony-girl harness, I knew Amber was going to punish me and utterly humiliate me. There was nothing I wanted more and, as I lay on the floor, my mind ran on what she might be going to do. I knew that it would be ecstasy but that didn't stop me being scared: scared and very, very excited. I would have liked to masturbate then and there, but Amber's last act before shutting the horsebox had been to strap my wrists together behind my back and fix my ankle straps to her pony-cart. She had also had me put my hobble on, a system of leather straps that linked my thighs and made it impossible to spread them properly. A thick collar of black leather with a ring at the front had also been put around my neck with everybody watching, marking me as Amber's.

Tied as I was, all I could do was lie in the dim interior with the smell of horses in my nostrils, squirm in my bonds and listen to Amber, Anderson and Vicky chatting in the front. I could only catch a word or two from their conversation, but I did gather that they were discussing the merits of different brands of mineral water. Having me strapped up in the back didn't even seem to warrant a mention, which made my feelings even more piquant. Somewhere between Wiltshire and Amber's house, she dropped them off, still ignoring me completely. The journey then continued in silence, my emotions growing stronger and moving in a direction I had never experienced before.

My body was completely under Amber's control: hers and hers alone. I trusted her or I'd never have let myself get into the situation. It was that trust that kept the situation so intensely erotic and, as time slipped by, I found it building into a reliance. I felt I was her pet, treasured but ultimately owned. Being in the harness provided a name for this emotion: pony-girl. If the physical sensation when I first went in harness had been more intense than I had anticipated, then this new mental aspect to it was richer still.

At a deeper, more rational level of my mind I realised that Amber was doing it on purpose. Her understanding of the fantasy made Matthew, and even Michael, look shallow. I gave up squirming, lying patiently on the floor with only the occasional stretch to keep my muscles moving.

The journey seemed to go on for an immense period of time, but objectively it can't have been all that long. I could still see bright sunshine through a crack at the side of the doors when the horsebox finally stopped. I heard Amber getting out to open the gates to her yard. When the vehicle stopped again, my trepidation returned, stronger than before. She didn't open the back and the last thing I heard was the sound of her kitchen door closing.

I lay still in the cool dimness, waiting for my mistress. Every sound and sensation seemed magnified: my own breathing, the slight jingle of my cheek and nipple bells when I moved, the dull ache in my muscles. The tension inside me kept building and I had begun to sob with need and frustration when I finally heard the grating sound of the bolt being drawn. Light flooded the compartment, stinging my eyes as the doors were pulled open. Then the ramp was being lowered and a surge of adoration went through me as I saw Amber.

She was naked but for knee-high boots of black leather. Her hair was caught back, giving her a severe look. In her hand she held a long whip, like the type a circus ring-master might use, and a coil of black rope. She stood looking at me and fingering the tip of the whip. The whip and her determined no-nonsense stance brought back all my misgivings about having humiliated her. It looked very painful and I knew I'd soon be feeling it across my bottom. I wanted to crawl to her feet and kiss them to say sorry, then be whipped anyway, but I could only look at her and beg with my eyes.

The ramp creaked faintly as she stepped forward and entered the horsebox. My ankles were unfastened and I was pulled to my feet, the end of the rope knotted in the ring of my collar. She walked down the ramp, the rope thrown casually over her shoulder. I was forced to follow, the hobble making me walk in tiny, precise steps. She walked across the yard, my eyes fixed on the muscles of her back and the movement of her bottom. Without once looking round, she went to the gap in the hedge and passed through, drawing the rope behind her. The hedge was double, blocking the view into the little paddock it enclosed.

I stumbled after Amber, who walked briskly across the paddock to a central post painted in red and white stripes. To either side were horse jumps and I recalled Ginny suggesting I be tied over a jump for my caning. Amber was heading for the post, adjusting the coil of rope in her hand as she went. When she reached it, she tied the rope to a large metal eye that was fixed in the top, then turned to me.

I thought she was going to tell me what was going to

happen to me, but instead of the hard, merciless look she had worn when taking me out of the horsebox, she was smiling and looked more happy than anything.

'Come out of role for a second, Penny,' she said softly, taking the bit out of my mouth. 'That may have been a bit hard; are you OK?'

'I'm fine; it was lovely,' I answered truthfully. 'I never realised how much feeling I could get from all this. Other than just being turned on, that is.'

'Good,' she replied, smiling. 'You want me to punish you properly, don't you?'

'Yes, please,' I answered.

'Good,' she said again. 'While you're with me, your slow down word is "Yellow", not "Amber", otherwise it just gets confusing. Say it if you need to, OK?'

I nodded, almost in tears at her tenderness after my earlier treatment. She kissed me and gave me a squeeze then stepped back, about to return to her role.

'Can I have a name, please?' I asked, voicing a need I had felt ever since hearing that Vicky was called Hippolyta when she was a pony-girl.

'Of course,' Amber replied. 'I'm surprised Matthew didn't give you one. Have you got your heart set on something?'

'You choose,' I said, knowing that being named by her would add to the pleasure.

She smiled, and then the smile became cruel, with just the tiniest of changes in her face. I hung my head as she took my reins, leading me out until the rope ran taut from my collar to the top of the post. Ahead of me, some few yards away, was one of the jumps, as high as a small hurdle. I waited with my head bowed as she unfastened my wrists and looped the reins back up to the neck strap of my bridle.

'Right,' she announced, stepping back, 'we're going to try a little test of stamina while I think of a suitable name for my new pony. You run, jumping the two fences on each circuit. That sounds easy, doesn't it? Very easy, even with my whip to make your bottom tingle if you don't keep your pace up. Of course, it's not that simple . . .'

She paused, reaching out to tap one of my nipple bells and make it ring.

'You have earnt yourself six dozen strokes of the cane, which I intend to take out of your plump behind after dinner. Just before we go up to the bedroom, that is. Now, every perfect lap you complete will reduce your punishment by one stroke. Should you complete seventy-two laps, then you'll just get the good spanking that is the minimum you deserve. If the rope touches the ground, or if you miss a fence, knock a fence over or any other error, then the lap doesn't count. You start when my whip connects with your bottom.'

She had been walking away as she spoke, but turned and flicked the whip the instant she finished. I felt a sharp sting as the tip caught the skin of my bottom and started to run.

Even if I'd been fresh, I wouldn't have done very well. The ground was dry but I immediately discovered that the second fence was a water jump; or, rather, a mud jump. I couldn't jump over it and, by the second lap, my legs were already splashed with it. Each time I passed Amber, she would taunt me with the whip, occasionally flicking it expertly across my bum. By the fifth lap, my legs were burning and I had started to stumble at the jumps. Somewhere around the tenth, I lost count and, not long after that, let the rope touch the ground for the first time.

Only the memory of my previous caning and the thought of my coming punishment kept me going, although I was determined to take it without using my stop word. On what must have been about the twentieth lap, I slipped and sat down in the mud pool, smearing my bottom and thighs with muck. As it oozed up between my legs and into my pussy fur, I considered giving up and just collapsing into the cool goo. It would have been so easy, cane or no cane.

It was seeing Amber pointedly counting on her fingers that made me go on, forcing myself into a kneeling position, standing and staggering on around the pole. The brief rest did me good and I started counting again, completing four more laps before feeling the warning twinge of a stitch coming on. I forced myself on but, when I reached the next jump, I knew I just couldn't do it and stopped, sinking to my knees and then to all fours with my head bowed to the ground.

I was covered in muck and sweat, my hair falling around my face in a bedraggled mess, my beautiful new harness filthy with mud. For a long moment I stayed still, panting and wondering how many laps I'd done; then I heard a sound and realised that Amber was standing in front of me. I looked up, finding her boots directly in front of my face and the scent of leather and polish strong in my nose.

'Lick, Calliphigenia,' she ordered curtly. I eased my bit aside and put my tongue out to touch the shiny black surface, tasting the bitter-sweet tang. I'd been named, the name implying a pretty yet plump bottom; flattering, yet humiliating and just right.

Raising my eyes, I could see her boots through my fringe. Her feet were planted slightly apart, a position of command with me at her feet, face down and licking her boots. My bottom was raised and my knees open, a pose of blatant sexual availability which I had adopted without thinking. The touch of her whip between my buttocks made me fully aware as she tickled the ultra-sensitive skin around my anus with the hard nylon of the lash.

I moved from one boot to the other, working slowly higher, then changing my licks to kisses as I reached the soft flesh of her thighs. I looked up for approval, but her eyes were intent on what she was doing with the whip between my bottom cheeks. Taking this for acquiescence, I carried on kissing a little higher each time, aiming for the golden fluff of hair that covered her pussy. She couldn't keep herself from giving a soft moan when my tongue found her pussy lips. Her spare hand took a grip in my hair and I found my face pulled hard against her belly. I licked obediently, burrowing my tongue in to find her clit and settling down to a steady rhythm against the hard little bud. Her scent and taste were strong in my head, feminine and musky.

What I wanted most of all was to make her come under my tongue. She denied it to me, suddenly pulling my head back and looking down at me. Our eyes met for an instant and then she pushed me away. Her pussy was moist with my saliva and her own juice, the pink flesh of her inner lips visible among the hair. I think we both knew that if she'd let me make her come, it would have broken the covenant of mistress and pet for the afternoon, perhaps for the rest of our precious twenty-four hours. It was at that instant, as I knelt back and looked up at her naked body, that I realised I didn't want to go back. I was in love with Amber.

She paused, perhaps sensing something of the depth of my feeling, then took me by the collar, pulled me up and set off across the paddock. After tying me to a convenient ring in the wall, she took off her boots and turned on the yard tap. She didn't say a word as she hosed the mud off me and then scrubbed me down with a stiff brush and a sponge. My harness was in a fairly sorry state, but nothing a bit of polish wouldn't cure. I stood naked, raising my hands to let her get at bits of me that were still muddy.

By the time she had finished I was pink and well scrubbed, with my skin tingling deliciously. Having her groom me was another new aspect of pony-girl fantasy for me, different again from what I had already learnt.

I suppose in its purest form, the groom would be someone other than the mistress or master, but I was more than happy to have Amber washing me and still felt myself hers, with no diminution of our roles.

The day was beginning to cool and I could feel the first taste of autumn in the air as Amber rubbed me down with a towel. She rubbed firmly, covering my whole body and treating my breasts and bottom with the same detached thoroughness as the less sensitive areas of my skin. Only when she came to my pussy did she break role, rubbing the towel well in and coming close to kiss my mouth as she explored between my legs. Her breasts felt firm and resilient against mine, both bare, the hard nipples rubbing against my skin. I opened my mouth under hers, eager to be fondled as we kissed, only to have her pull away and raise an admonishing finger.

'Later, Penny,' she chided playfully, her first words since outlining the details of my punishment. 'For now, you are going to serve me dinner and, when I've finished, I'm going to cane you. You could probably do with some rest first, so run upstairs and relax until I call you.'

I obeyed, turning as I entered the kitchen to see Amber start to run the hose over herself. Amber's room was large and comfortable, with a faint smell of some sort of aromatic wood. It was true that I was exhausted but, as I crawled naked on to the bed, I didn't expect to be able to sleep. The ache of sexual need in me was too strong, especially with the implications of lying nude on Amber's bed.

Lying face down, I reached back to stroke my bottom, feeling the smooth skin and wondering how many cane strokes I had coming. A mirror on her dressing table reflected part of me, including my behind. The last traces of the marks from my previous beating were just visible, along with two pale-red lines where the training whip had caught me. I may be vain, but I think I can reasonably claim to have quite a nice bottom: small, round and firm but fleshy enough to be girlish.

I rolled to the side to give myself a better view. The pose left the rear of my pussy visible, the lips pouting out from between my thighs. That was the view Amber was going to have when she beat me later: only more vulnerable still, as she would probably make me part my legs and stick it out more. I turned from the mirror and slid a hand between my thighs, wondering if I should sneak an orgasm.

The next thing I knew, I was being shaken awake, Amber looking down at me as I lay curled up, with my hand still between my legs.

'Dinner time, Penny,' she said. 'You've got ten minutes to get ready and dress.'

'In what?' I asked blearily as, to the best of my knowledge my clothes were a hundred miles away in Wiltshire.

'You'll see,' she answered and walked out.

I'd been expecting to serve naked, and when she left the room I was imagining perhaps a maid's uniform with an embarrassingly short skirt and no panties. It didn't surprise me to find that Amber had nothing so obvious in mind. It was a maid's uniform, but of the most conventional sort. While it was a little large for me, the outfit was complete to an obsessive level of detail. Of course, the same could be said for her pony-girl tack, so I don't suppose I should have been surprised.

Only when I'd been for a brief wash and began to examine the outfit did I realise that she had chosen a style that hadn't been in fashion since the beginning of the century. The underwear consisted of several petticoats, a corset and a combination chemise and drawers that opened between the legs. Knee-length stockings completed the underwear; a dress of coarse, plain blue wool, a pinny and mob cap made up the rest.

It was a nice touch, typically complicated, and I was looking forward to wearing it so much that I even began to stop worrying about the caning I was going to get after dinner. Only when I started to dress did I realise that there was more to her choice than simply dressing me in an old-fashioned servant's uniform.

Ten minutes, she had said, and she hadn't needed to add that being late would result in some new detail being added to my punishment. After ten minutes, I was still trying to get the corset laced up and was beginning to panic, which slowed my progress even more. A gong sounded once, downstairs, then again, impatiently. I wrenched the corset and tied the laces off any old how, hoping that I wouldn't have my uniform inspected and knowing I would. The petticoats were easier, although she didn't seem to approve of anything as simple as buttons and everything did up with draw-strings. After that it was easy, until the last moment when I discovered that the dress buttoned all the way down the back.

The gong went again just as I was adjusting the mob cap in front of the mirror. If Amber's intention had been to fluster me, she had certainly succeeded, but I determined to play my part as coolly as possible.

I came downstairs to find Amber seated at a mahogany table in a room I had not been in before. She was dressed in a crimson gown and gave me a single disdainful look as I entered the room and curtsied to her. Rich scents coming from the kitchen told me that she'd actually done all the cooking while I slept, so I left her and went to fetch whatever she had chosen.

I like to think I did it quite well. A place had been laid for me at the kitchen table and it was a simple matter to bring her dishes in, quickly eat my own and be back in time to clear and serve the next course. The erotic effect of serving her was subtle and slow, defining my position with respect to hers and affecting me with the subtle humiliation of my position and dress. Of course, if I hadn't known that I was dressed as a Victorian serving maid, it wouldn't have really worked. Amber seemed to assume that I would be educated enough to know this and also understand the implications of it. Actually, I don't know how widespread fantasies of class distinction and corporal punishment of servants are, but I do feel that there's something very English about them and, even fifty years after the end of service as a major trade, there's still an echo of it in our culture.

She ate without hurry and ignored me, except for giving the occasional order. As the meal progressed, my sense of anxiety increased, so that by the time she gave her mouth a final delicate dab with a linen napkin I was actually unable to stop myself from rubbing my thighs together in anticipation. She told me to pour her a brandy and sipped it slowly, while I stood by the sideboard with my hands behind my back.

'I believe we have a regrettable little duty to attend to, Birch,' she remarked as she put the empty glass down on the table.

'Yes, ma'am,' I answered quietly.

'Thirty-six strokes, I believe,' she continued.

'Yes, ma'am,' I repeated. Thirty-six strokes!

'Bend over the table,' she ordered.

'Yes, ma'am,' I managed. It was going to be now, over the table with my bum showing. A hard lump rose in my throat as I went to the end of the table and bent. I looked up at Amber, who was rising and pushing her chair back. Behind her a tall mirror in a gilt frame reflected the room and also a similar mirror behind me. I could see myself in the reflection, both my face and the back of my skirts. The mirrors were evidently placed intentionally so that girls could watch themselves being beaten. I was going to see everything: my skirts pulled up, my bottom exposed and the cane applied to it. Oh, Amber, I thought, you really know how to get to me.

I couldn't keep my eyes from the mirror as she stepped behind me. First my skirt came up, exposing my top petticoat. Just that filled me with shame, although the petticoat was considerably more demure than most of my ordinary clothes. When it came up and my shorter, lighter petticoat was laid bare, the feeling of shame intensified. That petticoat followed the first and my drawers were showing, then her hands were on them and my cheeks were burning with the humiliation of it. She drew the flaps of cotton apart and I could see my bum in the mirror, bare in a froth of cotton and lace. I was shaking as she made a few final adjustments to leave her target completely vulnerable.

'On your toes, girl,' Amber ordered.

I could see my bottom clearly in the double reflection, a tuft of black hair sticking out between my cheeks. Pulling my back in and raising myself on to my toes opened my cheeks so that my pussy and the hair in between my bottom cheeks showed. The pose destroyed my last vestige of modesty. My bottom-hole was showing and she was going to beat me like that, while she had not so much as a button disarranged.

Amber walked out of the room, leaving me to contemplate the indignity of my position and my approaching punishment. I knew she had gone to fetch the cane and waited in an agony of humiliation and desire.

If it takes a good imagination to get in the sort of state I had worked myself into, then you don't need any at all to benefit from the physical side of a caning. Amber came back into the room and my heart jumped when I saw the cane in her hand.

'Count,' she ordered as she got behind me and laid the implement gently across my bottom. It felt cold and hard, a line of potential pain across the softness of my bottom.

'Yes, ma'am,' I stuttered, my voice shaking.

I saw her lift the cane in the mirror and, the next instant, a line of fire sprang up across my bottom. I gasped and kicked, gritting my teeth and only calling out the first stroke when the initial sting had begun to die. The second followed as I spoke, making my bottom dance again. In the mirror, I could see two red lines on the white of my bum, parallel and laid across the plumpest part of the cheeks.

'Two,' I said in between breaths, and the third caught me immediately.

My bottom was beginning to warm properly by the fourth stroke and, by six, my whole body was responding. I was beginning to get that wonderful, sexual warmth that only a well-smacked bottom can achieve. Amber applied the cane evenly and quite hard, but never hard enough to cut. By twelve I was in a blissful haze, wriggling and lifting my bottom for the strokes. The effects of the subtleties of my dress and exposure had begun to fade, replaced by wanton pleasure but, when I tried to sneak my fingers between my legs, I got a sharp word and a cane stroke across the back of my thighs for my trouble.

I made my thirty-six, but I know I could never have taken so much with someone less skilled and tender than Amber. To call someone who had just given me thirty-six strokes of the cane tender may seem strange, yet Amber could have been a lot harder and just hurt me. Also, when it was over and my bum was a mass of red strips and throbbing with pain, she knelt down and kissed my bottom. A moment later, I felt something cool touch my burning skin and looked up to see that she had begun to rub cream on to my skin. That was bliss and, as I let myself go limp on the table top, I felt completely hers, to be done with as she wanted.

What she wanted was me. Her application of the cream quickly began to touch places that the cane had left unblemished. First the insides of my thighs, then down in the crease of my bottom, and finally my pussy and anus. That was too much. I turned and was in her arms in an instant, kissing her and trying to get at her body.

Her gown came down over her breasts as I pulled at it. One large breast was bare in my hand, the nipple stiff as she took my shoulders and pushed me on to my back. Her hand was under my skirts, tugging my petticoats up and sliding into my drawers to find my pussy. My knees came up and open, spreading my thighs for her. Her fingers worked in the wet flesh as she moved herself half on top of me. I kissed eagerly as her breasts came over my head, finding a nipple as my face was smothered in soft flesh. I suckled her for a moment as my arms went round her, then she was pulling upwards, lifting my shoulders from the floor.

'Come up,' she breathed, disengaging herself and helping me up.

She took my hand and I followed her up the stairs, letting her guide me on to the bed and responded as she once more began to kiss me. Her fingers were working on my dress buttons, flicking each open with deft touches. It quickly fell open at the back and she pulled the front down, trapping my arms and baring my front as the chemise was pulled open. I pulled my arms free as she laid me back and straddled me, my lower body invisible under the spread of her skirt. My knees were open and my skirts well rucked up, the air cool on my hot pussy and the coverlet rough against my well-beaten bottom.

Amber looked down at me, her mouth slightly open, her tongue wetting her lips. With her legs on either side of my waist, she had me pinned firmly to the bed, producing a deliciously submissive feeling in me. What I wanted best was to lick her, so I stuck my tongue out in clear invitation. She responded with a mischievous look and shifted her weight, turning so that she was still straddling me but head to toe, with her sitting on my chest.

I was even more firmly held in place and could only moan as she adjusted my skirts to bare my pussy and began to play with me. Despite having the wonderfully female roundness of her bottom just in front of my face, I could do no more than squeeze it through her dress while she explored my vulva in the most intimate detail.

'Please, Amber,' I begged, getting fairly desperate.

She shifted her weight again, raising her bottom as she began to pull up her skirt. I helped her, tugging at the crimson velvet until it was clear, revealing cream silk camiknickers, loose at the sides but stretched taut across her bottom. She edged back, my mouth was suddenly dry as she tugged open the poppers that closed the garment between her legs. Then her naked bottom was in front of my face, her cheeks wide, her musky, feminine scent rich in my nostrils. As she rocked back, she dropped her dress, leaving my head covered in the red velvet.

I put my arms round her hips and pushed my face into the warm crease of her bottom. She settled herself on my face, wiggling to spread her bottom over my mouth. I knew that all I had to do was poke my tongue out and I'd be licking her bottom-hole, something that had always seemed simply far too rude to do. If there was ever a time to do it, it was now, and as she gave another wriggle I kissed her anus and then stuck my tongue out, licking at the tight hole.

Amber moaned as my tongue touched her bottom-hole, taking hold of my legs and pulling them up so that my ankles were around her neck and gripped by her hands. I knew that my position left the lower part of my bottom cheeks visible, including some of the welts she'd given me.

'Make me come,' she demanded.

I could barely breathe with her bottom spread over

my mouth, but my attempt to transfer my attention to her pussy was met with more pressure on my face.

'With your fingers, Penny,' she said, her tone now more plea than order.

I managed to get one arm up between her thighs, finding her pussy and starting to frig her with my fingers. Her anus was moist with my saliva, and open enough for me to put the tip of my tongue in it.

'There, yes, do that,' she said, gasping out the words. 'Right in, Penny.'

I tried to push my tongue deeper up her bottom and began to circle her clit with a knuckle. She sighed and began to move up and down slowly. I knew she'd come soon. My tongue was well into the opening of her anus and it had begun to spasm. Her hands were locked tight on my ankles and she was squirming her pussy desperately against my knuckles.

She screamed my name and put her whole weight against my face, smothering me against her flesh. I kept licking until her shudders and the contractions of her muscles had subsided, only then pushing at her thighs to signal her to let me breath. She rolled off me, collapsing on the bed with a sigh of utter contentment.

I sat up to look at her. She was lying back, a happy smile on her pretty face, her breasts still bare were I'd pulled down her bodice. One eye was open and turned to me.

'Thank you, Penny,' she said quietly. 'Just let me get my breath back, and I'll return the favour.'

She did, not once but several times, and it was well into the early hours of the morning that we finally went to sleep, now naked and with my head cradled on her chest.

Seven

I've had my share of morning afters and have at least once woken up with a roaring hangover and a man I wouldn't normally have even considered. When I woke up and realised that I was in Amber Oakley's bed, it was very different. I'd never spent a night with a woman before and still felt a lingering guilt for what I'd done. Not much, though, even when I remembered that I'd actually licked her bottom, also something that I'd never done before. Other than that, my feelings were entirely happy and very, very satisfied.

She wasn't actually in the bed when I woke up, but I could hear breakfast sounds coming from downstairs and could smell coffee and toast. For all my acceptance of having had sex with her, I couldn't help but giggle when she appeared with a tray laden with breakfast. She just stuck her tongue out, clearly happy and completely at ease. Of course, I knew it wasn't the first time for her.

'It's gone ten, sleepy-head,' she remarked. 'I'm supposed to have you back in Wiltshire by two.'

I'd completely forgotten the background to why I was there and suddenly found my cheerfulness dissipating. Spending the day with Matthew could only be an anticlimax, after Amber. He was nice enough, and had been good to me, but he simply didn't have her understanding of my sexuality, let alone the affection I need after that sort of treatment. I mean, it's one thing to beat me and humiliate me until I have to come, but

I need a cuddle afterwards and Matthew's post-coital response was mainly guilt and insecurity. Not only that, but Amber was far more subtle and skilled at the beating and humiliation.

So I didn't want to go back. I wanted to stay with Amber, preferably cuddled up to her for the rest of the morning. On the other hand, I felt really bad about wanting to desert Matthew. It was he who had taken the trouble to follow me that day and introduce me to the thrills of being a pony-girl, after all.

I must have looked miserable, because Amber sat on the bed and put her arm around me, kissing me gently on the cheek. I smiled weakly and accepted a cup of coffee from her, wondering what to do. Honesty seemed the best idea and I began to explain things to her, praying to myself that her feelings towards me were the same.

They were. She listened patiently and gave me a hug when I'd finished. Her suggestion was to go to Wiltshire, make the most of the day with Matthew and then come and see her as soon as possible. Matthew, she pointed out, had no particular claim on me and could hardly expect me to see him as my full partner in the circumstances.

It seemed an odd thing to say, since being his girlfriend seemed to me to be more or less what he did expect. Other than the fact that our sex had been less than ordinary and that he was terrified of his tyrannical brother, our relationship had got off to a fairly straightforward start. I didn't pick her up on it, but took a piece of toast and reflected that she wanted me as much as I did her, which was the important thing.

I would have liked to have talked to her more on the way to Wiltshire, but instead fell asleep in the car. She didn't wake me up until we were nearly at Broadheath, and we were pulling up outside the Scotts' before I was really awake. Michael greeted us at the door, typically unaffected by the new intimacy between us.

We entered the house to the smell of roast beef, which made me realised just how hungry I was. Ginny was cooking and greeted both Amber and me with a friendly hug. All in all, it was a scene of rural domesticity that couldn't have been in greater contrast to what the same people had been doing just twenty-four hours earlier.

Matthew had apparently been held up at the farm, for some reason, but appeared just as we were about to start lunch. He was really affectionate to me, picking me up and kissing me, then ruffling my hair as I sat down at the table. This made me feel even worse at the thought of deserting him for Amber and I decided that her plan was the best. Eventually, I told myself, things would work out.

I had imagined that we would be going to play up at the park, after lunch, and had determined to give of my best to assuage my guilt. Nobody had mentioned anything though, and I was beginning to wonder if they had decided to rest for the day when the grandfather clock in their hall struck three.

'Ah, good, punishment time,' Michael announced, putting down his wine glass.

'Oh, dear,' Ginny replied and got up, fiddling with her jeans button as her husband pushed back his chair.

I watched as she undid her jeans and pushed them down around her thighs. Her panties were pink and quite tight, with a fair bit of her full bottom cheeks spilling out to either side. She shuffled round the table and bent over Michael's knee, looking thoroughly contrite with her head down and her bottom up. He pulled down her pants in a wonderfully matter-of-fact manner, then began to spank her. Her cheeks wobbled and bounced under his hand, her legs opening occasionally to provide flashes of golden hair and plump pussy lips. He had one arm around her waist to hold her still and a rather bland look on his face, as if dishing out bare-bottom spankings to his wife after Sunday lunch and in front of guests was completely normal. Knowing the Scotts, it probably was.

I was enjoying the show in any case, especially as I rather felt that Ginny had got off lightly since I had been around. Also, I was at her tail end and got the best view, or at least the rudest view, while Amber was evidently getting a kick out of watching the expression on Ginny's face. Matthew continued eating his pudding, only occasionally looking around to look at his sister's naked bottom as it was smacked to a glowing pink.

'Why is she being spanked?' I asked, partly from curiosity and partly because I wanted to humiliate her.

'Didn't we say?' Michael replied, stopping for a moment with a hand resting on one flushed cheek. 'This is for losing, yesterday. On the hour, every hour from when you arrived to when you leave.'

'Poor Ginny,' I answered in mock sympathy. 'Still, I wouldn't worry, you're well padded.'

'Hey!' she protested. 'That's not padding, that's all me.'

I reached out and gave her plump bottom a squeeze. Her skin was warm and had a slightly rough texture where the spanking had brought up goose bumps.

'You can laugh,' she answered. 'You're next.'

'I'm a bit too sore, actually,' I admitted.

'Let's see,' she answered, moving to get up from Michael's lap.

'No, you don't,' Michael said, tightening his grip on his wife's waist. 'Not until I've finished with you.'

'But . . .' she began, only to be silenced with a smack. There's not much modesty or dignity for a woman with her pants down over her husband's knee, in any case, but it's amazing how quickly she'll forget both completely once her actual spanking begins. Ginny certainly had. She was quickly kicking and wriggling again, her knees opening to give me an intimate view of her pussy, then the tight pink spot of her bottom-hole as her cheeks came apart. I could feel my own pussy moistening at the sight and remembered how I'd licked Amber between her cheeks, the previous night.

Michael finally decided Ginny had had enough and let her stand up; she pouted her lips while she rubbed at her smarting bottom. For all her show of displeasure, she kept her back to us and took care to make sure we all got a good view before pulling her panties and jeans up.

'Well, Penny?' Matthew said as Ginny sat down.

'I really can't be spanked,' I said. 'Amber caned me, last night.'

'May we see?' Michael asked.

I didn't reply but stood up and turned my back to them, lifting the dress Amber had lent me. I had a pair of her panties on underneath as well, comfortably loose over my extremely sore behind. There was a satisfying chorus of exclamations when I pulled the panties tight up between my cheeks.

'No spankings for you, then,' Matthew admitted. 'Do you want to take it easy today, then?'

I could have said yes, but it would just have made me feel worse about the whole situation. Also, having seen Ginny spanked, I was pretty keen not to spoil the chances of an interesting afternoon.

'I don't mind being punished,' I answered him after a pause, 'just as long as it doesn't involve my bottom getting smacked.'

'Nobody could ever call you a spoilsport,' Ginny remarked. 'You could take the cane on the front of your thighs, that's quite nice.'

'Maybe,' Michael put in, 'but I've got a better idea, at least for the four o'clock session. We'll have to go up to the park . . .'

'All in good time,' Matthew interrupted him, 'but for now I'd like a moment with Penny. Penny?'

He was holding out his hand and I knew full well

what he wanted. I stole a glance at Amber, who smiled back, and so I reasoned that I might as well take my fill. I'm not sure if he noticed, but there was something definitely proprietorial about the way he led me upstairs and closed the door of the spare bedroom firmly behind him.

I expected a show of passion, which would have been difficult to handle. As it was, his approach was straightforwardly sexual and I've never had a problem with sex for its own sake. No sooner was the door shut than he was guiding my hand to his fly. I pulled his cock out and felt it begin to swell in my hand as I leant up to kiss him.

Seeing Ginny spanked had triggered two fantasies in my head. Firstly, that of the view between the legs of a girl who's been upended: bottom fully on display, pussy showing, head down with her breasts dangling, a deliciously rude and undignified position. Then there was the thought of sucking a man's cock after he's spanked me; knowing that the act of punishing me has made him want an orgasm and helping him to have it, in my mouth.

Matthew sat down on the edge of the bed, his erect cock sticking up from his trousers like a mast, his balls bulging out at the base. I knelt, feeling utterly dirty as I took hold of his cock and began to kiss his balls. I was about to suck a man's cock, but my head was full of thoughts of another woman and it was the sight of a different woman getting spanked that had first turned me on. Knowing that many people would find my behaviour outrageous made it all the better, and I wished they'd all been able to watch while I sucked Matthew's lovely thick penis.

I started to lick at his shaft, but his hands came down and clutched at my dress, pulling it up. I leant back, letting him pull the dress over my head and leaving me in nothing but Amber's panties. I put a hand back and tweaked at the panties, pulling them down over my well-caned bottom for the benefit of my imaginary crowd. Matthew had me by the hair, my mouth open and his cock pointed at it. There would have been a murmur of approval when they saw that I'd been beaten, then sounds of disgust as I took the cock into my mouth, so obviously willing.

Matthew was holding my head and fucking my mouth, his shaft sliding in and out of my lips at a leisurely pace. I spread my knees until I could feel Amber's panties stretched taut between my thighs. My hands went back, one to pull open the crotch of the panties, one to go inside and cup my pussy, my middle finger burrowing down to rub on my clit. There would be more cries of disgust from the crowd as they saw that I had started to masturbate, but the men's cocks would be stiffening in their trousers despite themselves and the women would be feeling disturbingly warm between their legs.

My fantasy ran on as Matthew continued to hold me by the head and fuck my mouth. It gave me a wonderful feeling of being used, and I was already beginning to tremble and tense as his pushes became deeper and more urgent. I was hoping that he'd pull out and cover my face in sperm, even as my fantasy changed to an earlier scene that didn't include him at all.

I was in front of the same crowd as before, but in my Victorian maid's dress and about to be caned by Amber. I would be trembling with shame as my skirts were lifted; pleading to be allowed to retain my last scrap of modesty as my petticoats came up; then sobbing in utter humiliation as my drawers were pulled apart and my most secret places exposed to everybody. I'd wait, snivelling and begging as I was lectured, then kick and writhe as I was caned. The cries of the crowd would be loud in my ears: disgust at the sight of my naked bottom and open legs, approval at my being punished, and amusement at the way I kicked and wriggled so wretchedly.

The first time I'd sucked Matthew off, I'd come first. This time, we hit a peak together. Even as my fantasy hit its climax and my muscles began to spasm, his cock jerked in my mouth. He pulled my head back, the tip of his cock right in front of my mouth, shiny and wet with my saliva. I was coming, my mouth gaping as a jet of sperm erupted from his cock. It went right in my mouth, adding the final touch to my pleasure as I thrust my bottom out and my spine arched in orgasm.

I took his cock back in, making him groan loudly as my mouth clamped onto his erection while he was still coming. My mouth was full of sperm, so full that I doubt he'd come since the last time I'd done it to him. I swallowed all I could and then licked the rest off his cock. I felt like purring in the afterglow of my orgasm as Matthew slowly began to lose his erection.

I sat back on my heels, feeling too weak to rise. I managed a smile and got one in return, along with the slightly guilty look I'd come to associate with Matthew. We tidied up and I dressed in my own clothes, which had been washed, ironed and carefully laid out on the bed for me. Now that I was down from my sexual high, I began to think about the Matthew situation again. There was no doubt that he did a lot for me sexually, but there was little of the affection that I got from Amber. On a purely selfish level, I wanted Amber; but I still wanted my share of cock, especially as it had been a good three months since I'd had sex before meeting Matthew. Then again, it seemed likely that Amber's collection of sex toys included an artificial cock that she could strap on to fuck me with. Also, Matthew seemed a lot keener on putting it in my mouth than my pussy; and pussy needs her share. Still, I would feel mean, letting him down . . .

There's never an easier option than just going along

with the tide of things, and that's what I decided to do, hoping that it would all work out in the end.

The result of all this sex and philosophising was that when I came back down stairs I was in a thoroughly *laissez faire* mood. If Michael wanted to take me up to the park for some strange punishment, that was fine. In fact they could do as they liked, just so long as they spared my bottom.

Amber gave me a gorgeous 'I'm going to punish you for that' look as I came into the living room. Ginny was in a lively mood and obviously turned on, Michael cool as usual, and Matthew cheerful but excited or perhaps a little nervous.

'The park?' Michael asked me as I took a seat.

'Great,' I replied, 'but let me have a glass of wine first.'

'Of course,' he answered, and poured for me.

It was approaching four o'clock when we reached the park, Michael locking the gates behind us with his usual thoroughness. I was wondering what was in store for me as we parked and wandered down towards the lake. Ginny must have been thinking the same and I was looking forward to being punished side by side with her. She was obviously very excited and started to undress as soon as we reached the wooden boat house by the edge of the lake. Like the stables, it had been kept up and had a punt and a rowing boat tied to the little dock. Nothing immediately suggested an erotic purpose, although there was plenty of rope and I supposed that Ginny at least could be spanked with an oar. Also, we had bought our pony-girl harness, which made me wonder if I might be due for some new piece of punishment training, like Amber's combination of the pole and jumps.

There's more than one use for a pony-girl harness, as I found out. Ginny had pulled her panties off, by the time I'd finished looking around the boathouse, and had pointed out that I should strip too. I complied, undressing as I watched Michael fix her into her harness. My own followed; Matthew and Amber helped to do up the straps, buckles and lacing until I was in full kit.

The next part was left to Amber, who was always deferred to when things got complicated. She stood Ginny and I back to back, attaching the laces of our waist belts so that we were tied together. Our arms were then raised above our heads and the straps of our wrist cuffs intertwined. Our bridles followed, so that the back of Ginny's head was touching mine, the reins locked into the cheek rings and buckled into place. This left us completely immobile except for our legs, and that wasn't to be allowed us for long.

As Amber had been fastening our harnesses together, Michael and Matthew had been preparing long shanks of rope: thick, soft yachting lines. One of these was looped through our linked wrist cuffs and thrown over a beam, pulled up until we were on tiptoe, and cleated off on the wall. The second length went around our ankles, was passed back and forth around our legs like shoe lacing, and tied off on my waist ring.

The result left us completely helpless, tied in place with our breasts and bellies bare and vulnerable. I could feel Ginny's body warm against mine but couldn't see her at all. I'd never been so helpless and again was surprised by how strong a feeling it gave me. It wasn't just the physical sensation of being tied and helpless, but far more the feeling of being totally subject to another's will. Even in the back of Amber's horsebox, I'd been able to squirm around and could probably have got free if I'd wanted to. Now all I could do was wait: wait with my naked breasts stuck out and my belly and thighs bare.

Michael had left the boathouse, pulling gloves on as he went, which both surprised and alarmed me. Matthew had taken a seat on one of the benches that lined the walls, and was appraising my body with undisguised interest. Amber was invisible to me, on Ginny's side; from the way Ginny kept moving against me, I guessed Amber was playing with her, which immediately sent a pang of jealousy through me.

It wasn't long before Michael returned, holding a large bunch of greenery in his gloved hand. The plants looked pretty soft and, for a moment, I wondered what he was doing; then I realised the reason for the gloves. He was holding an enormous bunch of nettles, and it was suddenly quite obvious what they had in mind for us.

I began to squirm in my bonds immediately and was on the verge of pushing my bit out with my tongue and yelling 'red' as loudly as I could. Just the thought of stinging nettles on my bare chest had my nipples rock hard and my tits shivering. It must have looked good because Matthew's eyes were almost popping out of his head, and even the normally cool Michael allowed the tip of his tongue to moisten his lips.

Amber appeared in my range of vision, looking disapprovingly at the enormous bunch of nettles in Michael's hand. Suddenly I was determined that, if anybody was going to torment me with stinging nettles, then it would be Amber. Once I'd been put in an ecstasy of pain and submission I knew she'd hold me, and to my mind that was the only thing that gave her a right to do it.

'Yellow,' I managed, pushing the bit as far out as I could. 'I mean amber, or orange, whatever; slow down.'

'Are you all right, Penny?' Amber asked immediately, although, to be fair, both men looked concerned, if rather disappointed.

'Fine,' I said as her fingers took hold of my bit to make it a little easier for me to speak, 'but only you, please, and start very, very slowly.'

'OK,' Amber replied and kissed me.

‘What’s happening?’ I heard Ginny’s muffled voice from behind me and realised that she couldn’t see a thing but had only heard me use my stop word.

‘As we can’t spank Penny, we thought we’d use nettles on your titties, darling,’ Michael informed her, stepping to the side so that she could see what he was holding.

‘Oh, right,’ Ginny answered. ‘Don’t worry, Penny; it’s not too bad at all.’

‘Thanks,’ I answered, only partially relieved.

I composed my mind as Amber took a thick rag from the rowing boat and carefully selected three nettles from Michael’s bunch. He took the rest in one hand, for all the world like a bunch of flowers, and stepped out of my sight. Amber followed and I realised that they were going to do Ginny first.

‘Tell me, please,’ I managed, wanting to know what was happening rather than just have Ginny writhe against my back.

‘OK,’ I heard Amber say. ‘Michael’s got the nettles in his hand, right in front of Ginny’s tits. You know how big they are; well, she’s sticking them out like a brave girl. Her nipples are hard, too, but I can see her shivering. He’s going to do it now . . .’

I felt Ginny’s body arch against mine as the nettles were pushed on to her breasts. She was making whimpering noises in her throat and wiggling her bottom against me as Amber continued. ‘He’s put her breasts right in among the nettles and he’s twisting the bunch to get a good covering.’

‘Enough! Amber!’ I heard Ginny squeal. ‘Oh, my titties. I love you, Michael, you bastard! Oh, they’re burning! Come on, do it again, now . . . Yes!’

Ginny’s back arched again and she began to writhe, calling Michael every name under the sun but begging for more in between. Her struggles meant that her naked bottom was writhing against the small of my back, which alone would have been enough to have me wet and ready, without the fact that she was having her breasts stroked with nettles and that it was my turn next.

'She's rubbing her own breasts in them now,' Amber said as Ginny started to beg to be made to come. 'I'm holding the nettles and Michael's put his knuckles to her pussy so she can rub herself off on his hand.'

I could have guessed that. Ginny's hips and bottom had started to gyrate, bumping against me as she tried to masturbate herself against her husband's fist. Her back was moving wildly too as she moved her breasts from side to side in the nettle bunch. Her squeals were enough to lift the roof and I was glad we were in such a remote place. I was being shaken like a rag doll and was running with sweat by the time she came, screaming her passion out and calling Amber a bitch even as she begged her to move the nettles more.

Finally, it was over, and Ginny was telling them to stop. She continued to pant and squirm against me for a moment, then subsided with one long sigh. I'd had most of our combined weight on my toes and was exhausted just from her ordeal, but straightened myself and prepared to take it as Amber and Michael came around to my front.

'Oh, my poor titties,' I heard Ginny moan from behind me. 'Thank you, both of you; that was glorious. I'm sorry I called you so many names, too.'

'Don't mention it,' Michael answered her, eyeing my chest as Amber held out her three nettles towards my breasts.

They were quivering, bare and streaked with my sweat, the nipples sticking up, erect and expectant. She moved the stingers back and forwards in front of my face, then, without warning, stroked them across my breasts. I tensed my whole body, but only because I was expecting the same sort of pain you get from a cane stroke.

Instead there was a sort of tickling feeling, a bit like pins and needles and actually rather pleasant. I stuck my boobs out for more as Matthew walked over to watch; Amber brushed them again and sent a second wave of little prickles across my chest. I sighed, wondering what Ginny had made such a fuss over. OK, so her boobs were three times the size of mine and she'd had a whole bunch used on them, but still . . .

Then the stings started to throb. First gently, like a fingertip massage, then more painfully, with a burning sensation. I moaned out loud, realising that Ginny's reaction had been perfectly reasonable. Both my breasts were throbbing and burning, feeling incredibly prominent. The sensation was one thing; the extraordinary awareness of one's breasts was quite another. I clamped my teeth hard on my bit, arching my back and pulling at my bonds as Amber began to tickle each breast with a single nettle. The combination of agony and ecstasy was overwhelming and I knew why Ginny had been begging to come, even as she called her husband every name she could think of. I wanted the same, a hard fist against my pussy to rub my clit on while Amber tormented my boobs.

'Fist, please, Matthew,' I said, gasping the words out as I managed to push the bit down onto my chin.

'Go on, Penny, do it,' I heard Ginny encouraging me, her voice sounding tired.

He stepped forward and put his hand between my legs, but palm up, not with his knuckles. I tried to rub, getting some purchase but not really enough.

'The other way!' I gagged, wondering if I actually had enough energy left to reach orgasm. He turned his fist, but it was too late; I knew I'd never make it. I was in ecstasy, but every movement I made meant pulling Ginny with me. Also, I knew she must be making a big effort not to ask to be let out of bondage until I'd come, which was sweet of her, but I couldn't really relax while I knew she was hoping I'd get on with it.

'Red,' I said finally, and both Amber and Matthew stopped immediately. 'That's my lot. I'm sorry. It was lovely, but I just don't have the energy.'

Amber dropped the nettles and hugged me, Michael and Matthew moved quickly to the knots to let us down.

Two minutes later, Ginny and I were sitting sprawled in the boathouse. Her breasts were red and swollen, far more so than mine, which were just covered in nettle rash. She was squeezing cream on to them from a tube, making a good-sized dollop on each. The expression on her face as she began to rub the cream in was one of absolute, unrestrained bliss; her eyes were shut and her mouth a little open. My own breasts were throbbing and I took the cream, smearing it over them and rubbing it in. As Ginny's expression suggested, it was bliss.

'They'll throb all night, I'm afraid,' she told me, 'but you'll probably want to come at least twice. Here, let me do yours.'

I moved close to her, locking our legs together and reaching out to take her breasts in my hands, even as she did the same for me. Hers were heavy and soft, bigger even than Amber's and lovely to handle. Mine felt tiny in comparison, but Ginny made no remark and seemed to be enjoying creaming them. It felt more warm and friendly than sexual, sitting in front of her with my legs open and her big breasts in my hands. We were both completely naked, our pussies bare in front of each other and Amber and Michael, Matthew having gone up to the cars to fetch cold beers. It felt completely natural, relaxing and intimate.

I could not have been more off guard. Ginny had begun to giggle under my attention to her boobs and I was starting to wonder if I might not have that orgasm after all. There was a click at the door and we all thought it was Matthew coming back with the beer. I was thinking that he might be feeling a bit pushed aside after I had only let Amber use the nettles and then failed to bring myself off on his hand. To cheer him up a bit, I turned to the door to show off how open and moist my pussy was, only to find myself face to face with a woman I'd never seen before in my life.

We looked at each other for a second and then I hastily closed my legs while she went bright scarlet. Her eyes travelled slowly around the boathouse, taking in Ginny and me – naked and covered in cream and nettle marks. Beyond us there was a pile of discarded pony-girl harness and rope, stinging nettles and bits of nettle leaf strewn across the floor, the other rope hanging from the beam.

Her face was the colour of strawberry jam, her mouth wide open. The towel she had been carrying dropped to the floor. I knew my own face had to be much the same colour and Ginny's was no better. Amber managed a wan smile, but it was left to Michael to actually say something.

'Hi . . . Catherine,' he managed. 'I'm, er . . . afraid you've caught us at a bit of an awkward moment.'

That was an understatement, if ever there was one, but it broke the deadlock. I put the tube of cream down and started scrabbling for my clothes. Ginny got up and shrugged to the newcomer, giving an embarrassed smile as she picked up her top.

'Sorry about this,' Michael continued. 'We were . . . um . . .'

'Where's Matthew?' the girl asked. 'And who are you?'

The last question had been directed at me. In the circumstances, I think I did pretty well. I'd never seen her before in my life but, from her presence there and what she'd said, it was quite obvious to me who she was. She, and Michael and Ginny too, obviously felt she had every right to be there but they hadn't expected her. That meant she was family or at least close. She was of middling build and red-haired, probably not a Linslade or a Scott, and she was younger than I'd have expected Arthur Linslade's wife to be. Also, the first person she'd asked for had been Matthew. She had to be Matthew's girlfriend or even his wife.

I'm small and I've never pretended to be brave or aggressive or anything. Admitting to being Matthew's playmate was the last thing I was going to do. She clearly knew Amber and so I took the best way out I could see.

'I'm Amber's girlfriend,' I answered her.

'Oh,' she answered in a very small voice. 'Hi, I'm Catherine, Matthew's fiancée. Sorry, I didn't mean to . . .'

I'd obviously hit the right note. She must have known Amber was a lesbian and was more embarrassed than we were. What she made of her prospective sister-in-law's behaviour I could only guess at.

'I thought Matthew would be here,' she stammered. 'Look, this is really embarrassing, I'm sorry . . .'

We might have got away with it if Matthew hadn't chosen that moment to reappear with the cold-box of beer.

Eight

By the end of the week, I was beginning to cool down a little. I'd felt extremely hard done by, mainly because nobody had told me anything, even Amber. The fact that she hadn't known that I hadn't been told about Catherine was the only thing that saved me from being completely furious with all of them. What made it worse was that my quick thinking had saved Matthew from the full force of his girlfriend's wrath, but I was still the one who ended up on her own and feeling thoroughly used.

Term had ended, leaving me free of having to go into the labs every weekday and so I spent most of the week sitting in my flat. I was wishing Amber would ring and wondering what I would say to her if she did. I'd been fairly cold to her when I left, but I still wanted her, the more so as my initial anger and resentment began to wane. On Friday I felt so fed up that I almost asked to join a field trip to the Orkneys that the university was organising. Fortunately I didn't, because Amber rang that evening.

Her tone revealed that she was thinking I might not want anything to do with her, but my own voice betrayed my eagerness before I could even consider a show of being cross. From then on, it was all apology. I agreed to come and see her on Sunday, feeling immense relief and excitement that the whole thing wasn't over, after all.

I drove up, expecting to be invited either to bed or out to the paddock more or less immediately. Knowing her tastes, I'd put on a demure dress with a silk body and stockings underneath. My harness was in the back of the car and, as I'd packed it, I'd found myself trembling with the desire to be back in Amber's hands.

When I did arrive, I was surprised to find that she was on the verge of panic. I got the long hug and intimate kiss I'd expected but, instead of letting her hands wander or ordering me into the work room, she asked me to get into my harness to model for a customer.

'Of course,' I answered, slightly taken aback by the speed of things.

'Thanks, darling,' she answered. 'Vicky's ill, and the man's come all the way from the Czech Republic.'

'I didn't know they had pony-girls,' I remarked.

'Nor did I. Anderson put him onto me. He's some sort of businessman, apparently. From the way he was talking on the phone, he wants a huge order. Look, I'm sorry Penny; I'd planned a really nice day for just the two of us. You don't mind, do you?'

'No, really.'

'Thanks, you're really sweet. Could you get into harness, then? I'll help, but he'll be here any minute.'

I followed her into the kitchen and started to undress while she sorted my harness out.

'According to Anderson, he's incredibly fussy,' she told me as I peeled a stocking off. 'I like your underwear.'

'I was hoping you'd be helping take it off,' I replied.

'I will, later, I promise. Look, put the bridle on while I sort this out.'

She handed me the bridle and I took the bit between my teeth. The rest of the harnessing was done fast and Amber had me tethered in the yard when we heard a car pull up outside the gate. For all her hurry, she hadn't skimped on the extras and I was feeling a proper little show-off as she composed herself and walked over to the gates. She had pulled my waistbelt in to the maximum and tied it off in a bow, leaving my waist tight and my boobs thrust out. The wrist cuffs were done up behind my back and the reins looped on to a big iron hitching ring. She had joined my ankle cuffs to one another and put my thigh hobble on, leaving me pretty much immobile. There were bells on my nipples and at my cheeks, red ribbon bows tied onto my headstall, smaller bows clipped into my pussy fur and a black rosette attached to my left cheek ring. My little boots completed the ensemble, three inches of heel increasing my helplessness. He had to be impressed. I had seen myself in the double mirrors before coming out into the yard and I knew I looked cute.

I couldn't see the gates from where I was tethered, but I heard them open and a large, black car drew into the yard, stopping more or less in the middle. My idea of a Czech pony-girl master ran to a sort of Bohemian intellectual: tall, thin, grey-haired, humorous yet stern. I was quite looking forward to being put through my paces by such a person.

The man who climbed out of the car showed me just how unwise it is to have preconceptions. He was small, round and slightly balding, although as he walked over to me his expression did combine amusement and severity.

Amber came up behind him and introduced herself. He responded, calling himself Mr Novak, which I think is rather like calling yourself Mr Smith in England. They exchanged a few pleasantries and then turned to me, Mr Novak eyeing me with an expression more critical than admiring.

'I would have expected a boy,' he said to Amber after a while, his English perfect if a little formal. 'Still, she will do. What is her name?'

'Calliphigenia,' Amber answered.

‘A fine choice: a nymph with a fat behind,’ he remarked, quite casually reaching out and stroking my bottom, then taking a handful of one cheek and squeezing. I stayed still, letting him caress my bum and wondering if he had expected a boy because he thought it more appropriate or because he was gay. Bisexual, rather, I corrected myself as his hand slipped under the tuck of my cheeks and bounced my bottom. Amber glanced at me and we exchanged looks while his attention was elsewhere.

‘I see she has been punished,’ he said as he moved around to get a better view of my bottom. ‘Caned, I would guess. Some time last week. Twenty-four strokes, I would say.’

‘Thirty-six,’ Amber answered.

‘Ah, yes,’ he replied, his fingers tracing lines across my skin, presumably on the now fading cane stripes. ‘The tack looks suitable,’ he continued when he had had a satisfying fondle of my bottom, ‘but you should use a harder and thicker grade of leather.’

‘I feel girl’s tack should be soft but strong,’ Amber replied evenly, although I could just imagine what was going through her mind. ‘I can use any grade of leather, within reason, as you prefer.’

‘I am disappointed that she has no tail,’ he said, presumably having accepted Amber’s assertions as to leather types.

‘I was waiting until you arrived to put her tail in,’ Amber replied, lying, I was sure, as she hadn’t mentioned it to me. I had been looking forward to having my tail and was glad to hear that it was ready. Having it put in with Mr Novak watching was a different matter and would be extremely humiliating. I knew that it would make me nice and warm for Amber when he left, though, and decided to take his presence as part and parcel of being Amber’s pony-girl.

‘That will be a good idea,’ he replied and I realised

that, while his grammar was perfect, he had no idea whatever of English manners and tact. I had thought the impolite, almost insulting, way he phrased things the result of a high self-opinion and a dominant sexuality. He obviously didn't know the implications of his choice of phrase, but his attitude was rather in keeping with my fantasies of how a pony-girl should be treated.

He wasn't good-looking and he wasn't charming, but he was about to watch my bottom being lubricated and a tail inserted into my anus. My feelings of sexual humiliation rose sharply as Amber unhitched me and walked me over to the door of her workroom. I kept my legs straight and my paces even and just as long as the hobble would allow. Inside, she refastened my ankle cuffs and put my reins over a convenient peg.

I was left to wait while Amber showed various bits of tack to Mr Novak, pointing things out with a large tube of lubricating jelly she had picked up from the desk. I knew exactly where that jelly was going, and the mere thought was enough to have me trembling with expectation.

Finally she opened a drawer and produced my new tail. It was the same glossy, almost black colour as my real hair, in a thick hank some two feet long and tied with a red ribbon at the base. The stem was some six inches of what looked like stiff black rubber, ending in a curve and a conical plug of about the same thickness as a rather skinny cock. She showed him how the stem could be bent and would stay in place, then put the tail down and picked up the jelly tube again.

I watched in awful fascination as she stuck out a finger and laid a long worm of jelly along it, explaining quite coolly why it was important to use water-based lubricant as she did so.

'Turn. Stick it out,' she ordered me.

I did as I was told, turning my back to them and pushing my bottom out. Her finger went between my cheeks and I felt the cold lubricant on my anus. I stayed obediently still and quiet as the finger was pushed up my bottom, but couldn't resist a sigh when she wriggled it around inside me.

'Stay there,' Amber ordered as she turned back to Mr Novak and picked up the tail.

I looked back over my shoulder, watching Amber grease the butt plug. Mr Novak looked thoroughly pleased with himself and I was hoping Amber would make me bend over more in order to complete my humiliation by letting him watch it actually go in.

Sometimes, I thought, she read my mind. When the plug was heavily coated with jelly, she unhitched me and led me to the work bench, bending me over so that my face and chest were pressed against a pile of skins and my bum was high in the air. The scent of leather was strong in my nostrils as I felt her hand slide between my buttocks and ease them open to show him my anus.

I was breathing hard and shivering as Amber touched the tip of the plug to my hole and began to work it in and out, opening me slowly. It felt very like being buggered, only Amber was a lot gentler than any of the men who'd had their cocks in my bottom. I relaxed, letting her fill me with the plug and thinking of what he'd be able to see. I felt my anus stretch to accommodate the thickest part of the plug, then pop shut around the stem, and I knew it was in. Finally, I was wearing my tail, and it felt even better than I had expected.

I stood up and Amber fixed on a belt, consisting of a single strand of nylon line and a popper.

'Beautiful,' Mr Novak announced, impressed for once. I had to agree with him. I could see my reflection in a mirror, the tail hanging down over the curve of my naked bum. The way the shaft came up between my cheeks really did make it look as if it projected from the base of my spine, up and then down in a graceful arch, falling below the backs of my knees.

'You are very pretty, Calliphigenia,' Mr Novak told me and then turned to Amber. 'Does she perform as well as she looks? I would like to see her.'

'Certainly,' Amber replied, 'she's still in training, but she has a natural grace.'

I was in pony-girl heaven as I was led outside. They discussed my qualities as we walked out to the paddock, Mr Novak asking questions which Amber either answered truthfully or made up as she went along. She was obviously keen to present an image of skill and experience, and I did my best to help.

First he asked to see my gaits, which meant very little to me but turned out to be various types of walk. Their names – walk, trot, high-step, side-step and so forth – were fairly self-explanatory and I managed to respond to Amber's commands, without needing more than the occasional light touch of her whip across my bottom. A session on the pole and jumps followed that, after which he insisted on seeing more tack and Amber had to bring her cart out.

I was harnessed to it and driven around the paddock, first by her and then by him, giving my permission for him to ride by stamping my foot in response to Amber's questions. I had taken off my heels to do the jumps and was barefoot, managing a decent turn of speed on the grass. By the time he was satisfied, I was hot and sticky, with a warm bum from their whips and a wet pussy from the whole experience.

'Excellent, excellent,' Mr Novak announced as Amber led me back towards the yard. 'I must have many of the things you make so well; in the right leather, of course. I will pay you in pounds sterling; cash, of course.'

He did, as well – quite a lot and never questioning Amber's honesty. I was tethered in the yard, dripping wet after having had a bucket of water emptied over me, and could see them through the kitchen window. I watched as Amber noted down his order and put the money away, shaking his hand and then rising. I was hoping he would leave so that I could masturbate in front of Amber, which was what I most wanted to do but, when they emerged from the door, they walked over to me instead of the car.

If he wasn't going to go away, I told myself as they approached, then I hoped he would enjoy watching me come. All morning, I'd been getting excited by the added humiliation of having him watch me, best of all when he had seen the tail plug inserted in my bottom, so coming in front of him would actually put a nice finishing touch to it.

'Your pony-girl is very fine,' he was saying to Amber as they stopped in front of me. 'Yes, really very fine.'

He was looking at me with frank admiration and I found myself blushing, only to be let down flat by his next remark.

'Not as beautiful as one of my pony-boys, of course, but still very fine.'

So he did prefer boys, which didn't surprise me. His next remark did.

'Would she enjoy anal sex with me?' he asked Amber, as if it was a completely reasonable request.

That really put the cap on it. First to tell me I was second rate and then to ask if I'd like his cock up my bottom.

'I'm not really sure,' Amber answered, sounding less than one hundred per cent sure of herself for once. 'I suppose you could ask her.'

'I will ask her,' he replied, giving a little amused smile and raising his finger as if to admonish her for an error of etiquette. 'Calliphigenia, I am willing to have anal sex with you. Stamp once if you want that.'

Willing to! The arrogance of the man was extraordinary. He was twenty years or so older than me, hardly taller than me and would have obviously preferred it if

I'd been male. With all that, he expected me to be not just willing, but eager to be buggered by him; doubtless while he shut his eyes and imagined it was one of his precious pony-boys.

I do like it in my bottom, though, and was seriously turned on, especially with the way the tail plug moved as I walked. If he had been most men, I'd have been on my knees with my bum stuck up in the air on the spot. As it was, I hesitated, looked at Amber, received a look of mock despair and then stamped my foot.

'Good,' he answered. 'Perhaps over the bench in the first room we went to?'

Over Amber's work bench, with my face pressed into the leather skins seemed ideal. Once more, I was unhitched and led into the workroom, this time to be bent gently down over the bench and my legs freed to allow me to open them and present Mr Novak with a nice view of my bottom. They left my hands tied behind my back, which added to the submissive feeling as I waited. Watching over my shoulder, I saw Amber burrow into a drawer to find Mr Novak a condom. His cock was already out of his fly as she turned back: not too large, thankfully, and still limp.

'Perhaps if you could . . .' he addressed Amber, gesturing to his penis.

I wondered if there was any end to the cheek of the man as Amber glanced first at his face then at the limp cock that was being offered to her.

'A few moments in your mouth will be quite sufficient,' he continued, as if it wasn't obvious what he wanted her to do.

I remembered Ginny Scott saying that Amber liked to have an excuse to have sex with men and so wasn't that surprised when she shot him only a brief glance of disbelief and then knelt to take his cock in her mouth. She licked it and then gulped it into her mouth, easing his balls out of his fly as she began to suck. As he had predicted, it stiffened quickly and Amber was soon sucking on a hard little shaft; Mr Novak then pulled it out of her mouth to stand, glistening and ready for insertion into my anus.

They had to take my tail out first, which Amber did while Mr Novak rolled the condom down on to his erection. I clamped my teeth on the leather of my bit as she pulled it gently out, relaxing as much as I could to keep myself open and moist for Mr Novak's cock. The sour, sharp taste of the leather filled my mouth as a hand touched my hip. The other, I knew, would be on his cock, guiding it to the juicy, willing target of my bottom-hole. Then something was touching me, the head of his prick, in that most sensitive of places: nuzzling, pushing, then making me grunt as it found its way in. For a moment, it hurt, then there was the wonderful, breathless sensation that I only get from having a cock pushed up my bottom.

Most men expect to fuck a girl's bottom as if they were fucking her pussy, hard and fast. It's not the same, though; it requires more care and less eagerness. I'll say one thing for Mr Novak, he knew what he was doing. His strokes were slow and firm, each one ending with his balls nudging my empty pussy. If my hands hadn't been strapped tight behind my back, I'd have been clawing the leather with one and playing with myself with the other. As it was, all I could do was let my feelings build to an impossible peak as he buggered me expertly.

'Do you enjoy having my penis in your bottom, Calliphigenia?' he suddenly asked, not varying his stroke but taking his hands from my hips and starting to caress my buttocks.

It was obvious I did, because I was grunting and panting unrestrainedly, not to mention pushing my bottom back for more. I nodded in response anyway, assuming he was getting an extra thrill from talking to me. He was squeezing my cheeks and pulling them apart, which I knew meant he'd be watching his cock go in and out. I suddenly wished I had a mirror so that I could see it too, or that Amber would take a picture so that I could come later over the sight of myself being buggered over her work bench.

'And would you prefer me to be a big young man with a penis like that of a donkey?' he continued.

I shook my head. I wasn't just flattering him either. Young men tend to go too fast and not last long enough, while really big cocks are too much for me. Mr Novak was a real expert and the knowledge of where he'd got that expertise just added to the delicious humiliation of being buggered by him. He gave a pleased laugh at my response and planted a gentle slap on my bum.

His pushes were getting firmer and deeper, his attention to my buttocks more urgent. I knew he was going to come soon, and wished I could have done so too. It was then that Amber joined in, coming to stand beside me and slipping an arm under my belly, her hand finding my pussy. First she took me in her palm, then slipped her thumb between my sex lips to bring the hard knuckle against my clit. She began to rub and I began to let my mind run.

There was no need for any embellishment to my fantasy. I was bent over in full pony-girl tack and a middle-aged Czech businessman had his penis in my bum-hole. I'd been shown off naked in front of him. My anus had been lubricated and a tail put in my bottom as he watched. He'd seen me perform as a pony-girl, seen me whipped, insulted me, and now he was working his stubby little cock slowly back and forth in my bottom-hole. Not only that, he'd had Amber suck his cock. My beautiful lady, who had trained me, beaten me when I needed it, even had me lick her bottom – and she'd knelt to suck his prick and hold his balls in her hand.

It was that thought that made me come. Amber kneeling with Mr Novak's erection in her mouth while she tickled his balls. My back arched and I nearly pulled his cock out of my bum, but he took a firm grip of my harness and pushed his cock back up to the hilt.

'She has come to her climax; how beautiful,' I heard him say as my shudders subsided. 'Now I will, too. Ah what a pleasure, to take my orgasm in an Englishwoman's bottom.'

I tried not to giggle as he began to hump away, his strokes getting rapidly faster and deeper. Amber had sat up on the bench next to me and was stroking my hair as she watched him bugger me. I was wishing he'd hurry up but didn't have the heart to stop him. I relaxed and moved my hips with his strokes, hoping it would help him come. Maybe it did because, a moment later, he grunted and slammed his cock to the hilt in my bum, his balls slapping on my pussy and his stomach smacking against my backside. He held it there for a long moment, holding me hard against him by my harness.

Then it was over and he had withdrawn. I stayed slumped over the bench while Amber undid my wrist straps, then let her help me to my feet.

'Most kind. Thank you,' Mr Novak said – to Amber, not me – and speaking as if she'd just let him use the telephone or made him a cup of tea.

He left soon afterwards, promising to be back in a fortnight for his order.

'You are a disgrace, Miss Penny Birch,' Amber chided me playfully when she returned from fastening the gate. 'I should really beat you for being such a willing little slut.'

'Yes, please,' I answered, 'but later, in the bedroom.'

'I'll hold you to that. Seriously, are you OK?'

'Fine, other than having a slightly sore bottom, and I could do with a bath.'

'Have one while I make lunch,' she answered, moving towards the kitchen door.

When I came downstairs, once more scrubbed and presentable, Amber was sitting at the kitchen table with a glass of white wine in one hand and Mr Novak's order in the other. I poured myself a glass and sat down opposite her, watching the rather serious expression on her face.

'Look, Penny,' she said after a while, 'are you busy, next week?'

'No,' I answered fairly truthfully, 'term's over, so I can more or less do as I like. Most of my team's away anyway. Why?'

'I . . .' she began and then stopped.

I knew what she was going to ask, and what the answer was, but I wanted to be sure.

'I need some help with Novak's order,' she continued, 'and, well, actually, I'd like you to move in with me. If you like . . .'

'Yes,' I answered and reached out to take her hand.

She responded by squeezing my hand and smiling, then getting up and walking around the table to hug me. I snuggled into her neck, feeling warm and secure, staying there until she let go and kissed me gently on the forehead.

The rest of the day was spent in blissful relaxation. We stripped naked and sunbathed in the paddock, inevitably ending up in a clinch. We kissed for a while and then started a play-fight. Of course, Amber won easily and was soon sitting astride me with her bottom poised over my face, threatening to sit down if I didn't submit. I refused and was rewarded with her full, female bottom sat squarely down on my face.

'Kiss it or I'll sell you to Mr Novak,' she joked.

I kissed her bottom-hole and stuck my tongue in a little way, making Amber sigh.

'Do that again,' Amber asked, a familiar urgency creeping into her voice.

She had relaxed, expecting her bottom licked as I'd

done before. Instead, I nipped her thigh with my teeth and squirmed away from under her, running to the side in the hope that she would chase me and spank me before making me lick her properly.

I got what I wanted, although I managed to get as far as the kitchen before she caught me. Once caught, I was pulled sharply down over her lap and spanked. She had my arm twisted up into the small of my back, and didn't stop until my bottom was hot and smarting. Only then was I pushed to the ground and sat on again, only this time with her pussy facing me.

'Now lick,' she ordered, 'and don't stop until I tell you to.'

I flicked my tongue out obediently, but only to tease her sex lips with the tip, deliberately ignoring her clitoris.

'Do you want to be spanked again, madam?' she demanded.

'No, please, not that,' I answered coquettishly.

'Then do as you're told,' she replied, pushing herself forward so that her vulva was pressed against my face.

I began to lick again, properly this time, letting my tongue find her clit and flick against the little bud. She was quickly moaning, softly and insistently, then began to rock her hips back and forth over my face. Inevitably, that was the moment the phone had to ring.

Amber reached for the receiver, staying on top of me and she put it to her ear.

'Ginny, hi,' I heard her say. 'Fine, thanks. Yes, she's here actually. No, she's busy. She's still cross, but mainly with Matthew. I expect she'll let you off with a good caning, if you grovel to her sweetly. I'll tell her. No, pretty awful, I had to spank her . . .'

I started to lick again, making Amber giggle.

'. . . across my knee. No, she was already naked. We'd been sunbathing. Finishing her punishment, if you must know. In the kitchen. Yes, Ginny, I know the phone's in the kitchen, but you still can't talk to her. She's got her mouth full, very full . . . Oh, Penny! Look, Ginny, I have to go. No, you can't listen! Oh OK, I'll leave the phone on the side.'

Amber put the phone down and settled herself more comfortably over my face, cradling her boobs with one hand and balancing herself against the table with the other.

'Harder, Penny. Yes, like that, yes, push. That's perfect, just keep going . . .'

I knew Ginny could hear and wished she'd phoned a moment earlier, so she could have heard me getting spanked as well. Inevitably, Amber was putting on a show for her, moaning and talking to me more than she would normally have done, but the scream when she came against my tongue was genuine, as were the sobs and heavy breathing immediately afterwards. She stayed on top of me when she'd finished, sitting back so that she was straddled across my tummy as she picked up the phone.

'Yes, thank you, very nice,' she said as she got her breath back. 'Yes, you can talk to her now.'

I took the phone, suddenly finding myself completely unable to be annoyed at Ginny. She was full of apology anyway and was angling for me to suggest punishing her. Of course, she knew that, if I accepted her submission, then I'd have already forgiven her for real. I had, but settled for a dose of the cane and a drive with all its attendant pleasures and possibilities, to be taken when circumstances permitted. I was looking forward to punishing Ginny, but as I passed the phone back and looked up at my new girlfriend, straddling me and gloriously naked, I wondered if I might not also manage to turn the tables on her.

Nine

The course of the next week saw my affair with Amber Oakley turn into a proper relationship. For all my fantasies and occasional fumbles with other women, I'd never have believed I could actually have a full blown lesbian relationship. Really there was nothing to it. I've always preferred to follow rather than lead in a sexual role, and Amber was very much the dominant partner. Out of bed, we got on as good friends.

On the Monday, I'd driven to my flat to collect clothes and so forth. After that, most of my time was spent helping her out in the shop while she got on with Mr Novak's order. This meant meeting the locals and various other customers, all of whom were terribly respectable. In fact, I don't think any of them so much as guessed that Amber and I were lovers or that the arrangement was anything other than innocent. Nights were a different matter, with plenty of straightforward love-making and no shortage of more elaborate role play.

She treated me as a perfect equal, yet there was always an undercurrent of sexual tension between us, and there was plenty of erotic play. I got spanked a lot, anyway. Generally Amber would take me across her lap with my dress up and my pants pulled down. My bare bottom would then be slapped a dozen or so times before I was let down to kiss her feet. She preferred me in dresses, at least when it came to punishing me, presumably as it made it simpler to get me ready for it.

She was endlessly inventive, and fascinated with complexity and ritual for their own sake, as well as erotic embellishments; there was always some new fantasy to try out. I spent a lot of time in the evenings in my Victorian maid's outfit, serving her at dinner, helping her undress, bathing her and invariably finishing with a smacked bottom for me and the services of my tongue for her. She never seemed to tire of me licking her pussy, usually with her sitting on my face, but sometimes with me kneeling between her knees or while she stood in front of me. She also liked to raise her skirts for me to kiss and lick her bottom, which always brought out a particularly intense feeling of submissive pleasure in me.

In bed it was different: kissing, cuddling and taking turns to bring each other to ecstasy with tongues or fingers. She did own a strap-on penis, a massive black rubber thing cleverly built into a pair of tight leather shorts. She only fucked me twice during that week, though, once over her workbench when she first showed me the implement and once in the paddock after a spell of pony-girl training in the evening. It vibrated, and so was great for bringing me off as well. Having things in her own pussy didn't seem to particularly appeal to her, and I didn't press the point, as I was getting so much of the attention.

Over the course of the week I increasingly came to want her at my feet in return. Ginny had told me the key to Amber's submissive side, but the chance didn't come; by the end of the week, I was beginning to consider abandoning the subtleties and just telling her to fetch the cane and get over the table. I know she'd have done it, but I also know she wouldn't have taken full pleasure in it and so held back.

What she did do was offer me the chance to be mistress to a pony-girl tack customer who had arranged to come up on the Sunday. The bulk of her customers were men, which she accepted with moderate grace as long as they kept buying tack. Oddly enough, it was the dominant males that she preferred; submissive male sexuality irritated her. Her closer male friends, like Anderson, were all men who were happy either way, the important thing being that they accepted that her interest in them was limited.

She was explaining this to me on the Saturday evening as we lay together on her bed. I'd been spanked earlier, and was lying face down, fantasising about turning Amber's bottom the same cheerful pink as mine was. She was very gently massaging my back and telling me about Sunday. The man coming the next day, apparently, was young, claimed to be good-looking and worked in the city. His fantasy was to be made over as a pony-boy and driven until he couldn't go on, which Amber honestly admitted she couldn't be bothered to do. I could see what she was hinting at and volunteered my services without hesitation. I felt I had watched her enough to make a passable job of it and was eager to try my hand at being mistress to a pony-boy. As far as he was concerned, then, I would be the fearsome Mistress Amber and she would just be the woman who did the leatherwork.

The only difficulty, Amber explained, was that she had another customer coming in the afternoon. This was a woman called Anna Vale, who sounded absolutely terrifying, like Amber only without the softness. Amber had never met her, but they knew each other by reputation, both being lesbian and experts on old-fashioned clothing. So when Anna Vale – or Miss Vale, as she would expect me to call her – had decided to try a pony-girl fantasy with her girlfriend, Poppy, she had contacted Amber. Unlike Amber and me, Anna Vale's relationship with Poppy never left the realms of fantasy. She wore styles from the 1930s and behaved accordingly, with Poppy as her maid. How she squared this in her mind with wanting Poppy as a pony-girl was beyond me, but Amber seemed keen to impress and wanted me to be her maid while Anna Vale was there. Anna Vale also despised men, unequivocally.

I was perfectly happy with this, as long as I had Amber near me, but it would mean that we had to get the pony-boy, Chris Ford, out of the way and me changed before Anna Vale arrived at noon. I sleepily assured Amber that we'd manage, only to get a sharp smack on my unprepared bottom. Inevitably, this started the whole cycle of punishment and sex off again and it was another hour before we got to sleep.

In the morning Amber had me getting into role the moment breakfast was finished. The first problem was that very little of her clothing fitted me. She had an impressive range of stern-looking dresses, also leather and rubber outfits and even a full set of studded body armour. In the end, we had to settle for riding gear, of which Amber had plenty of stock in the shop. We went to town, with corduroy jodhpurs and shiny black leather boots, a white blouse with a turquoise silk cravat, the traditional coat in hunting pink, a whip and hard hat. When Amber had applied a few carefully considered touches of make-up and I went to admire myself in the dining-room mirrors, I had to admit that I looked about as fierce as it is possible for a woman of my size and build to do.

Chris Ford seemed to be impressed anyway, although he was so grovellingly subservient to us from the start that I suspect he'd have been impressed if I'd been wearing a gorilla costume. When he arrived, he was in the sort of expensive casuals rich young men affect nowadays. He looked every inch the confident, successful man-about-town: six foot odd; sharp, intelligent features; neat sandy hair and a Mercedes.

I dare say he lived up to his looks in everyday life, but his attitude to me was positively worshipful. It gave me an immediate, and wonderful, feeling of power. The fact that all of a sudden I was no longer the little new playmate added to this; after all, for all he knew, I'd been doing it for years.

He started by asking to call me 'mistress', but I refused him permission. Instead, I ordered him to address me as Miss Oakley, a bitchy touch I was sure Amber would appreciate. That seemed to cow him considerably, so I asked if he thought he was dressed properly to be a pony-boy. He obviously wasn't and quickly admitted it, leaving me with the wonderful prospect of deciding what a handsome young man should have on. Amber may have been bored by the thought of controlling him; I wasn't. I decided to have him strip, which appealed as I was already keen to see what his cock was like.

'Then you had better strip, hadn't you?' I ordered, standing with my fists on my hips but sparing a glance for the workroom door, through which Amber had just gone. I knew full well that, in due course, I would be punished and humiliated in turn. Once he had left, I'd be lucky to keep my jodhpurs up for five minutes. When the time came, I would submit as meekly as ever. For now, I was in charge, and what Amber didn't see, she couldn't punish me for. Not unless I decided to tell her, anyway.

Chris Ford, naked, certainly lived up to my expectations. He was lean and well muscled; his body was obviously toned by regular visits to a gym, not to mention a sunbed. He had nothing like the brute muscularity of Matthew Linslade, but then he didn't work a farm. I was impressed, but kept my expression deliberately disdainful as my eyes travelled down his body, letting it turn to amusement at the sight of his genitals. Actually, they were quite impressive and my immediate instinct was to get down on my knees and suck his cock. Instead, I turned away, marching swiftly across the yard and snapping my fingers to indicate that he should follow.

Amber had already made a harness for him, a straightforward affair that had actually been run up as a prototype for Mr Novak's design. The leather was thick and hard, with a curious semi-gloss finish, not at all what I would have chosen for myself. He made no complaint. In fact, he simply watched dumbly as I examined the harness with a critical eye. I'd done some of the cutting myself and had made one or two tiny slips with the knife. I pointed these out to Amber, who bowed her head and apologised, although I caught a dangerous glint in her eye as she did it.

'Harness him,' I ordered Amber. This hadn't been agreed on, but I was intent on working up a really good punishment for myself in the evening.

'What's your name, boy?' I demanded as Amber fixed the waist belt around him.

'Chris, Miss Oakley,' he answered, looking nonplussed.

'Your pony-boy name, idiot!' I snapped back. 'I know your real name. Do you think I'd forgotten? Do you think I'm an idiot?'

'No, Miss Oakley,' he stammered.

'We'll call you Flabby, then,' I stated, choosing the name on the grounds that such an obvious fitness fanatic would certainly hate it. I was enjoying myself hugely and had never realised I could be such a bitch.

'Yes, Miss Oakley,' he answered, looking crestfallen.

I immediately wanted to stroke his cheek and apologise. At the end of the day I'm not actually a very good sadist, but that didn't mean I couldn't act the part. Amber had fastened the waist belt in place and was getting the bridle ready. I watched as she pulled it over his head and began to tighten the buckles, the bit slipping between his teeth.

'Well, Flabby,' I continued, 'I believe that you are to take me for a ride?'

'Yes, Miss Oakley,' he mumbled through the bit.

I turned on him sharply. I had caught him with the oldest trick in the book. Well, not a trick really, because there's no way around it. If he'd not answered I'd have had him for insufficient respect. He had answered and so I had him for talking after the bit was in his mouth. Amber constantly played it on me, and I knew how frustrating it is to have to do something but know that whatever you do leads to punishment.

'You spoke,' I snapped. 'Are you completely stupid?'

He didn't answer, of course, and I could see the expression of consternation on his face.

'Well?' I demanded.

He still didn't answer. Amber was fixing the last bridle strap, a short piece of leather that ran down the back of his head in place of hair rings. For a moment I thought she was going to start laughing and spoil it, but she managed to contain herself.

'Right,' I continued. 'You will be punished for talking. You will be punished for insolence. You will be punished for stupidity. I suspect the whip will do little good, so I intend to drive you until you collapse.'

Pretty neat, I thought, giving him his fantasy as a punishment, especially when I had thought the idea up on the spur of the moment.

'Prepare the cart,' I ordered Amber.

'Yes,' she replied, 'of course.'

'Yes, what?' I snapped back at her.

'Yes, Miss Oakley,' she answered meekly, but again the look in her eye told a different story.

'That's better,' I said. 'Fetch a suitable whip as well, and you failed to lay out my gloves this morning.'

'Yes, Miss Oakley,' she answered.

'Silly little girl,' I remarked, not really addressing anybody. 'I must whip her more often.'

Amber went to fetch our cart, which we had got ready earlier. I threw Chris's reins, or rather Flabby's, over the hitching ring. There was a bit of a problem. We were more or less honour-bound to run Chris into the ground. He had, after all, bought his tack and we'd agreed to realise his fantasy. Unfortunately, he looked like the sort of man who ran up mountains for fun, while I weighed next to nothing. It was approaching ten o'clock, which meant I had two hours to wear him into submission before Anna Vale turned up. On the other hand, the men's marathon record was just over two hours and he couldn't be that good. Also, marathon runners don't have to do it pulling girls in pony-carts, which is a pity really.

We only had the paddock to drive in. It was enough for ordinary pony-girl games, but I could see myself getting bored just going round and round. Obviously something was needed to spice the event up and I was turning my imagination to the task as Amber brought the cart up. I accepted the pair of black leather gloves and the riding whip she had chosen for me, swishing it experimentally through the air as she attached his wrist cuffs to the cart.

There was one obvious option; take him out cross-country. Not locally, of course, but there were some big areas of public woodland within twenty minutes' drive, and if I put him in a pair of leather shorts we wouldn't actually be breaking the law. I took Amber aside and explained my idea to her. She was uncertain at first, but agreed as long as I wore a veil and stuck to the loneliest section of the woods.

Half an hour later, I was backing the horsebox into a lay-by and nervously checking around for watchers. Chris was in the back, invisible; to any casual observer, I just looked like a woman out for a morning's ride. Over-dressed, perhaps, but quite innocent of any suggestion of sexual misbehaviour. A broad footpath led into the woods, apparently deserted. Working fast, I let the ramp down, ordered Flabby and the cart out and slammed it shut. I mounted the cart immediately, cracking the whip across his tight backside and setting him off at a run.

I drove into the centre of the woods, my heart in my mouth but hugely enjoying the risk of being seen. Not that I could be recognised, as I now had a top hat and a black veil that completely hid my features. Actually, I quite wanted someone to see us, only not the sort of person who'd make a nuisance of themselves over it.

It was also my first experience in the seat of a pony-cart, and it felt great to be on the giving end for a change. I could sit back as he pulled, watching the muscles in his back, bottom and legs work as he took the strain. A flick of my crop and a sharp word and he sped up, despite the fact that we were going up a shallow incline, pulling at a pace I doubt I could have managed myself.

If the experience of being a pony-girl had been unexpectedly strong and had turned me on immediately, then the experience of being a driver was very different. I liked the feelings of power and control, even though they had been gifted to me. It was relaxing in a way, and certainly erotic, but with a far slower effect. Not that slow, though, and by the time we reached the centre of the woods I had begun to toy with the idea of taking my pleasure of my pony-boy in much the way Matthew Linslade had taken his pleasure with me on my first trip as a pony-girl.

Flabby had worked up a good sweat on the slope and was beginning to breathe heavily. I estimated that we had done over a mile, mostly uphill and on fairly rough ground. I felt cool and relaxed, although the first bump we'd hit had punctured my composure. A dose of the whip and a few sharp words had ensured that it didn't happen again.

There was an area of large trees with open leaf-strewn ground between them to my left, and I turned him on to it. I was still undecided as to whether I should have him or not. There were condoms in my coat pocket and I knew he'd be delighted, so it was simply a question of whether I wanted it. It was wonderful to simply have that choice and, given that I could take it or leave it, I decided I might well take it. I hadn't seen anybody at all, and so felt pretty secure as I drew the cart to a stop in the lee of a good-sized holly and dismounted.

It actually takes a lot less courage to have sex with a man in the countryside than it does to strip and masturbate. After all, as a girl, you know that anybody who does see you will just think you've been persuaded into it by the rude and pushy male. OK, so maybe not when you're dressed in riding gear and mounting a pony-boy, but I was probably going to do it anyway.

I walked around the cart, admiring my mount. He was flushed from the exertion and breathing with deep, even draughts. The shorts, which were Amber's, hung loosely around his buttocks but were tight on his waist and thighs – very tight over his cock. I remembered how good the same shorts looked filled with Amber's more generous bottom and thighs and how it felt to kiss the taut seat. That decided me. I was definitely going to have him.

Amber knew I had the option, she had even put the condoms in the coat pocket. The penalty for going ahead was being fucked myself, with her strap-on, another powerful inducement to go ahead.

How to do it was a different matter. It's easy to fuck a pony-girl. You order her to kneel and stick her bottom up and there pussy is, wet and ready to be filled. You don't even have to unhitch her from the cart. With a pony-boy, it's not so easy. I wanted to keep him in role and maintain my dignity, so I couldn't just unhitch him and lie on the ground with my legs apart. I considered the problem for a moment and then ordered him to sit with his legs stuck out and his back propped up against the cart. That way I would be able to get on top, even though he'd be less than comfortable.

He obeyed without hesitation and I came to stand over him, rubbing the tip of my whip against the bulge in the front of the shorts. His cock stirred inside the tight leather and I found my excitement rising fast. I leant down, popping open the button and easing the zip down. His cock sprang out, swelling quickly as it was released from restraint. To touch it would be to break my role, so I used the whip to stroke him. It stiffened quickly, rolling upright as it became engorged with blood, hardening into a rigid bar of flesh just suitable for my pussy.

There is no dignified way to take a man's cock in when you're wearing jodhpurs. They have to come down and that's it. I was going to have to squat over him with my knees up as if I was having a pee as well, an even less dignified prospect. I didn't even want him to see my pussy, so I simply took off my hat and pulled it down over his face, leaving me with a nice cock to sit on and no disturbance from its owner.

I pulled my jodhpurs down to the tops of my boots, listened for a final moment and then dropped my panties too. A testing finger found my pussy every bit as damp as it felt and so I squatted down on his thighs, his cock rearing in front of me, ready and waiting. As an extra treat I decided to use my panties to give him a little wank. They were stretched tight between my knees, his cock lying against the part that normally covers my bum. He shuddered when I folded his shaft in the soft cotton and, for a moment, I thought he was going to come. Fortunately he didn't and I began to jerk him into my panties while I slipped my other hand back between my legs and began to play with myself.

Knowing he really would come if I wasn't careful, I stopped after only a couple of dozen pulls and put the condom on him. I then took his shaft and raised myself, rubbing it against my pussy and then putting the head to my vagina. I had my eyes shut in bliss as I lowered myself on to him, my vagina filling with lovely hard cock until I was sitting on his thighs. My fingers found my clit and I began to frig, bouncing up and down on him to keep his cock moving in my pussy.

I took my time, working myself to the edge of orgasm several times, never allowing him enough movement to come in me. I was delighting in not just the cock in my pussy and the fingers on my clit, but the whole atmosphere of the place. The smell of the woods, the warm sun on my bare buttocks, the helpless ecstasy of my mount. Only when I could feel the entrance to my vagina start to get sore did I focus my mind for my climax. I pictured what I was doing, controlling and mounting a strong young man; his body my plaything. I'd had him pull me through public woods, used a whip on his buttocks, given him a humiliating name and now wouldn't even let him see my body as I used his cock to slide my pussy up and down on. It felt wonderfully powerful, me in total control. Of course when I'd used him, my lovely Amber would haul down my pants and spank me, then fuck me, maybe in front of him; yes, that would be the final humiliation. I'd be fucked over the kitchen table while he watched, with my bum up and a thick black strap-on dildo in my pussy.

My orgasm hit me on that thought, making me shiver and cry out in the warm half-light of the wood. Even as I was coming, I was thinking that in the end I'd come over a submissive, lesbian fantasy for all my enjoyment in being in control of a man. He didn't know, though, and that was what mattered. Even if he was my plaything, it seemed only fair to let him come, so I sat up straight on his cock and told him he could. He began to buck immediately, bouncing me up and down on his cock as if I weighed nothing at all. I had to grip the shafts of the cart to stay on as he got faster, then finally rammed himself right up me as he came.

I climbed off slowly, feeling sore and a little bruised but determined not to show it. I retrieved my hat and undid one of his wrist cuffs to let him clean up, turning my back on him in a gesture in keeping with my role. Only when he was once more presentable did I think to look at my watch. It was nearly half past eleven, a discovery that put me into an immediate panic.

My legs were aching from being on my knees for so long and I realised that the quickest way back would be to drive him. A moment later I was in the cart, jumping over the shafts without bothering to order him to kneel.

'Go, fast!' I ordered, applying the whip to his bottom.

He took me at my word and set off at a hell of a pace, bumping me over tree roots and bits of branch until we reached the smoother going of the path. As luck would have it, there was a party of walkers, naturalists I think because they were standing around in the path and looking at something in the trees. Their expressions were something I won't forget in a hurry when they saw the pony-cart. Chris faltered but I yelled at him and he made straight for the middle of them. We didn't really have any option and they got out of the way fast enough, staring in disbelief as we passed.

I couldn't resist the opportunity to tip my hat politely and bid them a good afternoon, then we were through and gathering pace on the open track. I knew who I wanted as my pony-boy if ever I got a chance to drive in a race. Chris (Flabby really was too unfair) went like the wind. Inevitably, I managed to take a wrong turning and we ended up in one of the main car parks with more people. They just gaped at us.

It seemed stupid to turn around and try and find our path, so I drove straight through the car park and out on to the road, turning left in the direction I knew our horsebox was. By good luck there was nobody else there when we reached it and I had driven Chris in and slammed the door in an instant.

My watch read a minute short of noon when I pulled through Amber's open gates. We had probably set some sort of speed record, certainly for pony-boy racing and maybe for driving a horsebox. It was barely enough. Amber was waiting for us, tapping her foot and glancing at her watch even as I drew to a stop in front of her.

'Quickly,' she whispered as I jumped down from the cab, 'the wretched woman will be here, any minute.'

'Sorry,' I answered, 'we got a bit lost.'

'I know what you've been doing, young lady,' she answered as we struggled with the ramp. 'Your jodhpurs are wet between the legs.'

I looked down to find that it was true. My pussy was outlined in a shape like an upside-down harp. That was me caught out with a vengeance, but for now the main thing was to get Chris out and change into a meek little maid before Anna Vale turned up. He was lying down inside the horsebox, although whether from exhaustion or the way I'd driven home wasn't clear. In any case, he was thoroughly satisfied with his experience and wanted to talk about it once he'd been taken out of role.

We couldn't be too impolite with him; after all, Amber hadn't been paid yet and I'd been pretty cavalier in showing him off to half the walkers in Hertfordshire. He needed to wash, then took forever dressing and writing a cheque but finally drove off at twenty-five past and there was still no sign of Anna Vale.

Only when Amber was actually shutting the gates behind his Mercedes did another car appear, a fifties vintage Morris which could only belong to our expected visitor. She honked imperiously and Amber again began to open the gate. The car came into the yard and stopped, a very pretty girl in a print frock and a straw hat climbed out and went to open the back door. This, I realised, must be Poppy; she was twenty-three or so, small, with short, curly black hair and a snub nose. I fancied her immediately and I knew Amber would fancy her. She curtsied to me sweetly and then opened the rear door. I watched as someone very different indeed climbed out of the back.

Anna Vale was perhaps thirty-five, tall, slim and ramrod-straight with a lean haughty face. An enormous amount of shiny brown hair was coiled and pinned under a small hat that hadn't been in fashion since the 1930s. The rest of her clothing was the same. A maroon dress in heavy velvet with lace at the collar and cuffs, brown leather brogues and gloves to match, a pearl choker at her neck.

'Ah, Miss Oakley, good afternoon,' she addressed me, extending a gloved hand.

Ten

Well, I certainly looked the part. Full riding gear, hat, veil, gloves – the works. OK, so I had an obviously wet pussy, but sometimes you just can't help these things. The real Miss Oakley, by contrast, was dressed in a baggy T-shirt with a pair of bright red knickers underneath. She had been planning to go for full late-Victorian dress in order to upstage Anna Vale but, thanks to me, there had been no time to change.

If ever I was going to get an opportunity of dominating Amber, it was now. Not only that but, judging by Anna Vale's reputation and appearance, I wasn't at all sure we'd be able to explain away the apparent anomaly without losing her as a customer.

'Miss Vale,' I replied, 'a pleasure to meet you.'

That was it, the die were cast. Amber was behind them and heard me. She winked and then shook a finger at me, simultaneously supporting the deception and assuring me it would not go unpunished. It was the sensible choice, after all, and she didn't know the use to which I intended to put my temporary position.

'I see you've been riding,' Anna Vale remarked. 'I must compliment you on your dress.'

'Thank you,' I answered. 'Just a brief morning drive. You said in your letter you were considering taking up pony-girl fantasy?'

'No fantasy, my dear,' she answered, 'the real thing.'

I decided not to quibble, although her attitude struck me as pedantic, if not pretentious.

'And I take it your charming maid will be your pony-girl?' I continued instead and then turned to the pretty girl who was still standing by the car. 'Poppy, isn't it?'

Poppy nodded and looked down with a shy glance at me. She looked good enough to eat and I realised that, whatever Amber might swallow, she would be genuinely upset if I didn't manufacture a chance for her to play with Poppy.

'Poppy is my maid,' Anna Vale answered. 'My pony-girl will be Hazel.'

'Fine,' I answered, feeling slightly puzzled, 'but you do know that I'll need to measure Hazel if you want any tack?'

'That will be quite acceptable.'

'Is she coming later, then?'

'She is here, Miss Oakley.'

'Amber, please. Is she in the village?'

'No, behind me. I thought we understood each other, Miss Oakley?'

There were two options; either Hazel was imaginary and I was dealing with a lunatic, or Hazel and Poppy were one and the same but Anna Vale was refusing to allow the slightest relaxation in role. I hoped the second answer was right.

'Right, of course, forgive me,' I answered. 'Perhaps you'd like to look at some harness designs while my maid measures Hazel up?'

'Certainly,' she answered, 'Hazel will be ready on the instant.'

I signalled Amber over. She had been doing things on the far side of the yard but I knew she would have had a keen interest in the turn of the conversation. As she walked over, Poppy began to undress. This put a bit of a lump in my throat, but I carried on as if nothing were out of the ordinary. Under the frock she had big white panties, stockings and a suspender girdle, old-fashioned but looking very sweet on her. She had high, firm breasts and the sweetest bottom; like a pear, with full cheeks in contrast to her tiny waist. I had to swallow when she demurely turned her back and pulled down her pants, bending just far enough to give me a cheeky glimpse of dark fur between her thighs. Naked, with her clothes folded carefully on the bonnet of the car, she looked very enticing indeed.

We walked over to the workroom, Amber and Poppy following behind Anna Vale and me. Inside, I began to show off the sample album while Amber took the necessary measurements. The measuring process caused a fair bit of giggling and the occasional squeak. The resemblance between Poppy and myself was not lost on me. The two of us could have passed for sisters without difficulty. She had perhaps an inch more flesh on her breasts and bottom and an inch less height, otherwise, we were very similar.

There was just a touch of jealousy as I watched Amber out of the corner of my eye. She was measuring Poppy's thighs, not strictly a necessary measurement unless a hobble was ordered, but one that obliged Amber to kneel with her face at the level of Poppy's pussy. It also seemed to involve a lot of caressing of Poppy's bottom. I shrugged inwardly, realising that the most dramatic thing that could happen was for us to end up as a *ménage à trois*, with me in the middle. My faith in Amber was absolute. Anna Vale, on the other hand, was getting increasingly irritable with every giggle or squeak from behind her. Finally, she broke off from her inspection of a picture of Vicky in harness and looked up to me.

'Miss Oakley,' she began, 'I must ask you to keep your maid in order.'

'I'm sorry,' I answered. 'She's rather fond of pony-girls.'

‘Well, kindly instruct her to keep to her work,’ Anna Vale snapped. ‘And do you always allow her to dress in such a slovenly fashion?’

‘Stop fondling Hazel, and get on with your work,’ I ordered Amber casually, then turned to answer the question. Amber was in T-shirt and panties because she had been waiting to change, but I could hardly tell Anna Vale that. Instead, I explained that she had only just been taken out of harness and it hadn’t seemed worth getting dressed properly. Anna Vale gave a haughty sniff at my answer but turned back to studying tack.

What I really wanted to do at that moment was gang up with Amber, drag Miss high-and-mighty Anna Vale across our linked knees, pull up her prissy dress, take her pants down and give her the spanking of a lifetime. Heaven knows what would have happened if we had, although there was a sneaking suspicion in my mind that she’d have ended up sticking her bum up and whimpering for more.

We couldn’t do it, of course, but there was an alternative that was nearly as much fun. Ginny had said Amber needed an excuse to enjoy submission; here, surely, she had the perfect excuse. Also, I could just imagine the intensity of her emotions at getting whacked in front of Anna Vale. Her erotic humiliation would be ten times as strong as when she’d sucked Mr Novak’s cock, stronger even than when I’d peed all down her front with people watching. Having Poppy watch would get to her too, more so if Poppy and I were to beat her together.

‘Would you like her disciplined?’ I asked, judging my voice to imply that it was a matter of no importance at all.

‘It would seem appropriate,’ Anna Vale replied stuffily.

I smiled to myself and changed the conversation back to pony-girl harness, knowing exactly what would be going through Amber's mind. She was going to be disciplined in front of a woman she regarded as a rival. She knew that I'd take her panties down. She'd even be wondering if I'd let Anna Vale beat her, although I wouldn't.

Now that I'd got my chance, the question was how to punish her. I wanted to make it as intense an experience for her as I could. For Amber, I knew this would mean combining subtlety and rudeness. Also, being punished in a way she had punished me would be effective, for both of us.

'I think this design,' Anna Vale was saying, pointing to the picture of Vicky she had been studying. 'It has a certain elegance.'

Most of the 'certain elegance' was Vicky and I felt the tack would look wrong on Hazel. Given that I had a certain interest in having Hazel as pretty as possible, I left Amber to stew and began to argue the point with Anna Vale. It took me a while to persuade her that a corset system would look better, but I succeeded. I omitted to mention that this meant that Hazel's tack would be near-identical to my own.

She confirmed the order and wrote me a cheque, adding a tail and a couple of pretty accessories at my suggestion. We left Amber to help Hazel dress and return to being Poppy, sipping tea in the kitchen where she could look out into the yard and ensure that there was no further misbehaviour. I took my time with the tea, then had a second cup while she quizzed me on pony-girl etiquette and training. Having just been trained myself, I was pretty good on this and she was fairly impressed by the time we finished. I returned the cup to its saucer and took a delicate bite from a biscuit; it was time for Amber's spanking.

I went to the cupboard where we kept the implements for domestic discipline, generally my domestic discipline. Most things were kept in the workroom, but we felt it was safe to keep a couple of canes and a strap indoors. That way we saved a trip to the workroom every time my bottom needed smacking with something a bit more formal than her hand or a hairbrush. Now it was Amber's bum that was going to feel the sting and I was actually rubbing my hands together in glee as I studied the choice.

The strap would be best, I decided, it makes a girl's bum bounce so prettily and I wasn't sure I could use a cane properly. I took it down from the peg, an eighteen-inch length of thick leather with a plaited handle, shiny from polish and use. Downstairs, Anna Vale gave the implement an appreciative look and put her cup down. Despite her cool exterior, I could tell she was thoroughly looking forward to watching Amber being punished.

We went outside and I fetched a length of rope from the workroom, beckoning them to follow me and leading the way into the paddock. I had decided how to punish Amber, and to do it in the same place she had given me my first lesson as her pony-girl.

She must have realised what was happening as we struck across the paddock, aiming for the tall post in the middle. I reached it and ordered her to take her T-shirt off. She obeyed, baring the large, firm breasts I had so often cuddled into. I stopped her as she made to take her pants off, wanting her to think she would be allowed at least that modesty.

'You can keep those on,' I said. 'Now fetch a jump and set it up close to the pole.'

She did as she was told, arranging the jump so that the top bar was level with her hips. Occasionally she would look at me and I realised that her eyes were moist and her lower lip was trembling. It looked like she was scared, but I knew her better than that. Anna Vale was standing with an amused smirk on her face, with Poppy at her side trying not to giggle at the thought of Amber's coming punishment.

When the jump was ready I had Amber hold her wrists out and lashed them together, threading the rope through the eye at the top of the pole. Being on the other side of the jump, this made her come forward, bending at the waist so that her breasts swung out beneath her. I looped the rope back and tied it off on the jump, leaving Amber helpless. The position made her bottom stick out and it looked very spankable indeed, with the full cheeks stretching out her bright red panties.

'Stand on the bottom rung and part your legs,' I ordered. 'Then pull your back in.'

I watched as she obeyed, Amber's legs opening and her back dipping to a graceful curve. We could now see the bulge of her pussy in her panties, a wet spot betraying her excitement. Her soft, full bottom cheeks were quite open, the flesh quivering gently as she waited for her punishment. Her head was up and she was looking back, biting her lip as she looked at the strap in my hand. Her tawny curls were disarranged, half-hiding her face, her arms raised and holding the top of the post to which she was tied.

'Aren't you going to thank me for letting you keep your panties up?' I asked, looking straight into Amber's eyes.

'Thank you, mistress,' she answered softly.

'Still,' I continued, 'just because I choose to allow you some modesty doesn't mean you should have any extra protection, does it?'

'No, mistress,' Amber replied, hanging her head.

'A little adjustment, then,' I remarked, stepping forward and taking hold of the waistband of her panties.

She gasped, thinking I was going to wrench them down and expose everything, but instead I pulled them sharply up between her cheeks. This left her with a tight strip of red cotton caught in between her pussy lips and in the divide of her bottom. There was plenty of tawny fur spilling out to either side, and the patch of darker skin that surrounded her bottom-hole was also visible. Her cheeks were completely naked, plump and pink and vulnerable in the sunlight.

I stepped back and brought the strap around to land plum across Amber's full bottom. Her bum bounced under the slap and she cried out as a broad red line appeared across her skin. My second caught her a bit lower, the third right across the very crest of her cheeks.

'Well upholstered, isn't she?' I remarked to Anna Vale, as Amber's bum wobbled under my fourth smack.

'Beautifully,' she answered. Her face was just a little bit flushed and her tone betrayed her excitement. She was holding Poppy's hand, too, and their fingers were working together.

'I can take her pants down for you, if you like?' I offered, laying another smack across Amber's behind.

'It might be better for her sense of humility,' Anna Vale answered, doing her best to stay haughty.

'Yes,' I replied, addressing Anna but judging my words for Amber, 'you're right. It's important for a girl who's been naughty to have her pants pulled down. I'm sure she'll be better in future if she's beaten with everything showing. Come on then, Penny, let's have pussy out of those silly panties.'

I wouldn't have been surprised if Amber had come then and there as I took hold of her knickers and eased them down over the full globes of her bottom. The material that had been caught up between her pussy lips was soaking, and the flesh of her vulva looked swollen and moist as I settled them around her upper thighs. Above it, the tight puckered flesh of her anus showed clearly, bright pink with a ring of darker skin. Anna's face was a picture as I stepped back and lined myself up for another swing. Her air of steely disdain was gone, replaced by a look of wide-eyed pleasure as her tongue darted out to moisten her lips.

The strap cracked hard against Amber's now naked bottom, making her moan deeply. That made six and I knew she was ready to come, but added three more before stepping away and admiring my handiwork. She had most of her weight on her arms, hanging from the pole with her head down and her hair in a bedraggled mess. Her breasts were dangling beneath her chest, the nipples stiff and the skin shiny with sweat. The surface of her bottom was covered with red marks, the full cheeks moving slowly with her muscles. I knew that what she'd be hoping for was a face between her thighs and a tongue to lick her clit and bring her to orgasm.

'She's excited, of course,' I said to Anna. 'Perhaps Poppy would oblige?'

I wasn't at all sure how Anna would take it. Poppy, I could see, was keen. She'd been giggly at first when she was just thinking of how Amber was going to look, but now might as well have had her tongue hanging out of her mouth with excitement. As I waited for a response, I saw a hand signal pass between Anna and Poppy, evidently the way they communicated their real wishes to each other.

'I think that would be a salutary lesson for both of them,' Anna answered me. 'For Penny, to express her shame at having become excited during punishment; for Poppy, as punishment for having aroused Penny in the first place. She is an incorrigible flirt; indeed, it is hard to get her to keep her clothes on at all, in the house.'

The depth of Anna's fantasy was rather beyond me, but her reaction was great. Poppy curtsied to her mistress, then to me. Amber was looking back between her legs, and I heard her sigh when she saw Poppy drop into a squat, her face beneath Amber's pussy. I watched with my own excitement building quickly as Poppy pulled Amber's panties off, then took her ankles gently and opened her legs again. She hesitated, looking at the open vulva she was about to lick, then buried her face in between Amber's thighs.

Amber started to moan as soon as Poppy's tongue touched her clit, but Poppy was a tease and obviously not a novice. Within a minute, she had Amber wriggling and squirming, trying to push her bottom back in Poppy's face but only getting worse teasing for her efforts.

It seemed pointless trying to stay demure, so I put my hand down my panties and started to play with myself as I watched Amber writhe. This was perfect: my mistress was naked, her bum was the colour of a ripe cherry and she was begging to be allowed to come. True, I'd enjoyed every second of the numerous punishments she'd given me, but revenge is revenge, even when the victim comes to orgasm over it.

Amber was begging and pleading, totally uninhibited in her need, but Poppy continued to torment her until a word from Anna changed her licks to full bodied slurps directly on Amber's clit. That did it, and a moment later, she screamed her ecstasy out in a voice that must have been heard for miles. The only trouble was, she screamed out 'Penny'.

Anna gave me a curious look but said nothing, instead coming up to help me untie Amber from the post. When Amber was free, I cuddled her, finding her shivering in my arms. The breathless 'thank you' she whispered in my ear was one of the sweetest compliments I have ever had. We kissed for a moment, as equals, indifferent to Anna Vale's opinion.

Back in the house, with Amber dressed again and serving tea, Anna began to explain her philosophy. It was a strange combination of feminist and authoritarian principals. The ideas were interesting but too rigid for my taste. Also, from the way I had seen Poppy transmit her hand signal when she wanted permission to lick Amber, I suspected that little Poppy in fact had a good measure of control.

'Each woman,' Anna was saying, 'has a natural level

of precedence, and so within any group of women a hierarchy is bound to exist. That physical discipline should be given by those higher in the hierarchy to those lower inevitably follows.'

I wasn't at all sure it did, but nodded politely in any case.

'Take us four, for instance,' she continued. 'All intelligent, mature woman, yet among us the hierarchy is clear.'

That was all she knew and I again wondered what she'd do if Amber just casually took her across her knee.

'Poppy is the one most suitable for taking punishment and least suited to giving it,' she asserted. 'Penny the next; indeed, I suspect that, in any relationship between Penny and Poppy, Penny would be the mistress.'

'I'm sure you're right,' I agreed, glancing over her shoulder to catch a wonderfully wicked look from Amber.

'Next,' she said, 'I feel, would be yourself, and finally me as a natural alpha dominant.'

So that was what all the philosophising had been for. She wanted my knickers down but thought I would be too much the mistress to agree if I were asked a straight question. I nearly laughed out loud. She was obviously turned on; we all were, and there was a strong atmosphere of sexual tension. I would have been delighted to take a spanking and then get on my knees and lick her pussy for her. Not like that, though; 'natural alpha dominant', indeed!

'I would argue the opposite,' I said. If there's one thing I had learnt from people with dominant sexual fantasies, especially Amber and Michael, it was how to appear cool when you're actually wetting your knickers. I was now so deep in role, I was sure that I could be as good as either of them. Also, Anna's philosophy implied that if she only had the right person she would happily submit herself, an idea that really appealed to me. If I went down for her, then I was sure she wouldn't for me.

'Really?' she replied in a voice that screamed for me to get on my knees.

'Very much so,' I assured her and began to spin the most outrageous train of lies. 'I was eighteen when I first caned another woman. She was ten years older than me and rather fancied herself as a dominant as well. Once I'd caned her, she was as meek as a lamb; I remember how she used to beg to clean my boots with her tongue.'

'That is one of Poppy's regular duties,' Anna answered.

'Very right and proper,' I continued. 'Do you know Virginia Scott?'

'No,' she admitted. 'Should I?'

'She's bisexual, so perhaps not. She runs a stable of pony-boys down in Wiltshire, at this wonderful park she owns. They believe her dominance to be absolute but, just the other day, she rang to ask if she could visit me for punishment. I'm the only person she'll submit to. She asked to be naked, except for a pony-girl tail and some rather sweet nipple bells I make.'

The look on Amber's face was wonderful, that on Anna's even better. Not only was she swallowing my propaganda but her sexual excitement looked to be approaching desperation. Poppy hadn't said a word, but her big eyes were round and moist and the skin of her neck was flushed red. Having them so turned on gave me a glorious feeling of power and I wondered if I could get what I wanted then and there. Poppy would be utterly willing, I could tell. Anna still had some control left.

'Possibly it is I who is the natural alpha dominant,' I suggested. 'I may be small but as you yourself admit, it's all a question of character.'

'Perhaps,' she admitted, 'but –'

'I can see you're excited,' I interrupted. 'You're very welcome to play with Poppy, if you like; or Penny could fetch you a vibrator. I'd enjoy watching you masturbate.'

'Would you?' she asked; it was almost an admission that she wanted to please me.

'Absolutely,' I assured her truthfully. 'Penny, go and fetch a vibrator; the black one.'

There was only one black vibrator and that was the one fixed into Amber's leather shorts to make a strap-on dildo. If I could get Anna so turned on that she let me fuck her, then that would make an incredible climax to the day. Amber winked at me and left the room. The thought of Anna's long legs and tight little bum bare over the table edge while she whimpered and squirmed with eight inches of black rubber in her pussy had me shivering myself. Maybe I should lay her back on the table instead, to make the best of her long legs, with her bottom sticking out over the edge. We'd pull her dress down over her tits, then I'd take her by her thighs and fuck her while Poppy and Amber kissed her breasts. I'd put the vibrator to her pussy and watch her come, utterly abandoned in front of me. Lastly I'd have Poppy finish me off, kneeling with her face to my pussy. Anna would lie on the table, exhausted but happy as she watched her girlfriend lick me to orgasm.

'I . . .' Anna began uncertainly, then abruptly changed to her usual style. 'Poppy, get on the floor, you may do your duty.'

'Yes, Miss Vale,' Poppy replied eagerly as she dropped onto her knees to kneel in front of her mistress.

I could see what she wanted: to come before I managed to persuade her to let go completely. It would have been easier if she hadn't been wearing a tight thirties-style skirt. This had to come up for Poppy to be able to lick Anna's pussy, and that meant Anna standing and rucking it up around her waist. I watched as she did so, revealing her stocking tops and suspenders attached to the bottom of a girdle. Her legs were every bit as good as I'd anticipated, long and sleek and running up to a neat rounded bottom. She was wearing white silk drawers, fringed with lace and open between the legs, like my Victorian ones but much briefer.

'What pretty drawers,' I said. 'The back looks really sweet. Show me properly.'

She couldn't resist it. I knew she was proud of her clothes and guessed she was proud of her body. She gave me a smile and turned her bottom to me, holding the skirt up over her drawers with her bottom pushed out just a little bit. The waistband was tight, the silk clinging to her hips and the upper surfaces of her bottom, pushed out by the swell of her cheeks but loose in the middle where they opened and around the legs; copious lace added to their femininity. There was just the cheekiest glimpse of bare bottom cheek.

'That's gorgeous,' I told her, 'Pull them open for me.'

She gave a rueful shake of her head but put her hands to the seat of her drawers. This meant bending further forward to keep her skirt up, so that her bottom was stuck out at me as she opened the drawers. Bare, her bottom was even sweeter than it looked in a casing of silk and lace. Apple-cheeked was the description that came to mind, small and so firm that her cheeks were open enough for me to see the dark spot of her bottom-hole. There was plenty of pussy on show, too, her lips pouting out in a thick nest of fur and the opening pink and wet. The sight just made me want to purr.

'You can lick now, Poppy,' I said, trying desperately to hold my poise. They couldn't see under the table, anyway, so I slid a hand down my jodhpurs and began to play with my pussy through the front of my panties.

Anna had meant to be licked sitting down, but she was too far gone to make an issue of it. As Poppy moved behind her, kissed her on a thigh and then the exposed cheek of her bottom, Anna bent fully over, offering Poppy her pussy to lick from behind.

'That's beautiful, Anna,' I told her. 'You too, Poppy. Anna, your bottom looks so spankable in all that lace and silk. I'd love to hold you around the waist and smack it while Poppy licks you.'

That was when Amber came back into the room, holding the leather shorts in one hand and the rubber strap-on in the other. If she was surprised to see the haughty Anna Vale bent over a chair with her bum bare and Poppy's face between her thighs, then she didn't show it.

Anna had raised no objection to me spanking her so I had got up and was walking around the table, eyeing the sweet little bum that was my target. At the sight of the enormous dildo in Amber's hand she gave a little gasp which sounded to me like resignation.

I'd have done it, I know I would. I'd have spanked Anna and then fucked her. The dildo would still have been in her pussy when Poppy made her come. She'd have been in absolute ecstasy and totally submissive to me. Then I'd have had Amber and Poppy give me the same treatment and shown Anna how much more fun it was if you switched roles now and then.

As it was the whole thing got totally ruined by the phone ringing. Just the sound broke the spell, but I answered it in the hope that it might be a wrong number. Maybe we could have got things back: after all, Anna was on the edge of coming. Unfortunately, it was Mr Novak, wanting to make some additions to his order. He recognised my voice and it was the most I could do not to give the whole game away.

By the time I managed to get rid of him the atmosphere was entirely broken. Anna had rearranged herself and was looking rather wary. Poppy looked really mischievous and treated me to a knowing smile when Anna wasn't looking. Amber shrugged and went to take the strap and the dildo up to the bedroom.

Anna Vale left rather hastily and was obviously uncomfortable with her feelings, not to mention the state of her pussy. I imagined that they'd be stopping in a wood on the way back and that Poppy would be getting a very sore bum indeed as Anna reasserted herself.

There was a major consolation. I'd put Amber in a seriously submissive mood and, when we'd shut the gates behind Anna and Poppy, she turned to me and asked to stay in role as my plaything for the rest of the day. This cheered me up no end and I took her by the hand and led her up to the bedroom.

By the time we went to sleep I'd come three times. Twice with her kneeling between my legs, and once in her own favourite position, but with me sitting on her face instead, my fingers on my clit and her tongue well in my anus. After the first orgasm, she served me dinner and I had her kneel to be spoonfed her own, then had my ice cream off her breasts.

I also fucked her, which was glorious, with the shaft of the dildo sliding in and out of her pussy as she knelt with her bottom raised and her cheeks still red from the strapping I had given her. At bedtime, I had her bathe and powder me. Then, as I walked into the bedroom, I saw the hairbrush she had so often used to spank me. I ordered her to kneel on the bed and gave her a dose of her own medicine. When her bum was hot and she was moaning softly into the pillows, I told her to open up her bottom-hole with a wet finger.

I watched in delight as she reached back between her buttocks, found the little hole and slid her finger in. I let her play with her anus for a bit, then had her take her finger out and replace it with the hairbrush handle. She groaned as it slid up her bottom, and I told her to come, naked on her bed, with the hairbrush sticking rudely out of her bottom. As a last humiliation, I took a photograph of her at the moment of orgasm, with her face pressed in the pillows, breasts dangling, sticky fingers working in her pussy and a hairbrush protruding from her anus.

Finally, we went to sleep with her head cradled on my chest.

Eleven

I woke up with my head cradled on her chest instead, which I suppose is deeply significant. Amber was out for the count, but I felt full of beans and was in a really good mood. The previous day had really put the seal on my relationship with Amber. I now felt perfectly happy and completely at home. The feelings of guilt I'd had before just seemed ridiculous, and my doubts about the sex not being completely fulfilling were gone, too. I went out to the yard to check that we hadn't left anything suspicious lying around, then tidied up the kitchen and started to make breakfast.

Just as the bacon was beginning to brown to my satisfaction, Amber came down. She was wearing a T-shirt and looked at me archly as I turned around.

'Good morning, Miss Penelope,' she said. 'I have a small bone to pick with you, this morning.'

'You do?' I asked, all innocence.

'Yes,' she replied, turning and pulling up the tail of her T-shirt to show me her bottom. She had no panties on and the results of her punishment the day before were still clear.

'Oh,' I answered. 'Might we wait until after breakfast before my first spanking, please? There'll be time before the shop has to be open.'

'Actually, I want to go into London,' she said. 'I'll spank you before I go, if you like, but I was hoping you'd look after the shop for me, this morning.'

'Sure,' I agreed, feeling slightly disappointed that we wouldn't be spending the whole day together. 'Will you be back for lunch?'

'Yes; I only have to go to Southgate,' she answered.

'What for?' I asked her.

'You'll find out,' she said. 'I just feel that, after yesterday, you deserve something really special. I haven't got the details worked out yet; anyway, I wouldn't want to spoil it for you.'

She left me with that – well, that and a quick over-the-knee spanking with my jeans and panties just far enough down for her to get at my bum. When she got back, she ate quickly and disappeared into the workroom.

For the rest of the week she was equally mysterious, twice disappearing in the evening, keeping the workroom locked and refusing to tell me anything. I was on during the middle of the week, but that only meant I took my spankings with my panties on. Other than that, things continued much as before, with plenty of sex and me submissive to her, except when we were actually in bed at night. If anything, she was more cuddly and friendly than during our first week together. It was perfect, yet there was the nagging uncertainty of just what she had in store for me at the weekend.

It started to rain on Tuesday, a warm, depressing drizzle that lasted for days. We spent a lot of time just cuddled up in bed together, watching the rain outside the window. By Friday morning the soil, which had been parched, was a sea of mud. That afternoon, the rain stopped and Saturday morning dawned clear and fresh.

Amber was in a very good mood indeed and suggested a trip out to the woods. She was dressed in green corduroys and a cream jumper, casual and not at all suggestive. I knew she wasn't wearing anything kinky underneath, either, and she had no tack on her, so I was completely unsuspecting when she pulled the car onto a track about twenty miles from the village and told me to undress.

'Here?' I asked. 'Isn't it a bit public?'

'Not really,' she answered indifferently. 'Anyway, do as you're told or they'll see a pink bottom as well as a bare one.'

I began to undress, trusting her, yet a bit uncertain about the location. The track led down into a wood, was deep in mud and well-rutted with tractor marks, obviously in constant use. It was one thing to give strangers teasing flashes of panties or to risk been seen making love. Strolling down a country lane without a stitch on was quite another.

'What are we going to do?' I asked.

'We're going to go and play in the woods,' she answered. 'And don't worry about being seen. This is forestry land and they won't be working on a Saturday.'

That reassured me, although I was still feeling nervous as I slid my panties off and threw them into the back with my other clothes.

'Put this on,' Amber ordered, taking a piece of black leather from her pocket and passing it over. It was my collar and had a lead of braided black leather attached to it. I slipped it around my neck, already beginning to tremble at the thought of being led by Amber.

A moment before, I'd been completely relaxed, expecting a walk in the woods and a pub lunch. Now I was sitting naked in the front seat of Amber's car with a collar and lead on.

'Now this,' Amber said and I saw that her hand was back in her pocket.

I obeyed, my trembling increasing as she took a black silk scarf from her pocket and put it on me, like a blindfold.

'Stay very still,' I heard her voice and a moment later

something cold and wet touched the bridge of my nose. It felt like a lip-gloss brush, but she applied the liquid in a roughly triangular shape around my nose instead of my lips and pressed something to my face. She was sticking something over my nose: something that obviously had holes in it, because it was stuck all the way round, but I could still breathe through my nose.

'Turn around and stick your bum up,' she said. Well, I knew what happened when I did that. Either it got smacked or something was put up my pussy or bum: frequently both.

I turned over to kneel on the seat and present Amber with my bottom, expecting either a smack or a caress. Instead, I felt the same cold, wet feeling in the small of my back, again painting a triangular shape but a larger one. Again, something was pressed to my skin and held until it stuck. This time I could guess what it was. As an alternative to her plug-in tail, Amber sometimes made one that stuck onto the pony's back, giving the same look but not half as much fun. That was presumably what I'd had put on me, only I should have been able to feel the tail tickling my bottom. Instead, there was just a slight sensation of extra weight.

'Stay still,' Amber ordered and I heard her door slam. My own opened a moment later and she helped me out of the car. She didn't let me get up, but led me out on to the grass on my knees. A tug at my lead pulled me forward and I began to crawl, acutely aware that I was stark naked by the side of a public track and on a lead. I couldn't see, but I was listening for the sound of an approaching car or voices.

Amber was doing something in the car, leaving me to the humiliation and uncertainty of my position. There was a thump as she shut the boot, then another noise and she was undoing the knot that held my blindfold in place.

In front of me was a mirror, with my face and body

reflected in it. I turned to look, to find that in place of a nose I had a snout; a little pink snout, upturned and with the nostrils at the end. I had a side view of my body, including the curve of my bottom, above it a curly pink tail stuck out at a perky angle. When Amber had stuck a nose and tail on me I'd thought she might be making me into a puppy-girl, a fantasy I'd heard of but which we hadn't tried. I wasn't a puppy; I was a pig.

It's hard to imagine a more humiliating image. Naked and permanently crawling, so that my rear view was just as rude as it could possibly be. For a girl to be naked and crawling is sexy; to be naked and crawling in a collar and lead is sexy and submissive; to be naked, crawling and collared with a snout and tail is sexy, submissive and just unbelievably wanton. It was everything a woman is taught not to be: immodest, undignified, naked in public, an available slut, a sexual plaything. Add to that the popular image of a pig – dirty, ill-mannered, fecund – and you had Amber's new creation, the piggy-girl.

That was what she called me as she stood over me with a long, whippy hazel switch in her hand. It should have been unendurably humiliating.

It was me to the core. Amber really understood me and had made the best of all the things that turned me on the most. Exhibitionism, because I was naked and in a position that left my pussy and bottom-hole showing all the time. Submission, because I was on her lead and naked at her feet. Punishment, because I knew full well that her hazel switch was there to decorate my bottom with some pretty red stripes. Sexual irresponsibility, because I was now a pig and could be expected to behave no better. It was humiliating, yes; deliciously, exquisitely humiliating.

Besides, as I looked at myself in the mirror, one thing was certain. I made a really cute piggy-girl. I'm small, with a round bum and little tits. As pony-girls, Ginny and Vicky looked much better than me, taller, more elegant and with lovely breasts to show off. I really came into my own as a piggy-girl: neater and more loveable.

I rubbed my face against Amber's trousers to show my appreciation, then turned my bum to the mirror and looked back over my shoulder. As I knew it would, my pussy pouted out from between my thighs like a little ripe fig, a wet, pink centre to a nest of black fur. My bottom-hole showed, too, a tiny dark dimple in puckered pink flesh, again with a good deal of hair around it. My bum cheeks were pink and fresh and parted, my tail curled above them, wobbling slightly as I moved.

It's vain, I know, but at that instant I wished I could fuck myself. My rear view was just pure sex. It made me want to stick my bum up in the air and offer myself publicly to anyone who fancied filling my little piggy rear with cock, a dildo, their fingers – anything they wanted, really, just as long as I got filled, and preferably in my pussy and bum-hole at the same time.

Of course I knew that an average member of the public wouldn't have the guts to just take me like that, even if it were offered, especially with Amber there too. Reality was that anyone who saw us would probably ring the police. I didn't think Amber would take that sort of risk and so far we hadn't so much as seen a car, so I began to feel more secure.

I rubbed up against Amber's leg again, wondering what she had planned. She had been admiring her handiwork and looking pretty pleased with herself. When I put my cheek against her leg she patted my head and reached into her pocket to offer me a chocolate. I nuzzled it off her hand: a rum truffle, which seemed appropriate and was better than being fed on acorns.

'Right, Pinky, we're going for a walk,' she told me, tugging gently on my lead.

There was immense satisfaction in her voice. Her greatest pride was always in sexual creativity, and this was her own creation and so a fantasy all our own. For now, anyway: I knew my lover and knew that she'd be far too pleased with herself not to show me off to like-minded friends. I knew Ginny would be delighted, Vicky too; Anderson would probably want to fill my fantasy of being taken from behind as a piggy-girl. The name was sweet, too, friendly and familiar, a good name for a pet pig.

Amber walked onto the track, my hands and legs sinking into the cool, squishy mud as I followed. The feeling made me want to wallow in the muck until my body was plastered with it. I made to roll over but got a smack across my haunches with the switch for my trouble. I still got a good coating as I crawled down the track, the mud often coming up to my thighs and once deep enough to smear my dangling breasts. I wanted to sit in it, but Amber wouldn't let me and, by the time we reached the bottom of the track, my bum had four red lines across it.

A little stream ran across the path, surrounded by oaks instead of the ranks of poplars that made up most of the wood. I was led onto a narrower path, floored with damp leaf mould instead of rutted mud. Amber strolled along, whistling and swinging her switch, only occasionally turning to look down at her piggy-girl.

I was sure that there would be more to it than just being walked and then having sex when we found a suitably lonely place. I was right. After a couple of hundred yards, the path opened out on to a little bowl-shaped depression where the wood ended. The stream ran through the middle, passing underneath a dilapidated barbed wire fence and a thick holly. Beyond the fence was a semi-circular area of thick lush grass. In the centre the stream spread out into a wide ford, heavily pocked with cow hoof marks. The resulting mud pool was about ten yards across and full of deep, oozing mud; rich brown and glutinous.

I knew I was going in it, the moment I saw it. Amber helped me under the fence, let me off the lead and went to sit on the trunk of a fallen tree. She had chosen well. The holly shielded us from the interior of the wood while the depression made us invisible from the field. Her head was above the level of the lip of the bowl and she could see the field clearly. Nobody could catch us unawares.

'In you go,' she said merrily as she settled herself on the oak trunk.

I put an arm out and it sank to the wrist in mud. The other went in halfway to my elbow. Another pace and I was in up to both elbows, with my titties only an inch from the surface. With my knees still on the grass, this left my bottom stuck up with the tail pointing up in the air. Amber laughed at the exhibition I was making of myself and I turned and stuck out my tongue at her.

'Get in it, Pinky,' she ordered, sounding thoroughly amused by the thought of me plastered in filth.

I took another pace, my knees now sinking in and my breasts brushing the surface, the wet muck cold against my nipples. I shivered at the feeling, hunching my legs forward into the deeper mud. My knees landed on either side of a ridge of firmer soil, making them slide apart and my thighs open to Amber. She laughed again at the sight of my spread pussy, her amusement at my plight adding to my humiliation.

The mud felt good and was obviously the perfect place for a piggy-girl to wallow. I went in further, rubbing my titties in the mud and then sitting up to put my bottom in it. It squelched up between my cheeks, wet and filthy against my nice clean pussy and bum-hole. Lifting my bottom, I stuck it out to show her the mess and looked back over my shoulder. I was in ecstasy, dirty and rude in front of my Amber, my body plastered with mud, my tits and bum filthy with it, my snout and tail marking me for what I was.

I rolled over and spread my legs, squirming in the muck and presenting Amber with my open legs. Stretching out, I rolled full length, covering my belly and coating my pussy hair. It was in my hair and up between my bum cheeks, sticking to my breasts so that they felt heavy and sensitive, coating every inch of my skin except my face.

'Pose for me,' I heard Amber say, and turned to see what she was up to.

She was undoing her trouser button and looking out across the field. I watched as she slid the corduroys down her legs to her ankles. She had on white panties with a flowery design and, as she opened her legs, I could see the plump swell of her pussy inside them. It looked very inviting and I wanted to crawl out and lick her, but she had other ideas.

'Crawl, show me your tail,' she said, her voice sounding hoarse as she slid her hand down the front of her panties.

I presented her with my bottom, lifting it and wiggling to make my bum cheeks and tail wobble.

'Perfect, just stay like that,' she breathed.

I glanced back, smiling at the sight of Amber with her eyes riveted on my bottom. She was holding out the front of her panties with one hand and masturbating with the other. I didn't know why she hadn't just taken them down, but it looked really sweet, rude yet innocent. It was as if she were too turned on not to play with herself, but too shy to pull her panties down while she did it.

I wiggled again and turned my upper body a little so that she could see my dangling, mud-smeared titties. She sighed and began to rub harder, then suddenly stopped to wrench her jumper up and pull her tits out of her bra, cupping them and squeezing the nipples before returning her attention to her pussy.

The bra and jumper were in a tangle of material above her breasts, which looked big and creamy and inviting. The sight of her masturbating was really getting to me. With her tits out and her trousers down, while her fingers were inside her pants, she looked the perfect image of an innocent country girl getting carried away. I imagined that it was completely normal to have a piggy-girl as a pet, and that what was improper was not me crawling nude in the mud, but her getting carried away and masturbating over the sight.

It was a lovely fantasy and I couldn't resist slipping a hand back between my legs and opening my muck-smeared pussy lips for her.

'You dirty little pig,' Amber gasped out and then began to come.

Her thighs locked around her hand and then spread again. She tore the front of her panties down, exposing the pink inside of her pussy. She screamed, as she always did, her breasts bouncing as her body spasmed with pleasure. Three times she called my names, twice 'Pinky' and then 'Penny', as she slipped forward from the log to sit panting in the grass.

I was face down, with my tits in the mud and my hands between my legs, one to spread my pussy lips, the other to rub my clit. I felt safe because she could see the field, so I wasn't hurrying; instead I waited for her to get her breath back so that she could come and beat me with the hazel switch while I brought myself off. There was also the question of how a piggy-girl should signal to her mistress that she wants her bum whipped. I turned to try and direct Amber's attention to the discarded switch with my eyes, only to find Amber looking not at me, but at the wood.

'Penny, we're being watched,' she said urgently.

I looked up at the wood as a great surge of embarrassment and shame went through me. Amber already had her breasts covered and was struggling with her trousers, but there was nothing I could do about my own nudity. Except, that is, sink down into the mud. This was hardly ideal and my piggy-girl snout and tail still showed, but it was better than crawling, not to mention masturbating.

At first, I couldn't see anyone in the wood, but then I caught a movement and realised that a man in a tweed suit was standing very still among some bushes, a little way up the slope. He didn't move and nor did we. Instead, we both looked at each other and waited for someone to do something.

I was a bit surprised he hadn't run away. Peeping Toms generally feel guilty, even if they come across something accidentally, like a man who'd seen my cousin Kate and me bathing naked in an old quarry. He'd had every right to be there, but he'd turned scarlet and beaten a hasty retreat. This man was made of sterner stuff, or possibly the blatant eroticism of what Amber and I were doing made him bolder.

He climbed over the fence and began to make his way slowly towards us. I could only gape in embarrassment and disbelief. I wasn't scared; he was none too young and portly as well. If we'd run for it we'd have been at the car before he'd got to the stream. Besides, I had Amber – not that she was being much help. Instead, she was adjusting her bra straps and waiting for his approach. I wondered what he thought he was doing. Was he going to tell us off? Was he going to ask to join in?

I am a slut sometimes, I admit it. Normally, if some fat fifty-year-old in tweeds came up to me and asked to fuck me, he'd get a knee in the balls. Then, I'm not normally a naked piggy-girl in a mud wallow, who's just watched her mistress come. Excuses aside, I knew that if the man had the guts to make a rude suggestion, he'd get what he wanted.

'Just what do you two think you're doing?' he

demanded as he reached the lip of the depression opposite where Amber was standing. His voice was strong and authoritative, for all the world like an old-fashioned schoolmaster telling off a couple of girls caught smoking. My immediate reaction was to start stammering an apology, but not Amber.

'Do you realise whose land this is?' she asked, answering his question with a question.

'Yes, mine,' he responded as firmly as ever.

That rather shut her up. I suppose she'd assumed he was a walker because he'd come out of the wood, which belonged to the Forestry Commission. Evidently, he wasn't.

'Oh . . . Well, in that case we'd better leave,' she managed. 'Come on, Penny.'

'Oh, no, you don't,' he remonstrated. 'I saw what you were doing, you pair of perverts. Why, I've a good mind to take a stick to your backsides.'

'You're not going to do that.' Amber answered with a dangerous edge to her voice.

He started to move around the lip of the depression. Amber stood her ground, which I thought was foolish. He must have weighed twenty stone and was heavily built. If he'd managed to get her across his knee, it would have been trousers and panties down and a smacked bottom for her, whether she liked it or not. I'm sorry to say that the thought turned me on, mainly because I knew she'd secretly enjoy it.

'You're not going to spank me,' she repeated with absolute confidence. 'But if it turns you on to punish girls, you can whip my pig. That's what you'd like, isn't it? You dirty old bastard.'

That stopped him. He turned to look at me and I saw that what I'd thought was anger was pure lust. He hadn't wanted to punish us at all, he'd just wanted to have us squealing while our bums turned red, then to jack off over what he'd done. As it was, he was clearly having trouble believing Amber's offer to be genuine. I wasn't surprised, but Amber knew me well enough to know that in the state I was in, I'd be more than willing to take a whipping in her place.

'You can fuck her, too,' Amber added.

That was the end of any pretence. He'd been watching us, so he knew we were far from innocent. What he hadn't known was whether we'd be willing to do it with him. Now he did.

'She's rather dirty,' he said, looking at me doubtfully. 'Couldn't I fuck you, instead?'

'No,' Amber answered, which was one hell of an understatement. 'Pinky, go in the stream and smarten yourself up. The man wants your pussy nice and fresh and clean for his cock.'

It sounded sarcastic, but Amber's choice of words made me realise that she was not just going along with it for my sake. She was enormously enjoying the prospect of watching him fuck me.

I waded down through the mud into the water. Neither he nor Amber said a word as I got into the clear water in the middle and began to splash cool water over myself. I was amazed at how well the tail and snout stayed on and began to wonder if I was going to be a permanent piggy-girl.

The atmosphere was uneasy but very erotic. I felt as if I was about to undergo some bizarre religious ritual, washing so that I would be clean for a whipping and to be fucked. It took me a while to get the mud out of all the little crevices, but after a while I was finished, my skin pink and flushed. I turned to find that he'd already got his cock out ready for me.

In sex stories, it's the handsome young man who has the enormous penis, while the fat old buffer who's always leering at the girls has a thing like a chipolata. This man completely destroyed that theory. His cock was quite as long as any I'd had before, but what was really impressive was the thickness.

It was already erect. I suspect he'd had it erect in the bushes when he'd been watching us. He was nursing it in his hand, keeping it stiff for my fanny, and his fingers didn't meet around the shaft. Amber didn't seem too bothered by this. She was sitting back on the oak trunk and watching him calmly. Still, she wasn't the one about to have it put in her pussy. One good thing, I reflected as I looked for a way to get out without getting muddy again, was that he hadn't expressed any desire to put the monstrous thing up my bum. If he had, I think I'd have run away and left Amber to accommodate him as best she could.

I got out on the grass and walked over to them. The man had picked up the hazel switch and was whipping it backwards and forwards experimentally, still stroking his cock with the other hand. He accepted a condom from Amber and peeled it on as I watched, then gestured to the ground.

'Not too hard,' I said as I got back on my knees and stuck my bum out for him. 'I do like it, but be a bit gentle.'

'I see you've already been done,' he said, gloating over the four red lines Amber had put across my seat. 'Were you a bad pig?'

I nodded and hung my head. The question had been just right, making him part of the game while enhancing my sense of erotic humiliation.

'And what were you whipped for?' he asked. 'Tell me.'

I knew I wasn't supposed to talk, but his questions were just what I needed to restore my desire to be punished.

'I wanted to sit my bum in the mud on the track,' I answered.

'Disgusting,' he answered.

The switch came down across my bum and I grunted at the sudden sharp pain.

'This,' he continued, 'is for trespassing on my field.'
Again the switch came down across my bum and again I grunted. The first line was already stinging.
'And this,' he said, 'is for filthy behaviour.'
I had closed my eyes and was bracing myself for the next stroke, but instead I heard a dull thud and realised he had sunk to his knees behind me. The next instant I felt pressure against my vaginal opening and his oversized cock was being pushed up me. The sensation made me gasp as my pussy filled with cock. It had me panting even before he started to thrust, and when he did it was all I could do to lower my chest to the ground and grunt and squeal and pant as he fucked me. Not only was his cock huge and his pushes like being rammed by a goat, but he had his heavy belly resting on my bum and I was supporting a good deal of his weight.
When I got over the initial shock and looked up, it was to find Amber smiling at me and looking thoroughly pleased with herself. I couldn't say anything because the breath was being knocked out of me with increasingly hard thrusts. Had I been able to, I would have told her to stop smirking and try it herself.
Well, I'd wanted to be fucked as a piggy-girl and now I was getting it, and from a man who could well have been a pig farmer. It was the piggy-girl fantasy I wanted my own orgasm over, but he was slamming into me so hard it was difficult to focus my mind.
Fortunately, he didn't take very long. Not that I didn't like it, but as it was I knew my hips and vulva would be bruised and didn't want to be out of action for the rest of the weekend. After probably a couple of minutes, he took a final vice-like grip on my hips and came in me, slamming his cock up me to the hilt.
When he pulled out, it was all I could do to flop over to my side, curl my legs up and reach back underneath me to get to my pussy. Now that I was no longer being stuffed senseless, the fantasy came together perfectly. I

was Amber's pet again, but had been caught and fucked by the farmer.

One hand was on my pussy, the middle finger rubbing at my clit. The other was exploring my bottom, touching the tail, caressing the whip marks on by bum cheeks, teasing my anus. I knew he could see everything and didn't care; in fact, it made it better. He'd be watching me as I frigged in helpless ecstasy from his vast cock. In my fantasy he had begun to molest Amber as he watched me frig, lifting her jumper and bra to get her tits out to play with. She would be feigning reluctance but giggling as her breasts were bared and he took one soft tit in each callused hand, fondling her while her piggy-girl writhed in ecstasy on the ground.

I felt myself coming and wanted to do something really rude in front of them, so I slid a finger into my bum-hole. I wiggled the top joint about in the tight hole, felt my anus contract along with my pussy, then was coming, whimpering and kicking in the grass, fully aware of the display I was making of myself.

Of course, I knew the whole thing had been a fix from the instant Amber had said he could whip me. If he had really been a stranger, there was no way she would ever have done that. Even before that, I'd been suspicious. Dirty old men run away when they're seen; they don't just breeze up and ask to more or less exactly fulfil the fantasy of the girl they've been peeping at.

'Who are you, then?' I asked as I rolled over and sat up, not bothering to cover myself, as he'd already seen everything I'd got.

He and Amber were sitting on the log, looking thoroughly pleased with themselves.

'Henry Gresham; a pleasure to meet you,' he replied, 'and may I say that you make a most beautiful piggy-girl.'

'And are you really the farmer?' I continued.

'Oh, yes,' he replied. 'Amber and I set the whole thing up in the week.'

'So you were watching from the beginning?' I asked.

'I'm afraid so,' he answered, smiling cheerfully. 'I'm Amber's godfather, by the way.'

'So what's the background to you two?' I asked.

'Until I was eighteen, he was nothing more to me than a card on my birthday and the occasional dolly,' Amber answered as I sat down next to her on the log. 'Then, when I left school, he offered to let me work on his farm for the summer. I took him up on it and I have to say he was the perfect gentleman. What I found in his library suggested otherwise.'

'There's nothing ungentlemanly about wanting to spank a strapping young lass,' Henry Gresham interrupted.

'Maybe not,' Amber continued, 'but bondage, uniforms, pony-girls . . . Especially pony-girls. That's what set Ginny and me off playing pony-girls, and eventually I plucked up the courage to ask him about it all. The result, you can see.'

'You didn't tell me this before,' I accused her jokingly.

'No,' she admitted, 'because I knew that before long I'd need somewhere special to treat you to a really powerful piece of erotic play. The wood is his, too, by the way. The stuff about the Forestry Commission was just to make you nervous. We made the tracks last week, with Henry's tractor. The piggy-girl idea was all mine; a fantasy tailor-made to your dirty, submissive, perverted little imagination, Miss Penny Birch.'

I caught Amber completely by surprise. One moment she was sitting on the log trying not to laugh, the next I had pushed her over and she was on her back in the grass. She struggled half-heartedly as I jumped on her and rolled her legs up, even as I grappled with her trouser button. For all her size and strength, there was nothing she could do; she was laughing too much. I pulled the trousers up her legs, taking her panties with them and baring her pussy. With her legs up, I could get at a fair bit of her bum and she was soon squealing in between her laughs as I began to spank her.

Henry just laughed at his goddaughter's struggles and watched as I applied stinging slaps from the ends of my fingers, turning what I could reach of her bum cheeks quickly red. When I'd finished with her bottom, I started on her thighs. Her pussy was sticking out between her rolled-up legs and it was more than I could resist not to slap that too, but I only got more giggles for my efforts. After a while, she gave up struggling and obligingly lifted her bottom for its full share of slaps, indifferent to the show she was making in front of him.

We went back to Henry Gresham's for dinner. This was magnificent, with four courses each accompanied by a suitable wine. By the end, I was stuffed to the brim and feeling extremely mellow. He then showed us around his library and the collection of erotica. This included pony-girl stories and images dating back to the last century, which surprised me. In practice, I suppose, it can't have been long after the invention of the wheel that some paleolithic pervert attached his wife to it. We went home at close to midnight, after I'd treated his splendid cock to a leisurely suck. Amber watched this approvingly, and even took him in her hand for a while. She did this with a familiarity that suggested to me that it wasn't so unusual, but rather that masturbating him was simply a part of their friendship. It was my mouth he came in, though, which put me in a thoroughly turned-on mood as we drove back to Amber's.

When we arrived, there was a message from Vicky telling Amber to call them when she got in. Despite the time, Amber took her at her word, but it was a sleepy Anderson who eventually answered the phone.

'Do you want to go carriage-driving tomorrow?' Amber asked me over her shoulder when they had spoken for a while.

'Carriage-driving?' I asked.

'Anderson's built himself a three-seater,' she continued. 'He wants to test it out.'

'Sure,' I responded, 'a three-seater pony-cart sounds fun.'

'Carriage,' Amber corrected me. 'Carts have two wheels; this has four. Yes, Anderson, we'd love to. We'll get down to you by about eleven. Yes. Oh, and, by the way, I've got a new invention of my own to show you. No, you can wait until tomorrow. OK. Bye.'

Half an hour later, snuggled up to Amber in bed, I was dreaming of a huge barn, entirely filled with piggy-girls and tended by fat men with impossibly large cocks.

Twelve

Sunday proved dry and warm with a light breeze. Ideal pony-carting weather, in fact, as a really hot day just tires us poor pony-girls out and we're not nearly so much fun. Vicky and Anderson lived in Surrey and we managed to get to their house at the appointed time. He shared Amber's enthusiasm for the practical side of pony-carting and they were soon involved in a highly technical discussion about tack and formations and team control. The carriage was impressive, an elegant vehicle with two seats at the rear and a higher driver's seat. Twin shafts projected from the front, although when I asked how they worked I was told it was 'pole gear' and not shafts. It looked the same to me, and I nearly said so, but Vicky took me by the arm and led me to the kitchen, pouring cold beers for us and then going out onto the lawn.

'Leave them to it,' she told me as she made for a rug that had been laid out in the centre of the lawn. 'They'll sort it out in the end.'

I followed her as she walked across the lawn, as elegant and languorous as a cat. She was dressed only in a scarlet bikini, cut high to show off her sleek muscular bottom. I'd forgotten just how athletic she was and was thinking that I would cut a very poor image as a pony-girl next to her. There was nothing superior about her character, though, and we were soon laughing together and comparing experiences, mainly sexual.

Eventually Amber and Anderson emerged from the garage in which he had the carriage. They were still deep in a technical discussion.

'The question,' Anderson was saying with absolute seriousness, 'is how to balance the team.'

'I don't think pulling weight will be a problem, not at that speed,' Amber cut in. 'I'm more concerned with an even appearance.'

'That's simply not practical,' Anderson objected.

'Nonsense; we could use an in-line formation, then the disparity in height wouldn't matter.'

'Maybe, if we had the swingletrees forking out from the pole gear, but the lead pony would be miles ahead of the driver.'

'You're obsessed with symmetry, Anderson. As long as the gear and tack is complicated enough and the ponies are balanced people will be impressed. So all we need –'

'What people?' I interrupted.

'The people at Bourne village fête,' Amber answered. 'Anderson here has booked us in as a side-show.'

'A village fête!' I echoed. 'Pony-girls, naked on a village green? We'll be arrested!'

'We'll be wearing bikinis, silly,' Vicky put in. 'Not to mention ostrich plumes, ribbons and goodness knows what else. We've told them it's like a circus act.'

'And they believed you?' I demanded.

'They went for it,' Vicky answered easily. 'Be fair, it's no more obviously erotic than some trapeze acts.'

'Yes, it is!' I protested. 'We're in bondage!'

'So's an escape artist,' Anderson pointed out.

'But I've got six whip-stripes on my bum!' I objected lamely.

'If you didn't want people to see that you've been punished you shouldn't have been naughty,' Vicky replied, with a complete lack of sympathy.

'Thanks,' I answered, 'you really know how to

console a girl. OK, but if we get put in the cells I'm just going to whinny; you lot can sort it out.'

'Relax,' Vicky answered, then paused and turned to me with a wicked grin. 'But remember, they think we're a circus act, but we know we're pony-girls!'

I had to admit that she was right. As long as we got away with it, the exhibitionist thrill would be something else.

'I've worked out the formation,' Amber announced, at which Anderson immediately looked obstinate. 'We'll have the swingletrees in conventional set with a free lead and linking traces.'

'Brilliant, only we need three pony-girls,' Anderson answered.

'I suppose I'd better be your third then,' Amber answered in the tone of mock resignation I'd come to recognise when she wanted an excuse to be submissive. 'It's just as well I brought some spare tack. Penny will have to lead, of course, or we'll look unbalanced.'

That bit I understood, which was more than could be said for the rest of her idea, even after living with her for two weeks. I had no objection to being lead; if I was going to show off, then I might as well do it in style.

We did it with a vengeance. I named Amber 'Honey', which I felt suited her colouring. She and I stripped and got into scarlet bikinis which Vicky 'just happened' to have spare. These knotted at the hips and looked really sweet, leaving most of our bums bare.

Amber's spare tack proved to contain not only extra harness but a golden tail that was actually part of Mr Novak's order and due to be collected that evening. It was obvious that she'd decided to be a pony-girl in advance, which amused me after the way she'd made it seem as if she were doing it for the sake of perfection. To put the tails in, all three of us got into a line and took hold of our ankles, presenting Anderson with our bikini-clad bums. He tweaked our bikini pants down and greased our bottoms, then watched as we put our tail plugs in. How he resisted getting his cock out and sliding it up Vicky's pussy was beyond me but, when the plugs were in, he just helped us adjust our bikini pants and put on the invisible belts.

Our harnesses went on after that, with complicated head-dresses of scarlet ostrich plumes on our heads and scarlet ribbons to complement them. The tack was immensely complicated, with traces leading between our cheek rings and a system of rope that made the one I'd used with Ginny look simple. Heels made up for Amber being shorter than Vicky, producing a smart turnout.

I felt wonderful when it was all finished, standing at the front with my bit between my teeth and waiting for Anderson's command to move off. We did look gorgeous, but I couldn't see how anybody could think we looked anything other then unashamedly erotic.

'Right,' Anderson said as he got into the cart.

Moving out onto the public road doubled my feelings of uncertainty. We weren't just taking a risk of being seen, we were actively going to show ourselves off, and to a crowd at a village fête. Despite my feelings, I just acted as a good pony-girl should, following Anderson's commands and drawing the carriage.

It was nearly a mile from his house to Bourne, along a small but not exactly deserted road. Several times, we were overtaken by cars but, in the nature of drivers, they seemed to regard us as more of a nuisance than anything. The road ran down a wooded slope and then turned sharply around a building. I came around the corner to find the green spread out in front of us, bright with bunting and stalls and tents. This is it, I thought, they'll take one look at us and have us arrested for indecent exposure.

Anderson drove onto the green and drew us to a stop in the very centre. We stood, straight-legged and motionless, waiting for his command as people turned to look at us.

'High-step, take it slowly,' Anderson commanded, tapping my shoulder with the whip in the command Amber had taught me for high-stepping. I started off, pacing slowly and evenly, taking care that the upper surface of my thigh reached the horizontal with each pace and angling my leg back and my foot down as I had been taught.

A gentle pull on my left cheek ring signalled me to turn and I angled my course to the side, the others following. He drove us in a full circle around the circumference of the green, ensuring that every single person at the fête saw us. The vicar was there, and a policeman, I was sure that one or both would soon object to what we were doing, but nothing happened.

Convention is an odd thing. If we'd done it on a normal day, there would have been hell to pay. As it was, it was the fête and it was for charity, and so everybody thought we were wonderful. Nobody minded that our bums were all but bare, and if anybody noticed the fact that I'd obviously had mine whipped, then they were too polite to comment.

After a bit more display, we gave rides at a pound a time and maintained a roaring trade throughout the afternoon. Even when Anderson started to apply the whip gently to our bottoms, the crowd just thought it was good, ribald fun.

I was thoroughly enjoying myself and getting gradually more and more turned on with the thrill of exhibitionism. As Vicky had said, everybody thought we were just being good sports in the name of charity; but we knew we were pony-girls, that we were under Anderson's control, his to caress and his to punish. Oddly enough, those who clearly did find us attractive didn't seem to realise that we knew exactly what we were up to. Several people took more than one carriage ride and one old boy even offered me a peppermint. I nuzzled it up with my lips, only to drop it because I couldn't get it around the bit. The second time I succeeded, only to have Vicky and Amber making restless movements and little snickering noises until they got theirs, too.

The finest moment undoubtedly came at the end. The crowd was beginning to disperse and we were a little tired, so Anderson called a halt and told us to kneel. As the three of us knelt, the vicar appeared. He was in his dog collar and cassock, all smiles and offering his hand to Anderson as he climbed down from the carriage.

'Ah, Mr Croom,' I heard him address Anderson, 'a splendid turnout; thank you so much.'

'Anything for a good cause,' Anderson replied and I heard the chink of coins as he handed over the takings.

'Most gratifying,' the vicar continued, evidently impressed. 'Good afternoon, Victoria.'

'Hippolyta,' Anderson corrected him.

'Hippolyta?' he asked.

'Her pony-girl name is Hippolyta,' Anderson told him, which took nerve as they actually lived locally.

'Ah, how imaginative,' the vicar answered. 'Good afternoon, Hippolyta, then.'

She whinnied, which rather unnerved him, but he was introduced to me as Calliphigenia and Amber as Honey. He then remarked on how pretty our tails looked, which made me wonder just how innocent he was. Anderson restrained himself from telling him that they were plugged up our bottoms.

He watered us and gave us a toffee apple each, feeding us with great patience and obviously enjoying the sticky mess they made on our faces. Rested, we set off for his house at a slow walk.

Throughout the fête, I'd been acutely conscious of the exhibition I was making of myself and also of the plug in my bottom. Anderson must have been getting pretty turned on, too, with three pretty bottoms moving in front of him for the best part of three hours. I was in a happy, sexy and thoroughly mischievous mood by the time we reached his house. When he halted us fifty yards short of the drive and got out, I was pretty sure what he was going to do and really liked the idea. Sure enough, he opened his gates, walked back, stopped for an instant to listen for cars and then began to tug open the bows that were all that held our bikinis on.

In an instant we were naked, as pony-girls should be, but naked on a public road. It felt so naughty to be standing like that, with the breeze cooling my naked body. As he remounted, I found myself determined to make the best of the experience, no longer concerned for modesty at all, but just wanting to show off.

I set off at a gentle walk as Anderson's reins flicked against my back and the whip tapped my right buttock, responding correctly without having to be told. The next command would be a tug at my reins to signal a turn into the gate but, when it came, I ignored it, instead smartening my pace to a trot and continuing down the road. The others could easily have stopped, but being good, well-trained pony-girls, they followed their lead.

'Calliphigenia!' Anderson exclaimed as he pulled back on the reins in the stop command. I ignored him again, only to have the whip smack smartly across my bottom. Instead of stopping I again increased my pace, this time to a run, the others still following my lead.

'Hey!' Anderson called. 'Whoa! Stop!'

Again he used the whip on me and this time I bolted completely, running down the road as fast as I could go. I knew I wouldn't be able to keep it up for long, after being in harness all day, but was determined to get my full experience of being a naked pony-girl on a public road.

One car was all it took to puncture my brashness, but the look on the driver's face was something to see. He came up from behind us and had to slow, getting the full view of naked, jiggling bottoms, bouncing tails and then bare tits and pussy fur as he passed and looked back. That was great, but it was enough for me and I let Anderson steer me in a three-point turn and then back to his house.

He parked us on the lawn and ordered us to kneel. We went down gratefully; even Vicky was puffing a bit with the effort. I waited obediently for the inevitable spanking: inevitable and well-deserved.

'Heads down, bottoms in the air,' he ordered as he climbed out of the cart.

We obeyed, but I turned my head a little so that I could see him. He stood there with his arms folded, admiring his team. As I watched, he took his cock out and began to stroke it. I can't blame him. It's not every man who gets to have three pony-girls kneeling acquiescently for him, bums up, pussies bare and ready, their tail plugs showing in their bottom-holes. He also knew he could do exactly as he liked. As long as none of us gave a slow or stop word, we were his for his sexual amusement. It must have given him an extraordinary feeling of power and I was sure he'd make the best of it.

I certainly wasn't going to ask him to stop. My only concern was that he might just fuck Vicky and leave Amber and I without our share of cock. Whatever he did, I hoped he would keep us in harness for it, as his bound, willing pony-girls. He continued to stroke his cock, then moved Amber's tail with the whip, presumably because it was obscuring his view.

'I wonder what the penalty is for bolting,' he mused to himself as his cock stiffened over the sight of naked bodies. 'Whipping certainly, maybe a cock in each pussy. You're all very moist, but I expect you know that.'

I certainly did, and Amber just had her eyes shut and her mouth open in pleasure, waiting for whatever he chose to do to her.

'Of course, it's a little tricky for a man to service three girls at once,' he continued. 'Whereas a girl can service three men quite easily: pussy, mouth and anus. You're so versatile. Hmm, that gives me an idea . . . First, your bottoms should be warmed for bolting. Three for Hippolyta and Honey, twelve for Calliphigenia, I think.'

That seemed really unfair, but I said nothing and watched as Amber's bottom was whipped. He put three hard, precise strokes full across her cheeks, each one making her gasp. Her breathing was deeper afterwards, her eyes still shut and her expression totally acquiescent.

I turned to watch Vicky being beaten. She had her face pressed to the ground and her haunches really high, her tail falling across her hip to leave her bottom fully vulnerable. He stepped over the shafts and brought the whip down on her bum with a meaty smack, making her jump and squeak. The second and third had the same effect, increasing Vicky's shivering.

The sight of his girlfriend's ready pussy was too much for Anderson. He dropped the whip and sank to his knees behind her, sliding his cock in and taking her by the hips. Vicky began to moan as she was fucked, raising her head and giving a little whimpering noise each time he pushed into her. I watched, wishing my own pussy was full and knowing that I had twelve strokes of the riding whip to come before it would be.

He was certainly doing his best to be fair, because he pulled out without coming. She accepted this and relaxed into the same sort of erotic docility that Amber was in. I watched as he walked around Vicky, burying my face as she had done and bracing myself for the whip. Instead, I felt his hand in my hair and my head was pulled up to find his cock being offered to me, still glistening with Vicky's juices. He pulled my bit down to my chin and put it in my open mouth. I sucked eagerly, tasting cock mingled with her pussy, wondering if he was going to come in my mouth.

He didn't, instead pulling out quickly and stepping around to retrieve the whip. I braced myself again, which was useless, as the first smack was as much of a shock as ever. The second came instantly, then the rest, a flurry of strokes that had me kicking, wriggling and gasping, utterly out of control. I must have made a fine sight, because he laughed and then reached down to stroke my burning bottom, exploring my open cheeks and wiggling the tail shaft in my bum-hole. I was hoping he'd fuck me like he had Vicky, or pull the tail-plug out and fill my bottom with his lovely cock. Instead he stopped and walked away, leaving me as docile and expectant as the others.

He went into the house and we waited with our well-smacked bums stuck in the air. I wished I could see the full sight we made, as well as being part of it. It was best to be part of it, though, one of three girls taking attention from a man who seemed determined to bring all of us off before coming himself.

My bottom stung and my tail was tickling me where the breeze was blowing the hair against my leg. There was a soft trembling in my throat; my mouth tasted of Vicky's pussy, and I could hear Amber breathing. Then there was the sound of a door shutting and I looked back to see Anderson coming back with a large black hold-all. He put it down and undid the zip, then drew out an enormous prick made of flesh-coloured rubber.

It was one of those huge ones, alarmingly thick and far longer then any pussy is deep. Pussy wasn't what he intended it for, and I watched in delight as he pulled out Amber's bit and offered the rubber monster to her. She gaped obligingly and he stuck it in her mouth, half-way to the enormous rubber balls. It looked incredibly sexy, Amber's pretty face straining around an impossibly large prick, her mouth as wide as it would go. I could see she was making sucking motions on it, her expression one of submissive bliss. This changed as he moved behind her and slid a good-sized vibrator up her pussy. Now she was in ecstasy, sucking wantonly on the vast rubber cock, her spine arching with the sensation of the buzzing vibrator in her pussy.

He served Vicky the same way, only with a big black dildo in her mouth and a vibrating egg in her pussy. She, too, began to squirm when it was turned on, a beautiful sight which I watched until he came round to deal with me. What he offered me was a life-like rubber cast, I think of his own cock, which I sucked with relish as he went behind me. Something hard touched my vagina and I pushed back to accommodate it. The vibrator slid into me and then clicked on.

It was powerful and sent shivers right through my lower body. I was in instant ecstasy but I knew it wouldn't make me come. Once before, I'd had the same thing done to me, my hands tied and a vibrator left on in my pussy. It's torture. To come I need to have my clit touched; there's no other way. That vibrator put me right on the edge, though, and I was left there, squirming and begging for orgasm for a full twenty minutes. That was the state I now found myself in, my whole body reacting to the vibrator but unable to come. My feet were kicking and I was clenching my bottom cheeks onto the tail: ecstasy, but never enough.

Anderson just laughed as he stood up, once more stroking a good-sized erection and watching his three females, now with mouths, pussies and bums all full.

'Very pretty,' he said, 'and I promise you'll all come soon, but I intend to take my pleasure with all three of you.'

He did, and I've never seen a man look so pleased with himself. It must have taken an effort not to come too quickly, but he seemed to be getting as much out of our submission as actual physical sensation. He started with our mouths, in each case taking the dildo out and replacing it with his cock, staying in only long enough to get the full intimacy of having a girl accept a penis in her mouth.

Vicky got her orgasm first, with the egg pushed against her clit while he fucked her with slow, smooth strokes. One hand was cupping the egg to her pussy, the other holding her tail up to keep it out of the way. She was rubbing her pussy against the egg, her mouth gaping around the black dildo, her hands clutching at the swingletree to which they were strapped, her bare skin wet with sweat and straining against the harness. It was the perfect way to fuck a pony-girl, rear entry with her tail lifted and a vibrator for her pussy. I watched her pleasure build and then my own anticipation was rising as she came.

The vibrator in my pussy was driving me crazy and I was desperate for it to be put to my clit and to have my pussy filled with his cock instead. As he pulled out of Vicky I put my face to the ground and waited, concentrating on the agonising tingling in my lower body. I felt the vibrator drawn slowly out. For a moment my vagina was gaping to the air, then his cock was in me and sliding up. There was a moment of wonderful release as the hard, tingling plastic touched my clit and I immediately felt the first shudder of my approaching climax. He lifted my tail, tugging at it gently to make me more aware of the plug in my bottom. Everything went red as my pussy and anus contracted on cock and tail shaft, my teeth locked hard on the model of the same cock that was in me. For a moment I was completely lost as everything seemed to explode at once. It happened twice, or maybe three times in quick succession, then he had pulled out and I had rolled over on to my side, exhausted and shivering with reaction.

By the time I could be bothered to open my eyes, he was well into Amber, mounted up on her and cupping her breasts in his hands. Vicky was sitting up with her legs curled under her, watching her boyfriend fuck Amber with a happy, satisfied smile. Amber herself was sucking away on the big rubber prick, her eyes still shut in bliss. Then he stopped and withdrew, peeling the condom off and replacing it with another, his eyes feasting on Amber's open bottom.

I knew what he had in mind, and so did Amber. She gave a little moan and stuck her bottom up. It must have been perfect for her; first volunteering to be a pony-girl and shedding her responsibility as she did so. Then being made a total exhibition of, first publicly, then privately; whipped, fucked, made to suck a dildo. Now she knew she was to do that most ignominious of sexual acts, take a cock up her bottom.

For all her obvious pleasure and my own state, she was still my mistress and it made me feel strangely vulnerable to know I was about to watch her being buggered. He pulled out her tail and put his cock to her anus. I couldn't see much from my position, but I knew it had gone in because Amber screwed up her eyes briefly then opened them wide as she took the full length up her bum.

'You dirty, filthy little boy,' Vicky said. 'You've always wanted to do that, haven't you?'

Anderson nodded, his expression one of unrestrained glee, his eyes fixed on the sight of his erection protruding from Amber's bum-hole. She had dropped the dildo from her mouth and was making odd little sighs and grunting noises as he eased it in and out. Her hands were opening and closing on the swingletree and I could hear the vibrator buzzing in her pussy. He had hold of her by the waist belt, working her very slowly.

I knew how she felt, and that in her position what I'd want most was my head cuddled by her. It was hard with my hands cuffed to the pole-gear, but I managed to wriggle around far enough to kiss her. She responded with passion, her tongue meeting mine. As we kissed, his pace increased; he was no longer able to resist his orgasm, but worked hard to get the friction he needed to come in her bottom. Each push came through her like a shudder and she was grunting with the strain of taking it.

I heard him call for Vicky, which I thought must have utterly humiliated Amber, but he was after something else.

'Tight enough, is it?' I heard Vicky say in response. 'Does Honey's bum-hole feel nice around your cock, darling? Tight and firm between those plump, fleshy cheeks that you've been lusting after for years? How does it feel to bugger her in front of me, while her little pet soothes her? Go on, Honey, squeeze his cock in your fat, girly bottom; go on, tighten the ring around his shaft. That's right, Anderson, put your hand on her cunt, have a good feel, rub her clitty for her. Just think, Honey, you've got a man's prick up your bottom, a man's prick up your ever so precious bum-hole that you like to make us girls lick. Well, now my boyfriend's cock's up it and you're not a virgin up there any more, Amber. Not a virgin. You've had your bum fucked . . .'

That was too much for Anderson; with a final shove he came, his cock wedged in her bottom to the very hilt. Amber screamed and then she was coming too, kissing me with an insane fervour as her orgasm tore through her. It lasted an incredibly long time, then she was pulling away and rolling over on the grass with Anderson slumped back behind her, both of them utterly exhausted.

There was a lot of cleaning up and so forth to do, but eventually we ended up sitting in on the lawn with cold drinks, chatting idly. Personally I was half-asleep, what with the combination of pony-carriage driving, sex, drink and the heat of the sun. Amber was surprisingly vivacious, as was Anderson. Vicky had turned the sprinkler on and was lying under it, still cooling off from her exercise.

Having had the three of us as his pony-girls made no difference to Anderson's attitude to us, which was a nice change after the men I was used to, either cold or possessive. Instead he was full of praise for Amber's skill both at training and carriage work. She, likewise, behaved as usual. Underneath, I could tell they were both thoroughly happy with what had happened and I suspected it was something that had been brewing up for a long time. He had, after all, made the same request after our race, but it evidently hadn't been the right time for Amber.

I forget who came up with the idea of having a meeting to include our entire group of pony-girl fantasists but, once mentioned it was taken up with enthusiasm.

'There's only one place to have it,' Amber said after all four of us had turned our attention to the idea. 'That's Ginny Scott's old park.'

'What about Matthew and Michael?' I queried.

'Could you face them?' she answered.

'I suppose so,' I answered. 'I just feel a bit cheated, still. On the other hand, I was going to dump Matthew so that I could be with you, anyway . . .'

She already knew that, but she still smiled, tenderly at me and then more gloatingly at Anderson and Vicky. It seemed incredibly petty to wreck the idea of a pony-girl meet because of my sense of pride as well.

'I don't mind,' I continued. 'Let's do it, or at least ask Ginny if we can.'

'Oh, there won't be a problem there,' Amber answered with absolute certainty. 'Are you sure you're OK with it?'

'Yes,' I answered firmly, 'but it would be good if I could perhaps talk to Ginny and perhaps Michael before.'

'OK, then, look,' Amber responded. 'Why don't you drive over on Monday and talk to Ginny, then see Michael when he comes in from work.'

'What about Matthew Linslade?' Vicky asked. 'Do we invite him, if he hasn't got a girlfriend who's willing to play.'

'We'd better let Michael and Ginny tackle that one,' Amber replied.

'Who else?' Anderson asked.

'Not Mr Novak,' I put in. 'I didn't mind playing with him when you were controlling things, Amber, but I like to feel admired and he always makes me feel second rate to his pony-boys.'

'Vanity like that usually earns me an afternoon as a puppy-girl,' Vicky remarked.

'He'll have gone back to Europe anyway,' Amber put in. 'I think we should stick to couples, in any case.'

'Anna and Poppy?' I suggested.

'Who?' Anderson asked.

'Anna Vale, the thirties fanatic,' Amber told him, 'she's taken up pony-carting with her girlfriend, Poppy; Hazel, as a pony-girl. Poppy's good enough to eat but Anna's a bit haughty and a bit too full of her own dominance. Besides, she thinks I'm Penny and Penny's me.'

'Eh?' Anderson queried.

'Don't worry about it,' Amber continued. 'It's a long story. I only think she should come if she's prepared to get off her high horse.'

'I nearly had her,' I put in.

'Nearly, but not quite,' Amber said. 'Incidentally, talking about puppy-girls, if Penny can face it, we've got a brilliant new fantasy to show you.'

I'd do anything for Amber, but I had to insist on half an hour's rest and another glass of cold beer before letting her make me up into Pinky piggy-girl. They loved the fantasy and I even gave Vicky's breasts a nuzzle, but we were all too far gone to really make the best of it. We promised them a proper piggy-girl treat another time, and then decided we had better leave in order to be back in time for Mr Novak.

I slept all the way home and would have gone straight to bed, if he hadn't arrived ten minutes after we did. He was delighted with his order but disappointed when Amber kindly but firmly declined his suggestion of testing some of it. We went to bed as soon as he had left; not even the job of applying cream to each other's sore bits managed to stir us enough for any more sex.

Thirteen

Driving over to Broadheath the next day, I had time to be alone and just think for the first time in a long while. Looking back on the previous day, I was astonished, not so much by what I'd done as by how easily I'd done it. The thing is, it was proving easy to be relaxed about sex and nudity and all the sort of things that would have had me blushing with guilt and embarrassment before I met Amber. It was being with her that had changed me, not meeting Matthew Linslade – although that had certainly gone some way to help. A moralist would have said that I'd lost my innocence, and doubtless would have preached at length on what a terrible thing that was. Actually, innocence is a pretty useless attribute to possess. The appearance of innocence may be attractive; true innocence is generally just frustrating.

In any case, I'd hardly been innocent beforehand. I'd been spanked before; I'd played with other girls before; I'd been buggered before. Not so much, nor with such intensity of feeling, but I'd still done it and I'd always known exactly what I was doing. No, what I'd lost was my sense of guilt.

I hadn't lost that delicious naughty feeling of doing something that people don't approve of either. I'd have still been embarrassed to be caught with my panties down, just as I would have been on the first day I saw Michael and Ginny pony-carting, and I'd still have been turned on by that very feeling. The difference was that now I wouldn't have had the slightest trace of guilt at wanting to go and masturbate over what I'd seen.

As I passed the King Billy, I was still thinking about that delightful afternoon, and seeing the pub filled me with nostalgia. Suddenly, the idea of an afternoon at Ginny's house didn't seem so attractive, even though there was an unspoken agreement that we'd probably go to bed together. Not that I didn't want Ginny, but I did want the feel of the open air on my bare skin and delicious tingle because you knew you might just get caught.

Instead of continuing to Broadheath, I stopped at the pub and rang ahead, arranging to meet Ginny in the park. I then ordered a snack and a pint of cider and sat down in the same window seat I had occupied the morning I'd met Matthew. A second pint followed and I then set off along the footpath that would eventually take me to the park, the same route I had taken the day I had first seen the girl I was now going to meet. The day was as hot and sultry as it had been over a month before. As I walked my feeling of nostalgia deepened, enhanced by the glorious summer's day and the pleasantly tipsy feeling in my head.

I never learn. If I hadn't overdone it on the cider in the first place, nothing would ever have happened. Inevitably, by the time I was walking along the wall that surrounded the park, I was desperate for a pee. Fortunately, it wasn't such a problem this time, as all I needed to do was nip over the collapsed section of wall and do it at leisure. I hurried on, making for the gap, but as I went a really mischievous idea occurred to me. What if there had been no break in the wall? Would I have made the maize field? Or would I have wet myself?

I wondered if the presence of the army boys in the distance would have put me off going into the maize field. I get nervous in the presence of gangs of rowdy, laddish men at the best of times. Perhaps I'd have wet myself rather than risk them knowing what I was doing. They'd been a good quarter of a mile behind me and would never have known if I'd just let go in my panties and jeans.

I'd have known though; I'd have felt it trickling down my legs, soaking into the material of my panties, making a big wet patch on the seat of my jeans. Then I'd have had the problem of getting back to the car. It would have been blatantly obvious that I'd wet myself and almost impossible not to be seen. When I was, I'd have been filled with embarrassment so acute that I'd probably have cried.

Now that I wasn't actually faced with the prospect of such utter and public humiliation, the idea was really appealing. Several of my fantasies have involved tears of shame while I'm given a public spanking; generally over a man's knee while passers-by just glance contemptuously at me being punished. I usually come at the point he decides to take my pants down and my bum gets exposed to a laughing crowd. Camera-wielding tourists, secretaries out for lunch, workmen, tramps: they'd all see my naked bottom turning pink under his slaps as I kicked and squealed over his lap. If I added wetting myself in front of them all to the fantasy, it would be just so much better.

It was a deliciously naughty thought and I found myself tempted to give in to the strain and fill my knickers on the spot. There wouldn't even be the problem of getting back. I could wash my clothes and let them dry in the park. When I got home, I'd tell Amber and she'd spank me for it. So would Ginny, with any luck.

The whole thing was too erotic. I had to do it, but for it to be perfect I knew that I would have to be genuinely unable to help it. I continued to walk, now with an exquisite feeling of expectation at what I was about to do. When I got to the bull's field I stopped and leant on the fence, admiring the colossal beast as the pressure built between my legs. The gap in the wall was just yards away, invisible behind its screening elderberry bush. To reach it and safety would be the work of an instant, but I was determined not to do it.

I had begun to wriggle, moving my thighs together in an automatic action that went some way to soothing the overwhelming need to pee. I love the sensation of being unable to resist a physical reaction, like the way my back arches and my thighs squeeze at orgasm. This was similar, with my toes wiggling and rubbing together, my legs going up and down in little step-like motions and my bum cheeks squeezing rhythmically. It was going to happen at any second, and there was nothing I could do about it.

A glance up and down the path showed that I was alone. No; a small figure had appeared back along the way I had come. It was now or never; if I wanted to wet my panties, I had to let go. It's extraordinary how strong the conditioning against this is. My mind was telling me to just do it and enjoy the sensation but, at a less conscious level, something was screaming at me to hang on, no matter what.

At the last second, I chickened out, deciding to go through the gap, only to turn and trip, ending up on my knees in the middle of the path. The momentary lapse of concentration was too much. Even as I landed, I felt an explosive gush and a warm, damp sensation against my pussy. The next instant my knickers were full of hot wet pee. It was running down my thighs and soaking into the taut material across my bottom; it dripped onto the path and made a puddle underneath me. The sense of shame burst like a bubble in my head, mixing with the utter bliss of physical relief.

I stayed kneeling, letting it all run out, savouring every second of the experience. I could hardly believe it; I'd actually done it in my pants, and on a public footpath as well. Amber would put me straight across her knee when I told her. If she'd been there, she'd have probably done it on the spot, maybe with my wet panties stuffed in my mouth to teach me a lesson.

The sensation was not a hundred miles away from orgasm, and I was groaning softly by the time I'd finished. Glancing down the path again, I saw that the approaching walker was still far too distant to have seen anything. I could tell it was a woman, now, and she must have been wondering what I was doing kneeling in the middle of the path. I got up, enjoying the dirty feeling of having wet jeans. It was warm and damp all round my bottom and pussy as well as down the insides of my thighs. My immediate urge was to strip from the waist down, very slowly and imagining I was being watched by someone who would then punish me for my disgusting misbehaviour.

As it was, it was time to get into the safety of the old park. Once there, I could do as I pleased, with no worse a prospect than getting a smacked bottom from Ginny. That was exactly what I wanted, as I composed myself and walked around the elderberry bush, only to find that somebody had repaired the wall.

For a second I just stood there gaping at the barrier, then gathered my wits and continued along the path. I was still safe. The corner of the wall was not too far distant and I could simply skirt it and come in by the main gate. The only difference was that I would now have to walk a mile or so in wet clothes, which just served to add to my humiliation. I set off, walking fast in case whoever was coming up behind me got close enough to see what I had done.

A long way ahead of me, the path disappeared into the shadows of a copse. As I reached the maize field, a group of people emerged from the trees. I increased my pace, still confident that I would never need to pass close enough to them to risk exposure. Only when I reached the corner of the wall did I really begin to feel panic. Well out in the field, a lone man was walking – slowly, nonchalantly almost, and in my direction. He was a long way away, but if I went into the field, he was sure to want to know what I was doing. If I stayed on the path, both the lone walker and the group would pass me. I was caught. I had no choice but to endure the real humiliation of being seen when I had very obviously wet myself.

I turned, reasoning that one was better than many. The woman was closer now and somehow familiar. Red haired, middling in height, she was Catherine King, Matthew Linslade's girlfriend. It could not have been worse. For all I knew, she had extracted the full story from Matthew and regarded me as a rival and as an absolute slut. Now she was going to see me in wet jeans and of course she'd want to know what I was doing by the old park. I heard brash male laughter from behind me and decided to make a run for it through the maize field.

The fence was square mesh, topped with a double strand of barbed wire, easy enough to get over when you're not in a total panic. I was in a panic and snagged my jeans getting over. I stopped as I felt the prick of a barb against my inner thigh. With one leg over and the other only just on the ground I was in a really difficult position. I needed to get the barb out, but I also needed both hands to keep the wire pressed down. As I tried to work out what to do, I was only too conscious that I was presenting the men coming up behind me with a fine view of my wet seat. The jeans were tight and showed off my bum. They'd been selected for Ginny's sake, but were now making a prime display for about a dozen young men.

I'd tried to get away, but it was too late. I couldn't even sit down and hope they wouldn't notice. I had to stay put, effectively flaunting my pee-soaked bottom to them. In my fantasy, they'd not just have caught me but laughed at me while I cried tears of shame and frustration. In practice, they'd probably help me and be nearly as embarrassed as I was by the state of my jeans.

In a couple more seconds, the tears would have been real but, by good luck, one of my wriggles managed to free the barb and a moment later I was among the maize and invisible to the path. If they'd noticed, they gave no sign, but walked past my hiding place talking loudly about this and that. It may seem ridiculous, but I was actually a bit put out. If I'd seen, say, Ginny or Poppy caught on a barbed wire fence in a pair of tight wet jeans, I'd have been really turned on. They'd seen me, but they'd just carried on talking about football.

That's reality for you. In my fantasy, they'd have had a good feel of my bottom and tits, then helped me off the fence and taken me into the maize field for blow jobs all round. As it was, I listened to their voices fade and waited until I was sure Catherine King was past. After a while I began to feel safe and was wondering if I could use the elderberry bush to climb the wall. Being so alone and squatting in my sodden clothes started me feeling naughty again and I began to consider masturbating. The fantasy would be sucking the men's cocks in the maize field. I'd be squatting, as I was, but I'd have stripped for them and one would have his cock in my mouth while his friends stroked their erections in readiness for my attention. One would be behind me, admiring my parted bottom and wondering if I'd accept his cock in it . . .

Then someone called my name. I could have jumped out of my skin, especially as the voice was female and could only belong to Catherine King. I froze, but the tone of her voice had been warm and friendly and puzzled: not at all what I'd have expected. She had obviously seen me, so continuing to hide seemed ridiculous. I stood up, but still couldn't see anything and so pushed my way to the edge of the maize, feeling faintly ridiculous and not a little embarrassed. Catherine King was standing at the point I'd crossed the fence, looking around her.

'Hi, Catherine,' I managed, drawing her attention with a wave.

'Hi,' she called back. 'It's Penny, isn't it?'

'Yes,' I answered.

'Are you all right?' she asked, looking concerned.

'Not really,' I admitted.

I'll say this for her, she didn't ask any stupid questions about why I was standing in a maize field. Indeed, she obviously realised what had happened and was full of concern for me. I was really surprised. I'd previously seen her first shocked and then furious. True, the fury had been directed at Matthew, but I'd imagined it would more or less have included me, by association. Instead she was being really friendly and even seemed slightly in awe of me, which is not something I'm used to.

The explanation came as we helped each other over the wall. Her fury with Matthew had, at heart, been because he had excluded her. She knew nothing about Matthew and I, thinking I was Amber's girlfriend and a dyed-in-the-wool lesbian. She even apologised for interrupting us, which made me feel rather sneaky, but it seemed best not to say anything.

With some gentle persuasion from Ginny, she'd made up with Matthew and even agreed trying out as his pony-girl. Ginny seemed to have presented me as confident, experienced, sexually aware. Hence Catherine's awe.

There was more to it than that, as I quickly discovered. When I had asked to meet Ginny at the old park, Catherine had been there and asked if she could meet me. Ginny had agreed but, when they'd arrived and found I was not yet there, she had decided to walk round and check that the wall had been repaired properly. She had recognised me as I tried to climb the fence and wondered what I was doing, then decided that I'd obviously had what she called an 'embarrassing accident'.

The description rather appealed to me, making me feel at once slightly shy and shamefaced but also mischievous because she didn't know the truth. In addition to the red hair, she had green eyes, a snub nose and freckles: a really sweet look. Although taller than me, she was hardly large, with nice hips and medium-sized breasts. I could see Amber fancying her, just from the way her bottom moved under her skirt. With any luck, we'd be seeing her naked before too long, and then . . .

'So how did you like being a pony-girl?' I asked as we came to the track.

'It was great, once I'd got used to it,' she answered. 'It was weird, at first. It just doesn't seem the sort of sex a modern girl is supposed to have. I mean, we're supposed to go on top, be up front about when we want it, be in control and not let men dominate us . . . Not that that really applies to you, I suppose . . .' She had trailed off, as if she'd said something she shouldn't have.

I hastened to put her back at ease. 'Just do as you like and don't feel guilty about it,' I told her. 'Power is not being like other people think you should. After all, what's the difference between a man telling you that it's perverted to be a pony-girl and a woman telling you it's degrading to be a pony-girl?'

'None, I suppose,' she replied. 'I enjoyed it, anyway. I'd like to try driving too, but Matthew won't do that.'

'You can drive me,' I offered automatically. It wasn't intended as a come-on, just as a friendly offer, but she blushed beetroot red.

'Penny, can I ask you a question?' she said. There was a tension in her voice. Combined with the blush, it was an immediate giveaway. I'd been there myself.

'Go ahead,' I told her.
'What's it like . . . with . . . with Amber?'
'Glorious,' I replied, deliberately taking a slightly wrong tack. 'She's really imaginative and she's brilliant at making things –'
'I mean in bed,' Catherine interrupted.
'Tender, cuddly, soothing,' I answered, which was true, even if the most soothing hugs always came after I'd been punished.
'But doesn't she whip you and things? I thought that's what you liked?'
'Yes, when we're playing. She's really loving, in general.'
'So you like being beaten?'
'By the right person, on my bum, or my thighs maybe; yes. It doesn't mean I like being hurt nastily or anything. Just the opposite, in fact; I'm really tender. Doesn't Matthew spank you?'
'He likes to, but I never feel quite right about it. I suppose I do like it, but –'
'I've always liked it. Now I feel I need to be spanked, it doesn't just turn me on, it makes me feel better about everything.'
'Like feeling better after you've been punished for something?'
'Exactly; I like to be caught and punished. It's no fun being naughty if you get away with it. Sexually, anyway; in the normal run of things, I'm no different to anyone else. I like to get away with it. But if you don't feel that way, what do you get out of being spanked?'
'I . . . I suppose I'm just a little flirt really. I like to feel that I'm showing off and that everyone's looking at me and thinking I look sexy but that they think I haven't chosen to show off. That, and the warm glow you get afterwards.'
'I agree, I sometimes fantasise about being spanked in a park. It has to be for something really trivial, like

walking on the grass, or dropping a bit of paper. The park keeper has pulled my panties down and everyone's looking . . .'

'That sounds good. Do you think about men looking, too?'

'Yes; it makes it even more humiliating. Tell me one of yours, now.'

If the conversation was having anything like the effect on Catherine that it was having on me, then her pussy would be soaking. She was obviously fascinated by the idea of lesbian sex; fascinated and guilty, just like I had been.

'My favourite,' she began, 'had always been about being caught trespassing. I suppose it's because I've always lived in the country and am always being told not to cross other people's land.'

'What happens?' I prompted her.

We had come to the yard but there was no sign of Ginny and so I turned the tap on and began to strip, trying to be as nonchalant as possible. I decided to go naked, hoping we might end up in a clinch.

'Well,' she was saying, not turning away as I pulled down my soggy jeans and knickers in one. 'I like to imagine I've been caught stealing something: eggs, usually. The farmer catches me and pulls me along by the ear into his kitchen, where his two sons are sitting having lunch . . .'

'What are they like?' I asked, wanting the full detail as I began to run the hose over my body.

'Big, strong lads: say eighteen and twenty. A bit like Matthew when I met him, actually. Their mother's there too, a really big woman with red cheeks and big heavy arms that are always bare and red-skinned. Anyway, the farmer pulls me over his lap and starts to spank me. I kick and shout at him but he's so strong, he hardly notices. I'm wearing a big skirt and the folds are getting in the way, so he pulls it up, and that really makes me angry because the sons are watching and they're laughing at me. They think it's hilarious and are egging their father on to pull down my panties, but the woman's completely indifferent and just carries on knitting. Finally the farmer pulls my pants down . . . I usually come, then . . .'

She broke off, blushing, but I was determined not to leave such a gorgeous fantasy without more detail.

'Why then, and what if you don't?' I teased.

'I don't really know,' she continued. 'There's just something about the exact moment that my bum's stripped . . . As if I've been spoilt in some way, once they've seen my bare bottom . . . It's hard to explain.'

'I understand,' I agreed.

'Then, just occasionally,' she added, blushing again, 'instead of spanking me himself, the farmer throws me over his wife's lap. She's much more matter-of-fact; she immediately hauls up my skirt and pulls my panties straight down, as if my bum being bare in front of her husband and sons is completely unimportant. They're getting really turned on, but she just keeps on bringing that big strong arm down, harder and harder while she calls me a brat and tells me to stop squalling about a little spanking. In the end, she pulls my panties right off and stuffs them in my mouth to shut me up. That always makes me come.'

The idea certainly made me want to come. My nipples were rock hard, and it wasn't just from the cold water. She was obviously very turned on, too, and I realised that it was now or never.

'Would you like me to do that for you, Catherine?' I asked breathlessly.

'Just call me Katie,' was all she said, but the answer was obvious from the way her lip trembled, so I stopped her mouth with a kiss before she could have second thoughts. There was an instant's hesitation and then she responded, opening her mouth and then letting her tongue touch mine.

She must have been fantasising about sex with another woman for years because, the instant she let herself go, she was like a wild beast. One hand went around my back, snaking down to the cleft of my bottom, the other to a breast which she fondled with a clumsy urgency. I stroked the nape of her neck to slow and soothe her, but I might as well not have bothered. One moment her kisses were hot and passionate against my mouth, the next on my neck. Then she was nuzzling and kissing my breasts, cupping one to put the nipple to her mouth as her other hand curled around one cheek of my bottom. The other hand joined it, kneading my cheeks as her kisses travelled down my belly.

I sighed as her mouth touched my pussy, the tongue burrowing in to search out my clit and lap as her hands explored my bottom. I felt she wanted to eat me, the way she was licking and mouthing my vulva. Her fingers kept stroking between my cheeks, never quite daring to touch the centre, an act that would have destroyed her last vestige of reserve.

I had wanted to have her slowly, warming her with a spanking conducted with all the skill Amber had taught me. Then she could have licked me, even as I licked her. As it was, I was going to come at any moment, just from the manic way she was slurping at my clitoris.

'Slower, Katie,' I gasped. 'I want you, too.'

She sat back, resting on her arms, open-mouthed and flustered. Her skirt had ridden up so that the front of her panties showed: wet white cotton, plastered against her pussy. I sank into a crouch in front of her, reaching out for the buttons of her blouse. She put her head back and closed her eyes as the first button popped open, her breathing coming fast as each one opened and exposed a bit more of the creamy white flesh of her breasts. Her skin was very pale, also smooth and soft. The last button popped open and I pulled her blouse apart, exposing her bra.

Her breasts were the size of big oranges and looked lovely, nestled in white lace with the pale nipples showing through. I stroked each, making her shiver and swallow, then reached behind her to unclip her bra and pull it up. I caught them as they fell free, heavy, yielding globes of flesh crowned by stiff nipples. I wanted to suck them and leant forward to take a nipple in my mouth, holding the breast up and nipping the hard bud of rosy pink flesh between my lips.

I continued to nibble, letting my other hand sneak between her legs. Her panty crotch was wet and bulging with soft pussy flesh, a fold of cotton caught between her lips. I stroked the front, then slid my hand down them and cupped her pussy, my middle finger working in between the lips. She groaned as I found her clit, arching her back to push herself on to me.

At that instant, she was completely mine, utterly abandoned to my touch and moaning softly as I teased her to ecstasy. It must have been all the time I'd spent at Amber's feet, because that was where I wanted her: kneeling with her head between my ankles and her bottom hot and smarting.

She moved without resistance as I rolled her over on to the hard cobbles of the yard and straddled her back. She gave a low moan as I started to pull her skirt up and realised that she was going to get the spanking she'd been angling for. Her bottom was lovely, a plump peach wrapped in white cotton, the cheeks tight in anticipation of her punishment. I put my thumbs under the waistband of her panties and eased them down ever so slowly. She didn't make a sound, but said thank you in the softest, meekest voice imaginable when they were around her thighs.

I waited a moment, admiring the slight trembling of her naked bottom, then planted a firm smack full across her cheeks. She squeaked and gave a little kick, for all the world like I would have done in her place. There was something incredibly sweet about that. When I spanked Amber, she often laughed and I always felt I wasn't making much impression on her bottom. Catherine was just like me, girly and pathetic: squealing like a pig at the first slap.

She certainly squealed when I started to spank her in earnest, wriggling and kicking underneath me so that it was all I could do to stay on. I managed, though, and her bum was soon a cheerful pink, while her wriggles kept giving me flashes of the ginger fur between her legs, sometimes even her bottom-hole and pussy. Seeing the white panties twist and stretch as she thrashed reminded me of a particularly humiliating detail of her fantasy. I stopped spanking and she immediately went limp, breathing heavily.

'Thank you, Penny, thank you,' she gasped. 'That was so nice; oh, my bum's so warm.'

'Who says I've finished?' I asked, taking a good grip on her panties and pulling them down her thighs and off her legs. 'It's not just fantasy, Katie, you are a squalling brat. Now open your mouth.'

'Please, yes,' she said, the instant before I stuffed her mouth with her own panties.

I took hold of her ankles and set to work on her bum again, her squeals were now muffled by her mouthful of knickers. Her bum was getting very red indeed and my hand was starting to smart, soft and well-padded though her bottom was. What I needed was a cane or a strap to take her right to the peak of submissive ecstasy. The best I could do was one of her shoes: flat leather-soled ones that promised well as spanking implements. My use of her shoe redoubled her kicks and struggles, each smack making her buttocks bounce and then part as she bucked.

At last something in the tone of her squeaks made me decide she'd had enough and reminded me that I should have given her a stop word. I stopped, laying the shoe across the reddened skin of her bottom and admiring the sight with immense satisfaction. This was how Amber must have felt when she had put me into the back of her horsebox for the first time, a trussed and docile pony-girl ready for her pleasure.

The question was, what to do with Katie next? It was like having a big box of chocolates and knowing you couldn't eat them all at once. I put the shoe aside and began to stroke her bottom, then leant forward and kissed one hot cheek. I could smell the scent of her sex, rich and inviting, overpoweringly feminine. It was too much to resist and I abandoned my plans of slowly teasing her to orgasm in favour of burying my face between her thighs and licking her until she came. Then it would be my turn and I'd sit on her face and make her kiss my bottom-hole, which she'd been too embarrassed to touch. I'd masturbate while she licked it and then come right in her face.

'Time for you to come, Katie,' I told her. 'Stick your bum up and I'll give you a good lick.'

She obeyed, raising her bottom and opening her thighs as I started to dismount.

Inevitably, Ginny had to turn up at that moment. I heard a noise and looked up to see her standing in the entrance to the yard, gaping at us with an expression of disbelief. 'Penny! What are you doing?' she exclaimed.

'Spanking Katie,' I answered cheerfully. There didn't seem much else to say.

On hearing Ginny's voice, Catherine tried to get up, nearly throwing me off my seat on her back.

'Don't, don't!' I pleaded. 'Relax; Ginny's no different. Don't you remember seeing her at the boathouse?'

She relaxed again and I stroked one red bum cheek thoughtfully, then gave her a hard smack full across her bottom.

'Anyway,' I continued, 'you must have known she might catch us at it. You did, didn't you, you little tart?'

Catherine squirmed beneath me in an agony of pleasure and shame. Ginny was walking towards us, her big breasts bare under a flimsy T-shirt, tight blue bikini pants peeping out from beneath the hem.

'I'm afraid there's no spanking left to do,' I told Ginny, indicating Catherine's upturned bottom.

'Yes there is,' Ginny replied in a surprisingly firm voice. 'Penny Birch, for three years I've fancied Catherine, but I've never dared do more than kiss her goodnight. When she caught us we talked nearly all night and I gave her a cuddle, but that was all. Now you meet her and in five minutes you're perched on her back, starkers and about to tongue her.'

I shrugged and smiled, after all, it wasn't my fault if she had never had the courage to make a pass.

'I want both of you, now, or I'll be really hurt,' she continued. I could tell she was genuinely hurt and immediately felt sorry for her, determining to make it up.

I nodded to Ginny and climbed off Catherine, who rolled over and took her panties out of her mouth. She was wide-eyed and excited but also very uncertain and covered her breasts shyly.

'Just follow me,' I whispered.

'Kneel and put your hands on your heads,' Ginny ordered. 'Backs straight, knees apart and look at the ground.'

I complied, but slowly so that I could watch Catherine. The position left her tits sticking out under the rolled-up bra and most of her thighs showing where her skirt was rucked up. Her hands were folded on top of her head, her panties lying discarded between her open knees. It made a very pretty picture, helping me to make the mental switch from dominance to submission because she looked so sweet yet I myself was stark naked.

'First,' Ginny said slowly and firmly, 'I'm going to tell Amber.'

'Yes, miss,' I replied, immediately getting the thrill of knowledge of coming punishment. Amber would certainly cane me for seducing another woman, and probably in some new and humiliating fashion. Catherine sniggered, either out of genuine delight at my discomfort or because she was learning to play the game.

'I don't know what you're laughing at,' Ginny told her. 'You're as bad as she is. Do you know what Amber's favourite punishment for little trollops is?'

'No, miss,' Catherine replied, sounding genuinely contrite.

'You'll be caned,' Ginny told her with relish. 'First she'll have you play some humiliating game, to decide how many strokes you get. Then she'll put six or twelve cane strokes across your fat white bottom. Then you'll say sorry and kiss her bottom-hole to show you mean it. I suspect you'd enjoy that?'

Catherine wasn't stupid. She immediately caught the implication of Ginny's question. If she said no, then she'd never be asked to do it, but if she said yes . . .

She couldn't bring herself to speak, but she did nod, blushing furiously as she admitted that she'd like to do it.

'And the cane, too, I suppose?' Ginny demanded.

'Yes, miss,' Catherine answered, clearly and openly this time, although I doubted she knew what being caned felt like.

'Slut,' Ginny answered. 'There'll be a spanking coming up from Matthew, too, I dare say, then his cock in your mouth.'

'Yes, miss,' Catherine repeated.

'First,' Ginny continued, 'you can both apologise to me for having sex in my stable yard. Penny, first.'

She had taken a pace to stand directly in front of me. I mumbled an apology and then bent forward to kiss her feet, immediately finding my head trapped between her ankles, exactly as I had planned to do to Catherine. Of course, that left my bottom stuck in the air, a humiliating position that made Catherine snigger again.

'Funny, is it?' Ginny demanded. 'Kiss her pussy, now.'

I saw Catherine move behind me and then felt the soft brush of her lips on my vagina, directly over the hole. It was so light as to be frustrating, a hint of what her tongue could achieve in that same place. I wondered if Ginny would order her to bring me off in that position.

'Now her bottom,' Ginny ordered.

I felt a firm, wet kiss on one bottom cheek, then the other.

'Is that all, Katie?' Ginny queried, still giving Catherine a chance to back out.

Catherine hesitated, then her lips touched my anus. The kiss tickled and sent a thrill right through me so that I couldn't resist a sigh.

'Sluts, the pair of you,' Ginny remarked. 'Good, right, off with your clothes, Katie.'

She kept my head clamped between her ankles while Catherine undressed, only releasing me when she, too, was naked. I knelt back, adopting the position I'd been told to before, with my knees apart and my breasts thrust out so that everything was on offer. Catherine was in the same position, Ginny standing over her two playthings with her hands on her hips and a knowing smile on her face.

'Follow me,' she ordered suddenly, evidently having decided on a suitable punishment for us.

We stood and followed as she left the yard and took the path that led down to the boathouse. Most of her bottom showed under her T-shirt, the gloriously full globes wobbling slightly as she walked, covered only by a thin strip of bright blue material. I'd never really had a play with Ginny's bottom and was hoping that whatever she had in mind involved plenty of attention to it.

She seemed hesitant at the boathouse, as if unsure how to punish us. She did make us kneel and kiss her bottom-hole, pulling the bikini pants aside and holding her cheeks apart and presenting us with her anus. I got a delicious submissive thrill as I knelt forward and kissed the tight little ring and then watched Catherine do the same. There's not much more you can do to acknowledge your submission to someone than kiss their bum-hole, but Ginny gave a most undominant sigh of pleasure as each of us did it to her.

'Actually,' she said as her bikini pants snapped back into place, 'what I'd really like is a good spanking from both of you.'

Ginny was never that good at being in charge; she could never keep her own lust in check long enough. Catherine accepted the change of role with all the innocent enthusiasm of a newcomer, smiling at the prospect of punishing Ginny. We sat on two chairs with our legs interlocked and put her across our knees. I pulled her top up over her breasts and slid my arm under her chest to take hold of them. They felt huge, two great handfuls of flesh, each tipped with a nipple the size of a fruit pastille. Maybe it's because my own breasts are so small, but seeing a full-breasted girl always gives me the urge to have a really good feel. There was certainly no shortage of Ginny and she moaned as I fondled them, marvelling at their weight and softness. Catherine was waiting patiently, one hand on Ginny's waist while the other stroked the gorgeous full moon of her bum.

You couldn't call Ginny fat; her waist was narrow with no more than a hint of roundness to her belly. Fat-bottomed, maybe, and it was amazing how such a luxurious bum managed to stay in such perfect shape. I remembered the first time I had seen her, the same plush bottom that I was now about to smack bouncing as she ran, her tail swishing from side to side over her cheeks.

Now that same girl was over my lap with her gorgeous rump quivering under my fingers as I planted a preparatory slap on the fattest part of it.

'You can pull her bikini down,' I told Catherine and then watched as the little scrap of blue material was peeled down, baring the deep division of Ginny's bottom with a hint of golden fur between the cheeks.

We set to work without further fuss, taking a cheek each. We quickly had Ginny kicking her legs, although she made less fuss about it than either I or Catherine would have done. I expect regular spankings from Michael made our efforts seem rather pathetic, but her fat peach was soon a glowing red while her moans were gaining a familiar urgency. Her hand went back to her pussy and she started to masturbate, begging us to smack harder as her pleasure rose. We did our best, but my hand was stinging when she finally came and I could see that Catherine's palm was red too. Her orgasm was long and noisy, leaving me with a strong need for my own.

Even as her shudders subsided, I was easing her down to the floor and opening my legs for her attention. She was breathing heavily, looking at my open pussy, her hair plastered to her forehead and her breasts heaving beautifully. As she came forward, I spread my legs as far as they would go and took a big heavy breast in each hand. I'd have liked them in my face, but you can't have everything and, when her tongue touched my clit, I knew it wouldn't be long until I came.

'Put your breasts in my face, please, Katie,' I asked, intent on getting the best of both worlds.

She complied willingly, rising and holding them together so that my face was pillowed in her cleavage. My position was rather awkward, but it felt exquisite, smothered in plump, female flesh while another girl licked at my clitoris. All three of us were naked or near naked, lost in the pleasure of each other's bodies. I took one of Catherine's nipples in my mouth, thinking of how sweetly she'd let me pull her breasts out of her bra, then I was coming, squeezing Ginny's plump breasts in my hands and gasping out my ecstasy onto Catherine's chest, my mouth full of nipple and tit.

'That leaves you, Katie,' I said, when I'd had a moment to recover. 'We'll do anything you like; but let me tell you something, first. You saw how I'd wet myself on the path?'

'Yes,' she answered.

'Were you turned on by how I looked and by thinking how I must have felt? Or did you just feel sympathetic because I'd had an accident?'

'Both, a bit,' she admitted.

'You wet yourself?' Ginny asked.

'On the footpath,' I admitted. 'I was a bit drunk and I got caught short. The idea of doing it in my pants was so naughty I couldn't resist it.'

'You did it on purpose?' Catherine exclaimed.

'Yes,' I answered, feeling a bit ashamed of myself, despite our intimacy.

'That's so dirty. Did you want to be punished for it?' Ginny asked, smiling knowingly from where she was sitting in front of me.

'I wanted you to spank me on my wet jeans and then tell Amber,' I told her.

Catherine had sat down, legs open and one hand on her pussy.

'You ought to be punished,' she breathed, spreading her pussy lips and putting a finger on her clit. 'You filthy little tart. Get down between my legs.'

I knelt hastily, leaning forward to lick her although I didn't really see pussy-licking as a punishment.

'Wait,' she said, my face just inches from her pussy. 'Maybe this'll teach you not to be so dirty.'

I thought she meant the licking and looked up to her eyes, my mouth open in preparation for her pussy.

Suddenly a stream of pee erupted from her, catching me full in the mouth. I swallowed, but nothing like enough and it splashed over, running down my chin. My mouth was full of the sharp bitter taste as I rose to catch the stream on my tits, rubbing them as she did it all over me. It ran down my belly and soaked my pussy fur, forming a pool on the floor. I knelt in it and went forward to catch more in my mouth. As the stream died to a trickle, I put my mouth to Catherine's pussy and started to lick.

Her hand locked in my hair and I found myself kneeling in a pool of her pee while I gave her oral sex. Suddenly, I wanted to come again and put a hand back to feel my pussy. Ginny must have realised because, a moment later, she came behind me and cupped my wet titties in her hands, stroking the nipples and whispering the dirtiest things she could think of in my ear. Her breasts were against my back, my bottom pressed to her belly.

'I'm going to come, Penny; lick me,' Catherine gasped as I felt her muscles begin to pulse. I lapped harder at her clit, feeling her tense in response. Then there was a new, warm trickle running down the small of my back and in between the cheeks of my bum. I came as Catherine did, one of Ginny's fingers finding my wet bottom-hole at the instant I climaxed and slipping inside. For an instant my mind went black at the sheer intensity of it all, then Catherine's muscles were relaxing and I was rocking back to join Ginny in a heap in the puddle on the floor.

There was a lot of embarrassed giggling as we cleared up, especially from Catherine, but there was also the wonderful sensation of sharing a really dirty secret. I'd tell Amber, of course, and take whatever she invented in the way of punishment, but neither of them felt able to tell their men.

When we'd finally made the boathouse respectable,

we began to discuss the following week's pony-girl meet. Catherine's attitude had now changed from doubt to enthusiasm, suggesting all sorts of imaginative subtleties that she had previously confined to her fantasies.

After swimming for a bit and then resting while we waited for my clothes to dry, we drove back to the King Billy, collected my car and then met at the Scotts' house in Broadheath. Michael was already home and greeted our suggestions with enthusiasm. I was a little nervous at the prospect of facing Matthew, but when he did arrive there was no difficulty. After all, I knew what his girlfriend had done that afternoon.

Fourteen

I went back to Amber's with a fair degree of trepidation. After all, I had got rather carried away, and while Ginny had made a big joke of it when she rang and told Amber everything, I wasn't quite sure if she wouldn't be genuinely angry or hurt. The first thing I did on arrival was give her a heartfelt apology if I'd upset her. She swore I hadn't, but I could tell that my assurances were gratefully received. Of course, that didn't mean I was going to get off, but she decided to sleep on it and contented herself with spanking me before bed.

In the morning, she told me that she was deferring my punishment until the pony-girl meet, adding rather alarmingly that I'd be let off for the rest of the week so that my bottom was nice and fresh for Sunday. We had overwhelmingly voted for her as Mistress of Ceremonies and she took to the task with a will. The main plan was to have several challenge races and a show, interspersed with suitable punishments and rewards for winners and losers. Various girls would also receive correction for misbehaviour, myself included.

She had rung Anna Vale and persuaded her to come, succeeding because the prospect of a chance to play with five pony-girls at once overcame her dislike of a male presence. If she couldn't handle the little deception Amber and I had played on her, then that was just too bad.

There would be seven women in all, and only four

men. Four because she had roped Henry Gresham in as referee, being a noted authority on pony-girls and known by more than half of us. He was also the official photographer, being both experienced and trustworthy.

That was how things stood on the Saturday evening as we set off for the Scotts'. By staying over, we would be able to make the best of the day and add the finishing touches to the organising, with most of us there.

From the onset, there was an atmosphere of suppressed excitement. Not so suppressed in Ginny's case, as she could barely keep still. The six of us sat round the table, balancing out the details until nearly one in the morning, then retired, each satisfied that she or he would be getting plenty out of the next day's events.

Personally, I knew that I could rely on the others to give me all the attention and sensation I needed, both as a pony-girl and in the way of punishment. My aim was rather different: to have Amber and Anna Vale as my pony-girls.

The morning was a bustle of activity, with everybody trying to sort themselves out and all of us praying that Arthur Linslade wouldn't suddenly decide to come over. The weather was firmly on our side, sunny with few clouds and a moderate breeze, perfect for pony-carting. Henry Gresham arrived at ten, Anderson and Vicky somewhat afterwards, and by ten-thirty we were driving up to the old park in a convoy of cars and one horsebox.

I felt light-hearted, excited and keen to play, a mood echoed by the others as we set up the three carts and Vicky and Anderson's carriage. Amber had also filled the horsebox with paraphernalia: a pillory, a whipping stool, various punishment implements and a great pile of spare tack. When we were finished, the yard was a true pervert's paradise. Three pony-carts stood at one end, the carriage behind them. To the side, the whipping stool and pillory stood ready, next to a table laid out with devices for just about every sexual curiosity imaginable.

All we needed to start was Anna and Poppy, on whose arrival Amber intended to read out the order of events and kick off the meet. The first spectacle was to be my long-awaited punishment of Ginny, a prospect that I was looking forward to with relish. She was already giving me nervous, excited glances as I stood admiring the selection of goodies that were spread out on the table. I was just trying to choose between cane and strap when Amber hailed us from on top of the carriage.

'It looks like they've chickened out,' she announced, 'so let's start. I think all the introductions have been done. I will be leading the ceremonies and would like to thank you for your support for the post. As referee, we have Mr Henry Gresham, my godfather and a man who trained his first pony-girl before most of us were born. His knowledge is extensive and his decision final, so we'll have no arguments about tactics, Michael Scott.

'In between pony-girl events, there will be a number of spectacles designed to correct the behaviour of some of our number. The first of these will be the punishment of Mrs Virginia Scott by Miss Penelope Birch. Penny, you may proceed.'

'Thank you, Amber,' I called out to her, then turned back to the table. Ginny was a strapping girl and used to Michael, so I didn't really need to hold back. On the other hand, I had no idea if she had any particular favourites. She was waiting with Michael, dressed in a simple white dress, naked underneath but for her panties so that she could quickly become a pony-girl. I walked over to them, smiling cheerfully at both and getting a nervous grin back from Ginny.

'What does she like best?' I asked Michael boldly.

He gave me the cool, amused smile I'd always enjoyed and put his chin in his hand. 'Hmm, let me see,' he said evenly. 'It's more a question of what she doesn't like. You could try giving her an enema.'

'Michael!' Ginny protested, the first genuine objection I'd ever heard her make.

'A dose of the strap usually keeps her in line,' he continued casually.

'I'll strap her, then,' I replied. 'Does she ever come without her clit being played with?'

'Not really,' Michael told me. 'In fact, no; never.'

'Good,' I answered, 'then I have an ideal punishment for a girl like her; fat-bottomed, that is. Come on, Ginny.'

I took her by the hand and she followed me meekly across the yard, the others making themselves comfortable to watch her being punished. In practice, I wanted to make it spectacular and effective but I didn't want to make her too sore to be spanked and whipped later, as she undoubtedly would be.

The pillory was my chosen piece of equipment, a solid wooden affair designed not to be upset by a victim's struggles. Amber had built it deliberately low so that instead of the conventional position, the offender's bottom would be higher than their head.

Ginny looked at it apprehensively but bent down to put her head in the central hole submissively enough. I cleared her long golden hair from her neck so that it fell around her face, running my nails gently along the exposed nape before shutting the pillory and clipping the catch into place. A leg-spreading pole completed her position and there were murmurs of appreciation from the onlookers as I threw up her dress to expose her for punishment. I walked around her, admiring my handiwork. She did look beautiful, her eyes big and moist, her mouth set in a sullen pout, hair cascading down around her face. Her big bottom looked great, raised up with her pale blue panties stretched taut across her seat, the shape of her pussy showing because her legs were as wide apart as they would go.

'You should have had her take her knickers off before you put the leg-pole on,' Anderson pointed out from the crowd.

'Not at all,' I answered. 'You'll all see plenty of her pussy later, but for now her panties have a function.'

I pulled them down as far as they would go anyway, leaving Ginny's bum bare with the panties in a taut line just below her cheeks. It also seemed a pity not to show her tits off, so I adjusted the dress to leave them swinging bare beneath her, on full view for everybody. She now looked even better and I signalled Henry over to take a few photographs while I went to choose from the table. Ginny squirmed and pretended embarrassment at being photographed in such a position, but also made an effort to stick her bum further out and turn to give a suitably remorseful look to the camera.

It was Anderson's treatment of us as pony-girls that had inspired my idea for Ginny's punishment. The difference was that I intended to beat her while the vibrator was actually in her pussy. With a skinny girl, it wouldn't be safe, because you might catch the base of the vibrator with the strap. On Ginny's big firm bottom, there would be plenty of flesh to cushion the smacks. The purpose of leaving her panties on was to hold the vibrator in place, otherwise her wriggles were bound to push it out.

I chose a thick cock-shaped vibrator made of rubber. It also had a rubber prong above the main shaft, designed either to tickle a girl's clit or fit into her bum-hole, a feature that real cocks would certainly be improved by. For a strap, I chose a genuine Lochgelly tawse, a heavy leather implement made for use on Scot and Amber's pride and joy. I had felt it across my own bottom and knew how much it stung, while there was a satisfying weight to the smacks that was a particular turn-on.

Ginny watched me as I walked back to her, looking uncertainly at the vibrator and tawse. Once behind her I laid the tawse across the crest of her bottom and pulled her panties open to get at her pussy. I made sure the crowd got a good view of her full sex lips and moist, pink vulva. I sucked a finger and slid it into her, making her groan as the flesh of her pussy tightened on the intruding digit. Amber was never that keen on being fingered, and the sensation of having mine in another woman's vagina was still unfamiliar enough to make me want to explore for a bit. Ginny moaned again as I wriggled it inside her, enjoying the sensation of the tight wet tube of flesh clamped around my finger.

When I had finished opening her, the vibrator slid in easily enough, only needing to be pulled back a couple of times until it was deep inside her. I couldn't resist a quick lick of her anus to help the little probe in; Amber and, I think, Anderson laughed at my readiness to lick a bottom. Lastly, I tweaked the panties back into place, the taut elastic holding the vibrator well in her pussy while there was perhaps an inch and a half of finger-width rubber probe in her bottom-hole. I turned it on, immediately drawing a sigh of pleasure from Ginny.

'Could you just take a couple of close-ups of that for my album?' I asked Henry, a suggestion that made Ginny squirm until I told her to keep still.

As he backed away, I hefted the tawse over her naked vulnerable bottom, then brought it around in a full arc to land across her seat with a meaty smack. She jumped and squealed, her bum bouncing and wobbling prettily. The tawse had left a broad red mark across her bum, which I inspected before standing back for the second stroke. The onlookers were quiet, concentrating on Ginny's beating, each taking their own pleasure in the spectacle.

After the second stroke, Ginny was panting faintly from the beating and beginning to pull her back in and tense her buttocks rhythmically from the effect of the vibrator. I knew how she felt, exposed, punished and teased all at once but unable to come, an exquisite torment that would put her on a sexual high for the rest of the day.

As the third stroke smacked down on Ginny's plump posterior there was the sound of a car horn from the direction of the gate. I stopped, waiting while Michael went to investigate and returned with Anna Vale and Poppy. This meant that Ginny had five minutes just stuck there with the vibrator running and, by the time they had got out of the car, she was writhing her bottom from side to side and begging to be allowed to come.

I ignored her, greeting Anna with a peck on each cheek and Poppy with a kiss on the lips. Anna was in a uniform; WRAF, I think, from about 1940. This was very neat and bore an officer's insignia, giving her a cool, commanding look. Poppy had on a light summer dress that showed her legs in the bright sunlight. For an instant the wind blew it against her bottom, showing an outline that told me she was pantyless underneath. Anna smiled to the women and gave the men formal nods as she walked across the yard, Poppy following.

Of course, the scene was exactly what Anna would have expected to see. The ultra-dominant Amber Oakley strapping some remorseful female across the bare bottom while the others looked on respectfully. The real Amber had agreed to maintain the deception until lunch, so that was how long I had to seduce Anna into submission. After lunch, I was due a punishment that would destroy any illusions she had about me being untouchably dominant.

Strapping Ginny was a good start and, as I returned my attention to her bottom, I noticed that Anna took care to stand where she got a view directly between

Ginny's legs. It takes concentration to apply a tawse properly, so I gave Ginny her fourth smack and then went round to talk to her and stroke her cheek. I know how good it feels to have the person who's punishing you come and soothe you in between strokes, and that was mainly what I was doing. It also gave me a chance to watch Anna. She looked cool and poised, an officer observing a just and necessary punishment, but in my mind I was already rolling the tight skirt up to inspect her underwear.

I gave Ginny two more, both hard enough to make her bottom wobble and draw a gasp from her lips. I then took her around the waist and fucked her with the vibrator until she was once more begging for her orgasm. It was nice watching it slide in and out. Her pussy was soaking and took the thick shaft easily, while the little probe forced her bum-hole open with each push. The little ring would tense, then open to the pressure and reluctantly admit the rubber finger.

I was considering trying to fit the main shaft in her anus when she started to call 'Amber' and I realised that I really had taken her to her limit. I turned the vibrator off and pulled it gently out, then hurried round to talk to her. I knew she was all right when she gave me a big happy smile, so I kissed her and offered her the vibrator to suck. She took it, savouring her own juices with her eyes shut as I fed it in and out.

That was it; I had no intention of letting her come, but instead took the vibrator away and unclipped the stocks. She had to wait while I released her from the leg-spreading pole, but I got a lovely warm hug when she was free. Everyone clapped when we started to kiss, with Ginny's leg up so that her hot pussy was against my thigh. I broke away and sent her to Michael with a smack on the bottom, bowing to the crowd as she snuggled into his arms.

Our little show had put everyone in just the right

mood, myself included. Whether anybody else was scheming quite as much as I was, I doubted. From her previous behaviour when she'd been really turned on, I knew Anna would enjoy submitting to me, if she could only justify the act in her own mind. Once she made that all-important initial gesture I was sure she'd be mine, and, if the intensity of Amber's passion in similar conditions was anything to go by, the results should be spectacular. Then again I could always cheat . . .

As Amber announced that Henry was now taking challenges for racing, I sidled over to where Vicky was getting into her pony-girl gear. Anderson was across the yard, talking to Michael and Ginny, so Vicky asked me to help her.

She was already naked, and I kissed her and squeezed one firm buttock before starting to lace the waist belt of her harness.

'I'd like to make a deal,' I whispered. 'Are you willing to lose a race?'

'Maybe,' she answered doubtfully.

'How about a nice bribe?' I offered.

Her mouth broke into a mischievous grin, telling me that a bribe was exactly what she wanted.

'A piggy-girl to play with?' I suggested.

Her eyes lit up. I'd known she liked the fantasy from her reaction at their house, even though she'd been exhausted.

'Maybe two, if I can pull it off,' I offered. 'Look, throw out a challenge that anyone who can beat you on a single lap, with the driver of your choice, can punish both you and the driver. Make it girls only and ask Anna Vale to drive you, then add a heavy punishment for the challenging driver if she loses. Lose, and I'll do the rest.'

She nodded, glancing over to Anna, who was standing rather aloofly, admiring the carriage. I helped Vicky with the rest of her tack, leaving only her bridle off so that she wasn't technically in role. She then walked over to Anderson, who in turn spoke to Henry Gresham to arrange the challenge. I strolled away nonchalantly, heading for where Catherine, Matthew and Amber were standing.

As I reached them, I saw Anderson slip Vicky's bit into her mouth and give her reins to Henry. Both men then made for the centre of the yard; Vicky, now Hippolyta, paced behind them.

'Ladies and gentlemen,' he announced, 'we have our first challenge. Mr Anderson Croom challenges any all-female team to beat his pony-girl Hippolyta over a single lap. Mr Croom will not be driving and would like to offer his seat to Miss Anna Vale by special request from Hippolyta. Miss Vale?'

I glanced over to Anna. She was clearly flattered, as who wouldn't be if a beautiful pony-girl wanted to be driven by them.

'And the prize?' she demanded haughtily but not without real curiosity.

'The prize,' Henry continued, 'should you win, is the submission of both pony-girl and driver of the losing team. To your desire, subject only to stop words. The stop words, incidentally, are "yellow" for slow and "red" for stop. Should you lose, the winning driver will have the right to spank you and to drive Hippolyta herself.'

That wasn't quite what I had said, but the offer was good and surely had to tempt Anna. She got to drive Vicky anyway, and if she won she would have the submission of two other women. I saw her glance cautiously around, wondering if it was too obvious a trap. She was lighter than everybody else except myself, Poppy, and maybe Catherine. Also, among the girls, only Ginny and Amber had anything like Vicky's muscle and neither were built as sprinters. Anyone who accepted the challenge was clearly going to end up as her plaything. It occurred to me that she might have seen me speak to Vicky but, if she had, it might have seemed that I was manufacturing an excuse to submit to her myself. I shot her a coy glance to reinforce that theory in her mind. She responded with a knowing look and I knew I had her.

'I accept the challenge,' I announced.

'A challenge from Miss Amber Oakley!' Henry responded, fortunately getting the names the right way around. 'Who, then, will be your pony-girl.'

'Calliphigenia, of course,' I answered, reaching out to stroke Amber's head. I hadn't explained to her what I was up to and she shot me the most wonderful 'I'm going to get you later' look. The expression on Henry's face was splendid, too, as he evidently hadn't expected to see his one time *protégé* as a pony-girl.

Amber was a good sport and began to strip immediately. As I helped her harness up, I saw Anderson buckling Vicky into place and wondered if they might not have decided to pull a double bluff on me. It seemed unlikely, as Vicky would then lose her piggy-girls, and anyway, there were worse fates than being Anna Vale's plaything.

A naked Amber was a rare sight for most of the men and she had no shortage of admirers as I put her into harness. I had dressed in riding gear as part of my deception, and I like to think that when we were finished we made an exceptionally fine turnout.

'We're going to win, Honey,' I whispered as I pulled a bridle over her head.

'Are we?' she answered doubtfully.

'Yes,' I assured her, slipping the bit into her mouth and cutting off communication.

I had my beautiful Honey in harness as I had wanted, and there was a good chance I'd soon be naming Anna as I strapped her in alongside. Everything was going perfectly, but there was one other detail that I couldn't do without.

'Aren't we racing with tails?' I asked loudly as if the idea had only just occurred to me.

'We don't, usually,' Michael pointed out. 'It slows you down.'

'Referee?' I queried.

Ask a fifty-year-old pony-girl enthusiast if he'd like to see two girls wearing plug-in tails and the answer is not going to be no.

'Yes, tails it is, I think,' Henry said, as if on cue.

Amber gave me another of her looks. I smiled and kissed her.

'Is poor little Honey going to have a tail up her bottom?' I teased her, letting my hand slide down over the curve of her bottom to prod meaningfully between her cheeks.

I had her kneel and stick her bum out while I fetched Ginny's tail and pulled a condom over the plug. A well-greased finger opened Amber's bum-hole.

'Come and watch,' I announced as I put the plug to her anus.

A little crowd gathered around us and Amber hung her head as the plug popped in and her bottom-hole closed around the shaft. She looked really sweet and I promised myself to make sure she made herself a tail for regular use. Vicky was served the same way but with less ceremony, accepting the tail without fuss.

Anna lacked the experience to know how much a tail was going to slow her pony-girl down. Vicky did, but she was now Hippolyta and so not allowed to say anything even if she'd wanted to. Both pony-girls would be slowed, but the race was now more even, especially as we had more experience over the course.

I climbed into the cart and ordered Amber to rise. She was now Honey, or Calliphigenia maybe, the naming having got somewhat confused. In any case, she was my pony-girl, sleek and strong and beautiful. I know I'd got my wish rather sneakily, and the setting was erotic more than romantic, but at that moment I loved her more than ever.

A rush of adrenalin overcame my momentary sentimentality as I steered her in a wide arc to bring the cart to rest beside our rivals. Vicky looked lovely, with her long black tail hanging down over her neat little bottom. So did Anna, haughty and confident enough to make me want to submit to her, but not until I'd had my pleasure.

Henry took his place to our side, raising a handkerchief of the most startling vermilion silk as a flag. I tensed, then yelled to Honey as he brought the handkerchief down. We set off fast but they had a lead before we reached the carriage sweep in front of the ruined house, and we came into the wood a good ten yards behind.

Racing is very different from ordinary pony-carting. Normally you can sit back, admire the view, hold the reins in one hand and the whip in the other. You are in complete control of your pony-girl, who can be commanded at leisure. When racing, the best thing you can do is take a tight grip on the cart and pray your pony knows what she's doing. The lower the seat of the cart, the better, but minor potholes and stones in the path still become terrifying obstacles.

As Honey belted after our rivals, I was sure I was going to be thrown at any moment. I had only gone so fast once before, with Chris Ford, and his weight and strength had made the cart much more stable. It must have been worse still for Anna, in a higher-seated cart and close to equal in weight to Hippolyta.

At the low point of the track, we were twenty or so yards behind, but the rise was ahead and that would be to our advantage. We started to gain and I saw Anna take a smack at Hippolyta's rump. The unexpected sting of the whip only broke her stride and helped us.

I know Hippolyta could have kept her pace up and beaten us fairly, even with an inexperienced driver. As it was, she was brave enough to become more fretful with each smack of the whip on her bottom, so that we had managed to pull up right to their rear when we reached the big nettle patch.

The path was tight but we just had room to overtake, only Anna started to steer Hippolyta in a weave, blocking our path.

'Give way!' I shouted, not really expecting Anna to take any notice. We could actually see the stable yard gate and, for a moment, I thought I might have been betrayed. Then their wheel struck the edge of what had once been the lawn. Hippolyta stumbled, slowed and then righted herself. It looked real to me and made Anna clutch the cart to avoid being pitched out.

Honey dashed forward, her thigh brushing the nettles back as she overtook, but never losing speed. They were still trying to regain full speed and we had five yards on them before Hippolyta began to gain on the last stretch of flat path. It was too late and we came through the gate with the best part of a length to spare.

I drew Honey to a stop in the centre of the yard, feeling absolutely elated as Henry gave me his arm and then held my hand up as the winner. Behind us, the other cart came to a halt, Anna ordering Hippolyta to kneel and then climbing out.

She look seriously discomfited and I thought she would back out but, instead, she stood to her full height and put her head up with absolute dignity.

'I have lost and I accept your right to punish me,' she announced, addressing me. 'However, I must ask that no one watch, especially men.'

'I can respect that,' I answered coolly, although inside I felt like skipping. Anna Vale was actually going to submit to me; to accept her virgin spanking over my lap; to allow me, little, submissive Penny, to chastise and humiliate her.

I was prepared to spank her alone, but not to take my moment of triumph completely without an audience.

Marching briskly up to her, I took her by the ear and led her out of the yard behind me. I knew that at the back of the stables was a fallen tree, and it was to this I led her. Tangled rhododendrons and overgrown holly bushes screened the location effectively, creating a nicely private atmosphere for us. She had made no protest at my rough treatment and so I pulled her smartly across my knee and tucked an arm round her waist to keep her in place. Her bottom made an inviting ball under the material of her skirt, ready for spanking.

Having her across my knee felt absolutely glorious. Spanking Catherine or Ginny, Amber even, had been a blend of sex and the pleasure of accepting their submission. This had all of that, but also a sense of achievement and of having been a sneaky little brat to get my way. I knew it wouldn't last long but, for now, I had Anna Vale as my plaything and I intended to get the most out of the experience.

'Right, Anna,' I told her, 'now I'm going to spank you. Have you ever been spanked before?'

'No, Miss Oakley,' she answered in a meek, penitent voice, far different from her normal tones.

'You've done it to plenty of other girls, though, haven't you?' I continued.

'Yes, Miss Oakley.'

'Well, now you're going to find out how it feels. First I think we'll have this pretty bottom bare ...'

She hung her head as I said that, obligingly going up on her toes so that I could get the tight skirt fully over her hips. There was no reluctance, but genuine submission. I pulled her skirt up slowly, savouring the exposure of stocking tops, then the soft, creamy skin of her thighs and finally the seat of her panties. Her bum was sheathed in tight ivory silk, which was clinging to the swell of her bottom and fringed with lace, very feminine and just the sort of garment I would have expected her to wear.

'Think of all the girls who've lain over your knee with their panties as their last shred of modesty,' I told her. 'Did you ever think how they felt, as their bums were stripped? How do you think Poppy feels, as you ease her pants down over her chubby little pear of a bottom? Well you're about to find out, because yours are coming down right now, Miss Fancy-pants.'

She gave a little gasp as I took hold of her waistband, but I stopped with only the first inch of her bottom crease showing. Her whole body was trembling and I knew I was really getting to her.

'Actually,' I continued, 'I think you are getting off rather lightly. Let's make a few adjustments.'

I began with her hair, fishing for hair pins in order to take the little hat off, then release the full bulk of it. It was long, straight and a lustrous brown, faintly scented with some perfume I didn't recognise. She let out a little sob as it cascaded down around her head, falling to the earth and leaves beneath her. I hadn't been expecting such a strong reaction to this relatively minor humiliation and I paused for an instant, in case she wanted me to slow. When nothing was said, I slid my hand under her chest and started to undo the buttons of her blouse. Her trembling increased as the first one popped open and she sobbed again as my arm brushed the tip of a breast.

'I think bare breasts add a certain something to a girl's punishment, don't you?' I asked. 'No one will see, not even me, but you'll know they're bare, won't you, Anna?'

'Yes, miss,' she answered in a breathless voice more common after a spanking than before.

I continued to fiddle with her blouse, opening it and then tugging her bra up to free her breasts. I caught one, heavier and fuller than I'd expected, the nipple small and hard as I rubbed at it with my palm.

'On second thoughts,' I added, 'stand up and put your hands on your head.'

She obeyed instantly, standing as I had directed, her fine breasts stuck out for my inspection. She looked exquisite. The bra matched her panties: big and old-fashioned but very feminine. With her skirt up and her blouse open and strands of hair falling across her naked breasts, she made a fine picture of dishevelment. Her tummy was showing, too, a gentle bulge of flesh, with her tummy button a neat dimple in the middle. My slight disarrangement of her panties had also left a wisp of dark pubic hair showing at the front, with a tell-tale damp patch lower down. Best of all was her face. Her eyes were wide and moist, her mouth slightly open, the lower lip pouted and trembling, her tongue moving nervously inside.

'You are pretty,' I told her, which was true. The disarrangement of her hair and the stripping of her breasts and belly had softened the lines of her face and body, which I had thought a touch too austere to be called pretty. 'Almost as pretty as Poppy,' I added out of sheer malice. 'Come back across my knee, now, and we'd better have those panties down.'

She obeyed and I made myself comfortable with one arm tight around her waist. I grabbed a handful of her panties and tugged them unceremoniously down over her bum, then inverted them neatly around her thighs. As she was exposed, I again caught a hint of the same unusual perfume, but mixed with the musky smell of her sex.

'There we are,' I said, 'that feels better, doesn't it?'

'Yes,' she sobbed.

She had started to sob quite hard, which was disturbing me. Her naked bottom and trembling flesh had me really turned on and, I have to admit, so did the sobs. I reasoned that she had a perfectly good stop word if she wanted to use it and placed my palm against the crest of her bottom. Her skin was soft and lightly downed with tiny hairs, the flesh yielding underneath.

Virgin, I thought: a virgin bottom, so beautiful and all mine.

'Here goes, Anna darling,' I told her and lifted my hand, bringing it down hard across her seat, then again, and again, spanking her with the pace and firmness that leaves the victim kicking, squealing and utterly out of control.

I knew full well how it felt, and how a good spanking can leave a girl trembling in her lover's arms in an ecstasy that can be achieved only through punishment. For me, anyway, and I was sure it would be the same for Anna. She certainly squealed enough, and kicked too, but I was taken aback after about thirty smacks when she burst into tears.

I stopped immediately, only to have her beg me to carry on. If she needed to cry while she was beaten, then that was up to her, so I started again, this time using my fingertips to smack each cheek in turn. As she was slim and soft-bottomed, spanking her had quickly made my hand sore, and this was a technique Amber had taught me to use on less well-upholstered bottoms.

'Harder, Amber, like before,' she gasped, 'but right over my fanny.'

It would have been easy to exert my dominance and carry on as I liked, but there was a desperation in her voice that made me wonder if she wasn't actually going to come. I decided to compromise, planting a hard smack at the point where her buttocks and thighs met, even as I began to rebuke her.

'How dare you tell me how to spank you?' I demanded angrily. 'I'll spank you how I please, you snivelling little brat!'

I began to lay in with all my strength, each slap aimed so that my palm caught her pussy. She quickly burst into tears again, harder and mingled with choking sounds, then she screamed and I knew that she was actually coming, just from being spanked. My palm stung like anything and my shoulder muscles were beginning to hurt, but this was no time to stop. The irony was not lost on me. She was the one being punished, but it was now me who was under her physical direction.

'Harder, Penny, I'm coming,' she screamed, then gave a yell that must have made the people in the stableyard wonder what we were doing.

I gave her one last resounding slap and then cupped her pussy in my hand and rubbed hard. She screamed once more and locked her thighs hard around my hand, grunting in abandoned ecstasy as her orgasm peaked again. She slipped from my lap, collapsing at my feet with her scarlet bottom raised and her fingers working the last drops of pleasure from her pussy.

To my surprise, the first thing she did when she rolled into a sitting position was pull her panties off her legs. She put them neatly to one side, then began to take off her stockings. I watched, happy to go along with whatever she was doing but acutely conscious of one thing. At the very peak of her orgasm, when she was completely given over to her pleasure, she had called me Penny.

She stripped completely, never saying a word, then turned and knelt between my legs, as if waiting for something. It was obvious that she wanted a cuddle, so I held my arms out and let her come into them, naked and trembling, her head pressed against my chest as I stroked her hair.

'Thank you,' she said, then, 'could I be your pony-girl now, please, mistress?'

It was an offer I was not going to resist and so I took her by the hand and led her back to the stables.

'What about the men?' I asked, stopping as we approached the gate.

She shrugged. I accepted this on face value, having given up trying to understand her. Most women I can empathise with, easily enough. Ginny was down to earth and playful, Amber complex but open with me, Catherine not dissimilar to myself. Anna was unreadable and often contradictory. She was fun, so I didn't mind so much, but there was one question I had to ask.

'You called me Penny, just now,' I said.

'Sorry, Miss Birch,' she answered. 'You can spank me again if it was presumptuous.'

'How long have you known?'

'Amber called your name when she came, that first day. I thought it odd and so I rang a few friends. They told me Amber Oakley was of average height with tawny curls and a fairly full figure, not petite and dark.'

'Why did you let me have you, then?'

'No one had ever had the courage to try and make me submit, before. I wanted to do it for you, even though you deceived me: maybe because of it.'

'And if you'd won the race?'

'I'd have had you and Amber both stripped and caned. Begging your pardon, mistress. Oh, and, by the way, you are an exceptional spanker.'

'I've had plenty of practice,' I said, pulling on her hand to lead her into the stable yard. 'Most of it over the real Amber's lap.'

The others had been getting on fine without us. I'd obviously put Amber into a submissive mood, because she was still Honey pony-girl and was lead in a magnificent five in hand that was still having its system of traces attached. Or at least she soon would be, because Anderson and Michael were still arguing over how to set the carriage up.

'We did this last week,' Anderson was saying, 'only with three instead of five.'

'Make it six,' I called as we came into view.

It was wonderful. Everyone turned, including the pony-girls. The men in particular looked astonished to see me leading a naked Anna Vale by the hand, a shy smile on her face and her bottom cherry-red from spanking. The one I looked at was Poppy, expecting to see a satisfied smirk. Instead, she was looking directly at me, her eyes wide with surprise.

I smiled back, then turned to Anderson, who was holding a swingletree and a piece of rope.

'Could I drive that contraption?' I asked.

'Contraption?' he echoed. 'Yes, you can have a turn after me.'

'Fair enough,' I answered.

'What's the new pony's name, then?' he asked.

'I'm not sure,' I replied. 'Let me see.'

I took a step back from Anna and let go of her hand. She immediately put her hands on her head, standing for everyone's inspection.

'Quite beautiful,' Henry remarked.

It was tricky. Anna was tall and slender but she lacked the athleticism that made 'Hippolyta' suitable for Vicky. She had moderately full breasts, which her slim build accentuated. It should be something that suited her, flattering yet subtly humiliating.

'Dumplings,' I said confidently, her immediate blush confirming that it was a good choice.

Anderson smiled as Henry nodded sagely.

I led her away, going to the table to look for spare tack. There was enough there to put her in full harness, mainly my own, which I put on her while she stood patiently by. I included my nipple bells and a bow of red ribbon in her pussy hair. When I had finished one of the few bits of pony-girl tack left was my tail, a few shades darker than her own hair, which I had tied into a long pony tail with a red ribbon and a set of hair rings.

Anderson was calling to me to hurry up but I ignored him, instead picking up a tube of lubricant and waving it meaningfully in front of her face. She gave me a startled look but turned her front to the others and stuck her bottom out. As I prepared the tail, I noticed that Poppy already had her curly black tail in and I wondered who had put her in harness.

I had Anna pull her cheeks open and hold them like that as I slid a lubricated finger into her anus. She sighed as it went in and I wiggled it a bit before substituting it for the plug. She took it fairly easily, only squeaking slightly when the widest part went in, then standing upright and holding the tail while I attached the fishing line belt.

She was finished, and looked gorgeous, the more so when harnessed into place beside Poppy on the left-hand swingletree. I then stood back to admire the formation: six girls, all naked but for their harness, four with tails, all with ribbons and bells and all looking good enough to eat.

'Exquisite,' Henry remarked as he fiddled with his camera, 'and I believe it to be a first. We must have a group photograph like this, mounted and with the names and so forth in silver ink, like a team photo. Actually, could you just run through the names please, Amber?'

'It's all right; you can call me Penny now,' I answered. 'Yes, Honey and Hippolyta are on the lead swingletree. Dumplings and Hazel to the left, to the right . . .'

I stopped, looking to Michael and Matthew. I didn't know Ginny's pony-girl name and I had no idea if Catherine had one at all.

'Venus,' Michael informed me.

'You choose; you seem to be good at it,' Matthew offered.

'OK,' I answered, trying to think fast but not disappoint my friend. 'Pepper will suit Katie, for her red hair.'

'Splendid,' Henry remarked, 'now if we could have the three gentlemen standing by their seats I'll put this thing on automatic. Penny, perhaps you could stand at the front and take the reins in your hand. I'll come round to the back when I'm ready.'

He took that photograph and a couple more, then

Honey stamped and I took her bit out to let her speak. As Amber, she asked for Henry and whispered something to him which I didn't hear, then went back to being Honey.

We spent the next hour playing with the six-in-hand, which was tricky to control but really the last word in pony-carting. Anderson took the first turn, with Michael and Matthew as passengers, a combined weight that said a lot for the engineering of the carriage. When my turn came I took them out onto a section of lawn that was still mostly grass and taught them to high-step in unison, a difficult task that gave me plenty of opportunity to apply my whip to their bottoms.

Only when I was satisfied with their performance did I relinquish my seat, ordering all six to kneel with their heads to the ground and their bums up before Michael took the driver's seat. I adjusted the four tails to leave six bare pussies showing, then asked Henry to take a close-up of each. I think the way a kneeling girl's pussy pouts out from between her thighs is particularly sweet, also humiliating when a man takes a photograph in which every single tuck and fold of her lips will show clearly. I half-expected Anna to object, but she never even flinched as he photographed her virgin pussy from no more than a foot away.

I was laughing and teasing them as the photos were taken, commenting on Poppy's curly tail and kissing Honey's bottom after her pussy picture had been taken. Henry had been working from left to right, and finished with Pepper. I remarked to Henry on how ginger her pussy was and leant down to stroke it, feeling wonderfully dominant and in control. It was the last dominant thing I was to do that day.

Fifteen

Even as I took my hand away from Pepper's pussy, I heard Honey give a muffled snort. The next instant, I felt powerful arms wrap around me from behind and Michael had taken me in a bear hug. Matthew and Anderson were closing in on either side of me, Henry winding the camera on.

There was nothing I could do as I was upended and stripped, my boots and jodhpurs pulled off, my blouse torn open. They were far stronger than me, and I couldn't stop laughing anyway, and so gave in completely. Matthew actually held me upside down and clear of the ground as Michael undid my bra and Anderson pulled my pants off.

I was naked, less than a minute after I been strutting confidently in my riding gear. They carried me round to where the six pony-girls could see me, nude and wriggling in Matthew's grip. As he put me down, I grovelled at his feet and kissed his boot, expecting his riding whip to be applied to my bottom at any second. Instead, he bent down and took me gently by the chin, Anderson kneeling beside him and taking something from Henry. It was my piggy-girl nose.

Michael rested a booted foot gently on my back as my nose was stuck on, then my tail, completing my transformation. The comedown from mistress to piggy-girl was immense and had me feeling utterly humiliated. As Michael allowed me up into a crawling position and a collar was buckled around my neck, I was on the verge of tears, but had no desire whatever to use the stop word.

'She's called Pinky,' Henry informed them. 'It was Amber's idea and I think it rather suits her.'

It was true. No one could say I'm not versatile but, at heart, I'm a piggy-girl. The first thing I did was snuffle up to Honey and kiss her. I nuzzled her face, my feelings starting to balance out as we played. After a minute or so, I was all right and felt in role and curiously relieved in a way. Other than Anderson, Vicky and Henry, no one had ever seen a piggy-girl, which meant that all the attention and admiration were suddenly on me.

I started to feel really exhibitionistic when Henry took a photo of me nuzzling Honey. I like being in control, but I adore being out of it, and this was perfect. A pony-girl is expected to show certain standards of behaviour; a piggy-girl can hardly be expected to be anything other than dirty.

Michael had my lead and took me to each pony-girl in turn so that I could kiss her and nuzzle her face. Each responded playfully, but it was only when I got to the end of the line that I really got into piggy-girl behaviour, crawling around Hazel, pushing her tail aside and burying my face in her pussy. She squeaked in surprise and delight as I pushed my snout against her vagina, lapping at her clit as I forced the piggy nose into her hole.

She tasted of sex, and her plump pussy lips and soft buttocks felt wonderful against my face. I lapped greedily, wanting to make her come in my face, only to have Michael pull me away and tug me towards Dumplings.

'Don't spoil Hazel, Pinky,' he admonished me as he lifted her tail. 'Fair shares for all of them.'

Anna's pussy was tighter than Poppy's, but with her

inner lips peeping out from between the outer. I poked my tongue out and licked gently and teasingly against her labia, just enough to taste her pussy and tease her into arousal.

Straddling the shafts brought me to behind Ginny, now Venus, her full bottom stuck up and her thighs well apart. She had been watching me lick the others and knew what to expect, wiggling her bum expectantly as Michael guided me towards her. I feigned reluctance to tease her, only to have Michael take me firmly by the hair and push my face firmly in between his pony-girl's bottom cheeks. I licked obediently, first her pussy, then her anus before being pulled away as Michael tossed my lead to Matthew.

He gave me the same treatment with Pepper, first having me lick her pussy then pulling my head up to tongue her anus. This time Henry photographed me: a close-up of my face with the piggy snout and my tongue actually touching Katie's bum-hole.

I was taken to Vicky next and made to kiss her cheeks before licking her. I'd promised to be her piggy-girl, but hadn't expected it to be so soon, nor to have my face pushed into her vulva while she was still Hippolyta, pony-girl. Amber came last, her tail held up and the sweet, full-lipped pussy I'd licked at so often presented to me. Matthew let me take it at leisure, which was just as well, because I was dizzy with the scent of pussies and getting that familiar feeling of just wanting to lift my bum and hope someone would do something dirty to me. Matthew let me give Amber a good, long lick before pulling me away. I sat back on my haunches in the grass, aware that my face was sticky with pussy juice.

'Doesn't she look a happy little pig?' Anderson remarked. 'Anyway, that was fun, but how about some lunch?'

There was a general chorus of agreement, but Henry pointed out that we first needed a group photo, only with me as Pinky piggy-girl instead of as a mistress. We got back into position for him to do this, with the stable gates as background and me on all fours at the front. The pony-girls were then taken out of role. I wasn't, but was taken by the lead to one of the stalls in the old stable. He left me kneeling on a pile of straw after attaching a chain to my collar and padlocking it around a pillar. The upper part of the door was open, allowing me to hear what was happening in the yard and see the occasional person walking past. They ignored me, and got on with washing, dressing or helping to lay out lunch.

Being left tied up had really turned me on, before. Now, it was just frustrating. I'd just kissed and licked six very aroused women and the taste was still in my mouth. I wanted more, but it was when the smell of barbecuing steaks reached my nose that I finally called out 'Yellow' and Amber came to see what was the matter. She was dressed again, in full riding gear, and once more looked every inch the pony-girl mistress.

'Are you OK?' she asked, sinking down to stroke my head.

'Could I have some lunch, please?' I said, my own voice sounding pitiful in my ears.

'Of course,' she answered, 'I'll bring some in a minute. Did you enjoy the morning?'

'It was excellent, but I thought I wasn't going to be punished until after lunch?'

'I thought it would be nice to introduce Pinky to everyone while all the females were pony-girls; besides, you were getting just a bit too cheeky.'

'I suppose I was,' I admitted. 'How's Anna behaving, now she's no longer in role as Dumplings?'

'You've certainly done something, there. She's just asked if I'd like to spank her and Poppy side by side.'

'Can I watch?' I asked, delighted by the prospect.

'Maybe,' she replied evenly and left the stall.

She came back after a few minutes, not with a plate but with a zinc bucket which she put in front of me. To be fair to her, it wasn't full of the slops I probably deserved, but of a mixture of what everyone else had been eating. It was still humiliating to be fed it out of a bucket and by the end it was smeared all over my face.

Amber laughed and left me again, only for her head and shoulders to reappear above the door but well out into the yard. She raised her hand and the babble of voices died away.

'Ladies and gentlemen,' she began, 'the afternoon's programme will commence shortly with a training session for our novice pony-girls, Hazel and Pepper, and under my own direction. However, we also have the second of today's punishments. I am ashamed to admit the miscreant is my own girlfriend, Penny, whom I have all too clearly failed to discipline properly. She has been unfaithful to me and also to Matthew and Catherine . . .'

I swallowed, realising just what a slut I was about to be made to look. All of it was true, but not really fair. There was no point in whining, as it was obvious that nobody was genuinely cross with me. That didn't mean they weren't going to enjoy punishing me, and my arousal was joined by fairly serious apprehension as Amber continued.

'She has deceived Anna and Poppy, peeped at Michael and Ginny and trespassed on Henry's land. All of us therefore have earnt the right to punish her. Unfortunately, I can't think of anything she's done wrong to Anderson and Vicky, but it seems unfair to leave them out. Therefore I have had Pinky chained in a stall and she will remain there for the rest of the meet, her only purpose being to serve our sexual needs. Any questions? No? Well, let's get on with the training, then.'

That was it. Amber disappeared, presumably as she stepped off the carriage, and I was left, a naked piggy-girl, chained for the sexual amusement of ten people. Even if I hadn't been excited already, the idea would have had my pussy running with juice. As it was, all I could do was start to masturbate very gently while I waited for my first visitor.

The bastards completely ignored me, giving their full attention to Hazel and Pepper. I could hear laughter and murmurs of appreciation from outside, but not one of them had the decency to come in and fuck me or make me lick her to orgasm. I kept wanting to bring myself off and then stopped, knowing that it would be better to wait. I was squatting down with my legs open, in the state of uninhibited bliss that comes with being a piggy-girl. I sucked a finger and slid it up my bottom, then sucked it again, indifferent to who saw or what they thought of my behaviour. Not that there was anyone to see and it wasn't until the training session was over that I got my first visitors.

The door at the end of the stables slammed and I heard footsteps approaching. They sounded masculine and, sure enough, it was Michael, unzipping his fly as he came into my stall. He sank to his knees and offered his limp cock to my mouth, the door slamming again even as I took it gratefully in and began to suck.

The newcomer was Ginny, who just laughed when she saw me with her husband's cock in my mouth. She was naked except for Amber's leather shorts, which were unbuttoned at the front and still almost bursting around her bottom. I watched out of the corner of my eye as she fitted the dildo into place. I spread my knees obligingly as she went to kneel behind me. A moment later, the tip of the dildo nudged my pussy, then slid in, filling me with the thick, rubber shaft. Michael's cock hardened quickly as he watched his wife fuck me, his hand tangling in my hair as he came to full erection.

Ginny had me by the hips and was fucking me with slow, even strokes, pushing the dildo to the hilt with each one. Michael paused to take his balls out, had me kiss them and then put his cock back in my mouth.

'Spread her cheeks, darling; I want to watch it go in,' he said hoarsely.

She obliged, pulling my bum cheeks apart as he began to masturbate into my mouth.

'Yes,' he gasped, 'that looks so nice. Go on, darling, fuck the little slut; oh, Ginny.'

His cock started to jerk and my mouth was suddenly full of come, making me gag on his erection as he pushed it to the hilt in my mouth. He kept it right in for what seemed like ages, his come squeezing out around his shaft and dribbling down my chin. Ginny pulled out as he did, only to offer the dildo to my mouth. I sucked, the taste of my own pussy juice mingling with the other.

As they left I sank my face into the straw, breathing heavily and feeling utterly soiled. The stall was hot and rather stuffy, my head spinning from sex and heat, yet I was strangely sensitive, aware of the touch of individual blades of straw, the wet feeling of come around my mouth, the slight weight of my tail bobbing over my naked bottom.

My next visitors were Matthew and Catherine, he fully dressed and wearing his normal friendly, slightly shy grin, she still in pony-girl harness but for her bridle and streaked with sweat. As she turned, I saw that her bottom was decorated with several scarlet tramlines.

'We've come to give you some pudding, you two-timing little tart,' she told me blithely. 'Get on all fours.'

There had been no malice in her words, just the taunting tone of someone who knows that they're going to punish you. I watched as she pulled his cock and balls out of his trousers and began to stroke them lovingly. He stiffened quickly under her caresses and was soon proudly erect with his balls bulging out underneath his shaft. I moved forward, hoping to be allowed to take the lovely thick penis in my mouth, only to have Catherine cuff me gently away and begin to masturbate him by hand.

'Behave yourself,' she chided. 'That's not for you.'

With that she leant forward and took him in her own mouth, sucking greedily until I was sure he would come, then pulling her head away as I realised what she meant by pudding.

'This is,' she said, grabbing his cock and aiming it right at me. The jet of sperm caught me full in the face, half in my open mouth and half over my snout and cheek. She caught the second spurt in her hand, making a pool of sticky white.

'Lick it up,' she ordered, holding her hand out to me.

I put my tongue in the little pool of sperm, tasting the salt. Catherine made a disgusted face; Matthew watched with relish as I lapped it up. When I had finished, she wiped her hand on my tits and rose with a laugh that mingled delight and repulsion. Only as she stepped aside did I realise that Henry, Anderson and Vicky had all watched me humiliate myself from the yard.

'I cannot resist that little bum,' Anderson remarked. 'Doesn't it look tempting, with her little curly tail?'

'Truly delightful,' Henry remarked. 'Shall we?'

'Why not?' Anderson answered. 'Vicky?'

'Sure,' she agreed.

I wanted to come and didn't care what they did. My fingers were on my pussy as they entered the stall, rubbing my clit. Vicky took both men's cocks out, rubbing them and then sucking Anderson as Henry offered me his oversized prick. I opened wide and took it in, my mouth gaping around the shaft. He began to fuck my mouth as someone's finger slid up my bum-hole. I heard Vicky giggle and felt her boyfriend's cock against my anus, pushing, breaking into me and then sliding up my bottom with what must be the rudest feeling of all.

My bottom-hole was stretched around one erect cock, my mouth full of another. Vicky mounted me, leaning forward to kiss me and lick at Henry's shaft, her weight on my back. Her bum was towards Anderson, presenting him with two female bottoms to admire as he buggered mine. My eyes were shut and my head swimming, orgasm beginning to well up in me as my fingers ground against my clit.

'Me, too!' I heard vaguely, finding a soft body trying to get under mine. The others moved to accommodate the newcomer and helped me. It was Poppy, the thick black curls of her pussy hair appearing under my face as my hand was pulled gently away from my clit and her tongue substituted. Henry pulled his cock out of my mouth and slid it into Poppy's vagina, making her gasp against my own. I licked at her, tasting her, then finding my mouth once more filled with his enormous cock, now sticky with Poppy's juice. My anus was on fire, Anderson's hips slamming against my buttocks. Henry's cock exploded in my mouth without warning, and then I was coming, too. I could barely breathe as my muscles spasmed, my anus clamping tight around the intruding cock. I caught an image of Poppy's pubic hair covered in white semen, then my vision went red as my orgasm peaked, purple as a second hit me, then black as it all finally got too much.

I came round in the yard. Amber had a cold rag to my face and the rest of them were standing round looking concerned.

'Penny? Are you all right?' she asked.

'Sort of,' I managed, after a moment.

'You should have used the stop word,' she chided me gently.

'I didn't want to,' I admitted. 'Can I have some water?'

Ginny passed a bottle to me and I drank deeply,

returning more or less to normal as the cool fluid trickled down my throat.

'I'll be OK,' I assured them. 'Leave me propped up with the bottle and I'll just watch.'

That was how I spent the rest of the meet: propped up in the shade with a string of concerned friends waiting on my every need. I felt weak and not a little bit sore, but very satisfied. They'd taken my piggy snout and tail off, but I was otherwise naked, which seemed completely natural. I just wanted to rest, but that didn't stop me enjoying the view.

When I had fainted, Anna had been giving Amber a drive and the next item was the joint spanking of Anna and Poppy. This was done with both girls naked and kneeling side by side on the rear seats of the carriage. She spanked them both, then gave each six strokes of the cane, Anna obviously no longer caring what the men saw of her body or behaviour.

There was another race after that, with Ginny and Catherine pulling Michael and Matthew. Ginny won and Catherine was duly put across her knee and spanked in front of everybody. Matthew and Michael also took turns, leaving poor Katie's bottom looking very sore indeed.

Anna asked why none of the men had been anything other than dominant, but it was Amber who teased Michael and Anderson into being her pony-boys and hitched them to the carriage to offer the girls rides. From there, things became less organised, with people playing more gently and couples tending to stick together more. I could tell people were getting tired and, soon after, Amber stood up and asked if anybody had any final requests before we called it a day.

I'd been resting for over an hour and was beginning to feel a bit more alive. Not only that, but, for all the intensity of my period as a piggy-girl, I'd neither been spanked properly nor been a pony-girl.

‘Me,’ I chirped up as Amber looked around. ‘I’d like a gentle spanking from someone small: Poppy, if she’d like to. After that, I’ll be your pony-girl for a lap of the park.’

‘There’s energy for you,’ Amber said. ‘Come on, Poppy, put her over your knee.’

Poppy smiled shyly and came over to offer her hand. I took it and walked behind her to the centre of the yard, where a chair had been placed for an earlier spanking. Poppy kissed me as she sat down and pulled me gently across her lap, putting her hand on my bottom and stroking for a while before starting to spank me. We were both naked and happy to be naked, the spanking purely erotic rather than punishment, done as much to show off for everyone else as for our own pleasure. My bum was pleasantly warm when she finished and I knelt to kiss her feet, making a very public show of submission to the least dominant girl among us.

Somehow that act was immensely satisfying and I knew that a quick run as Amber’s pony-girl would put the final touch on the day. For all the general air of exhaustion, Amber harnessed me properly, putting my tail in and adding nipple and cheek bells along with plenty of ribbons. When I was ready, she had me kneel and she mounted the cart, putting me into motion with a command and a touch of the whip to my right buttock.

I walked smoothly and evenly, deliberately wiggling my bottom to make the tail swing for Amber’s pleasure. I was totally happy, easy and confident as a pony-girl and deeply in love with my driver. We crossed in front of the ruined house and entered the wood, Amber putting me into a trot on the downhill slope.

As we passed the point at which I had first seen Michael and Ginny earlier that summer, I couldn’t resist a glance to the side.

There was a face looking at me. Female, freckled and blonde, with glasses, her mouth open in an expression of shocked amazement. If she wasn't in the same bush I had hidden in, then it must have been a neighbouring one. I shied and stopped, but the girl had gone, only the tell-tale crack of a twig telling me that I had really seen her.

'Calliphigenia!' Amber ordered sharply. 'Walk on!'

I obeyed, wondering if I had looked quite so shocked the first time I had seen a pony-girl. Maybe, but probably not.

NEXUS NEW BOOKS

To be published in November

PET TRAINING IN THE PRIVATE HOUSE

Esme Ombreux

£5.99

When Jessica moves from the city to the exclusive Hillingbury estate she fears that she might find life in the suburbs rather dull. But the local shop is owned by the forbiddingly attractive Mrs Morgan, and it stocks a surprisingly wide range of collars, leads and whips. At the Health and Exercise Club Jessica is drawn to Matt, a young man on the staff who, as her personal coach, sets her a strenuous and strict exercise regime. And then one of her neighbours, pretty, blonde, Mel, sets out to seduce her. As Matt, Mel and Mrs Morgan compete for Jessica's devotion, she discovers the depths of her suppressed desire to be dominated.

ISBN 0 352 33655 2

SEE THROUGH

Lindsay Gordon

£5.99

In US Air Force intelligence, Frank Defargo was called many things: Psychic, clairvoyant or remote-viewer. From secret military installations, he was able to see the activities of many, friend or foe, regardless of distance. But Frank's burnt out, and he finds relief in putting his phenomenal skill to use looking at women in uniform. When his voyeurism is discovered, he's recruited to 'the agency', a mysterious intelligence organisation that monitors sexual subversives – wretched lovers in thrall to 'the Bond', driven to any extreme to find those of their kind. What Frank sees in their bizarre SM punishment rituals makes him understand that his gift is truly both a blessing and a curse.

ISBN 0 352 33656 0

NEXUS BACKLIST

This information is correct at time of printing. For up-to-date information, please visit our website at www.nexus-books.co.uk

All books are priced at £5.99 unless another price is given.

Nexus books with a contemporary setting

ACCIDENTS WILL HAPPEN	Lucy Golden ISBN 0 352 33596 3	☐
ANGEL	Lindsay Gordon ISBN 0 352 33590 4	☐
THE BLACK MASQUE	Lisette Ashton ISBN 0 352 33372 3	☐
THE BLACK WIDOW	Lisette Ashton ISBN 0 352 33338 3	☐
THE BOND	Lindsay Gordon ISBN 0 352 33480 0	☐
BROUGHT TO HEEL	Arabella Knight ISBN 0 352 33508 4	☐
CANDY IN CAPTIVITY	Arabella Knight ISBN 0 352 33495 9	☐
CAPTIVES OF THE PRIVATE HOUSE	Esme Ombreux ISBN 0 352 33619 6	☐
DANCE OF SUBMISSION	Lisette Ashton ISBN 0 352 33450 9	☐
DARK DELIGHTS	Maria del Rey ISBN 0 352 33276 X	☐
DARK DESIRES	Maria del Rey ISBN 0 352 33072 4	☐
DISCIPLES OF SHAME	Stephanie Calvin ISBN 0 352 33343 X	☐
DISCIPLINE OF THE PRIVATE HOUSE	Esme Ombreux ISBN 0 352 33459 2	☐

DISCIPLINED SKIN — Wendy Swanscombe ☐
ISBN 0 352 33541 6

DISPLAYS OF EXPERIENCE — Lucy Golden ☐
ISBN 0 352 33505 X

AN EDUCATION IN THE PRIVATE HOUSE — Esme Ombreux ☐
ISBN 0 352 33525 4

EMMA'S SECRET DOMINATION — Hilary James ☐
ISBN 0 352 33226 3

GISELLE — Jean Aveline ☐
ISBN 0 352 33440 1

GROOMING LUCY — Yvonne Marshall ☐
ISBN 0 352 33529 7

HEART OF DESIRE — Maria del Rey ☐
ISBN 0 352 32900 9

HIS MISTRESS'S VOICE — G. C. Scott ☐
ISBN 0 352 33425 8

HOUSE RULES — G. C. Scott ☐
ISBN 0 352 33441 X

IN FOR A PENNY — Penny Birch ☐
ISBN 0 352 33449 5

LESSONS IN OBEDIENCE — Lucy Golden ☐
ISBN 0 352 33550 5

NURSES ENSLAVED — Yolanda Celbridge ☐
ISBN 0 352 33601 3

ONE WEEK IN THE PRIVATE HOUSE — Esme Ombreux ☐
ISBN 0 352 32788 X

THE ORDER — Nadine Somers ☐
ISBN 0 352 33460 6

THE PALACE OF EROS — Delver Maddingley ☐
ISBN 0 352 32921 1

PEEPING AT PAMELA — Yolanda Celbridge ☐
ISBN 0 352 33538 6

PLAYTHING — Penny Birch ☐
ISBN 0 352 33493 2

THE PLEASURE CHAMBER — Brigitte Markham ☐
ISBN 0 352 33371 5

POLICE LADIES — Yolanda Celbridge ☐
ISBN 0 352 33489 4

SANDRA'S NEW SCHOOL — Yolanda Celbridge ☐
ISBN 0 352 33454 1

SKIN SLAVE	Yolanda Celbridge ISBN 0 352 33507 6	☐
THE SLAVE AUCTION	Lisette Ashton ISBN 0 352 33481 9	☐
SLAVE EXODUS	Jennifer Jane Pope ISBN 0 352 33551 3	☐
SLAVE GENESIS	Jennifer Jane Pope ISBN 0 352 33503 3	☐
SLAVE SENTENCE	Lisette Ashton ISBN 0 352 33494 0	☐
SOLDIER GIRLS	Yolanda Celbridge ISBN 0 352 33586 6	☐
THE SUBMISSION GALLERY	Lindsay Gordon ISBN 0 352 33370 7	☐
SURRENDER	Laura Bowen ISBN 0 352 33524 6	☐
TAKING PAINS TO PLEASE	Arabella Knight ISBN 0 352 33369 3	☐
TIE AND TEASE	Penny Birch ISBN 0 352 33591 2	☐
TIGHT WHITE COTTON	Penny Birch ISBN 0 352 33537 8	☐
THE TORTURE CHAMBER	Lisette Ashton ISBN 0 352 33530 0	☐
THE TRAINING OF FALLEN ANGELS	Kendal Grahame ISBN 0 352 33224 7	☐
THE YOUNG WIFE	Stephanie Calvin ISBN 0 352 33502 5	☐
WHIPPING BOY	G. C. Scott ISBN 0 352 33595 5	☐

Nexus books with Ancient and Fantasy settings

CAPTIVE	Aishling Morgan ISBN 0 352 33585 8	☐
THE CASTLE OF MALDONA	Yolanda Celbridge ISBN 0 352 33149 6	☐
DEEP BLUE	Aishling Morgan ISBN 0 352 33600 5	☐
THE FOREST OF BONDAGE	Aran Ashe ISBN 0 352 32803 7	☐

MAIDEN	Aishling Morgan ISBN 0 352 33466 5	☐
NYMPHS OF DIONYSUS £4.99	Susan Tinoff ISBN 0 352 33150 X	☐
THE SLAVE OF LIDIR	Aran Ashe ISBN 0 352 33504 1	☐
TIGER, TIGER	Aishling Morgan ISBN 0 352 33455 X	☐
THE WARRIOR QUEEN	Kendal Grahame ISBN 0 352 33294 8	☐

Edwardian, Victorian and older erotica

BEATRICE	Anonymous ISBN 0 352 31326 9	☐
CONFESSION OF AN ENGLISH SLAVE	Yolanda Celbridge ISBN 0 352 33433 9	☐
DEVON CREAM	Aishling Morgan ISBN 0 352 33488 6	☐
THE GOVERNESS AT ST AGATHA'S	Yolanda Celbridge ISBN 0 352 32986 6	☐
PURITY	Aishling Morgan ISBN 0 352 33510 6	☐
THE TRAINING OF AN ENGLISH GENTLEMAN	Yolanda Celbridge ISBN 0 352 33348 0	☐

Samplers and collections

NEW EROTICA 4	Various ISBN 0 352 33290 5	☐
NEW EROTICA 5	Various ISBN 0 352 33540 8	☐
EROTICON 1	Various ISBN 0 352 33593 9	☐
EROTICON 2	Various ISBN 0 352 33594 7	☐
EROTICON 3	Various ISBN 0 352 33597 1	☐
EROTICON 4	Various ISBN 0 352 33602 1	☐

Nexus Classics

A new imprint dedicated to putting the finest works of erotic fiction back in print.

AGONY AUNT	G.C. Scott ISBN 0 352 33353 7	☐
BOUND TO SERVE	Amanda Ware ISBN 0 352 33457 6	☐
BOUND TO SUBMIT	Amanda Ware ISBN 0 352 33451 7	☐
CHOOSING LOVERS FOR JUSTINE	Aran Ashe ISBN 0 352 33351 0	☐
DIFFERENT STROKES	Sarah Veitch ISBN 0 352 33531 9	☐
EDEN UNVEILED	Maria del Rey ISBN 0 352 33542 4	☐
THE HANDMAIDENS	Aran Ashe ISBN 0 352 33282 4	☐
HIS MISTRESS'S VOICE	G. C. Scott ISBN 0 352 33425 8	☐
THE IMAGE	Jean de Berg ISBN 0 352 33350 2	☐
THE INSTITUTE	Maria del Rey ISBN 0 352 33352 9	☐
LINGERING LESSONS	Sarah Veitch ISBN 0 352 33539 4	☐
A MATTER OF POSSESSION	G. C. Scott ISBN 0 352 33468 1	☐
OBSESSION	Maria del Rey ISBN 0 352 33375 8	☐
THE PLEASURE PRINCIPLE	Maria del Rey ISBN 0 352 33482 7	☐
SERVING TIME	Sarah Veitch ISBN 0 352 33509 2	☐
SISTERHOOD OF THE INSTITUTE	Maria del Rey ISBN 0 352 33456 8	☐
THE TRAINING GROUNDS	Sarah Veitch ISBN 0 352 33526 2	☐
UNDERWORLD	Maria del Rey ISBN 0 352 33552 1	☐